Tuesday and Annabelle live in the same state but in two different worlds. Tuesday, educated and independent, lives in the city; Annabelle knows only the harsh life of the mountain cabin, where she lives with her husband and two other women he has taken as wives.

Tuesday never knew that life could change so drastically in just a short time. When her car breaks down in sub-zero weather, she is faced with the choice between freezing or accepting help from a stranger. She chooses to trust the stranger named Jacob. Attracted to his good looks and quiet ways, Tuesday agrees when he asks to see her again. She tries to get to know Jacob and is both intrigued and put off by his secretiveness. Her friend, Cora, is uneasy about Jacob and asks Tuesday to be careful. Meanwhile, Cora continues an ongoing search for her daughter, who was kidnapped two years earlier. As this fascinating story unfolds, the lives of Tuesday and Annabelle become shockingly entwined, and the horrific activities of a baby-selling ring are exposed.

Set in the beautiful but treacherous mountains of West Virginia, The Cabin reveals the best and the worst of human nature.

# THE

## Cabin

## Misery on the Mountain

C. J. HENDERSON

International Standard Book Number 0-87012-633-4
Library of Congress Catalog Card Number 99-096292
Printed in the United States of America
Copyright © 1999 C.J. Henderson
Fairmont, West Virginia
All Rights Reserved
1999


Reprinted 2000


McClain Printing Company
212 Main Street
Parsons, WV 26287
http://McClainPrinting.com


Michael Publishing
P.O. Box 778
Fairmont, WV 26554

*For my two sons,*
*Johnny and Mark,*
*who are the center of my life.*

Far below the cabin, the town of Winding Ridge was nestled among the foothills. It had a population of 932. The townspeople wanted nothing to do with the mountain people, considering them to be ignorant, dirty, white trash, although most of the town dwellers were not much better educated than the mountain people.

Only a few families lived as high on the mountain as Annabelle. It was a hard way of life and few people chose to live in such a primitive environment. The few families living in the remote mountain area were scattered far apart and, for reasons of their own, wanted to live where others would not know their business.

Patty, who had lived even though her mother had bled to death in the time-forsaken cabin while giving her life, was still living there. She had arrived into the world with a birthmark on her otherwise pretty face; it covered most of one side of her face and was shaped like a map of South America done in purple.

Annabelle was sure that the birthmark was the reason her husband had not sold Patty. No one would pay a significant amount of money for a child with a disfigured face. She had suspicions of why he had not sold Joe and Sara, only time would tell. Except for Joe, Sara, and Patty, he had never kept a child past its second birthday.

THIS NOVEL WOULD NEVER HAVE BEEN FINISHED HAD it not been for the encouragement of my family and friends.

My mother was the first to read the manuscript and give me her glowing review. My sisters Fran, Edith, Karen, and my brother, Orval kept me writing by their praise of my work. Others who kept me from giving up in discouragement are my dear friends Nora Bloedow and Barbara and Tom Barnes. Also, many thanks to my original office staff, Fran and Debbie, and to my husband Jack for preliminary editing and support.

Thanks as well to Valerie Gittings, who edited this novel, and Dustin Merrill, who created the artwork for the front cover.

# 1

*S*HE DROPPED THE MATCH WITH A YELP OF PAIN.
Flame danced to life in the oil lamp, pushing
the black night further beyond the window. She fan-
cied that the dark shadows lay in wait for a chance
to invade the cabin once again.

Annabelle moved about the kitchen and prepared for the long day's chores, piling wood chips
and pages from an old Sears catalog into the belly of
the stove. Scraping a farmer's match across the potbelly's iron door, she held it to the paper. It caught
fire—burning her only window on a fantasy world
of beautiful people—and ignited the wood chips.
She added wood, watching as the fire burned
stronger, and basked in its warmth.

The faded dress Annabelle wore covered her huge
frame, the uneven hem falling slightly above her
ankles. Her hair was knotted back in a bun, and
frizzy strands had escaped from the hairpins, making her look like Weezie in the Snuffy Smith cartoon.

She left the close warmth of the fire and grabbed
her old standby sweater that hung from a spike nail.
Like hard-featured handicraft, the spikes protruded

1

from the walls throughout the cabin, serving as closets. Annabelle shivered as she plodded to the woodburner, her oversized slippers making slapping sounds as she went. She started the fire in the woodburner so she could cook breakfast. Working at the stove warmed her front, but her back stayed chilled.

Gazing beyond the window above the woodburner, Annabelle watched as the outside world slowly brightened, banishing the dark night. The snowflakes fell from the sky so thick she couldn't see the outhouse right out back.

She bent over to choose a few sticks from the wood box. She threw them into the woodburner and added more to the potbelly stove, endeavoring to warm the kitchen to a comfortable temperature. Warming the other three rooms was impossible. With a flip of her wrist she threw lard into the skillet to make the gravy. She had enough flour left to make biscuits for the next two days. It wasn't her wish to send the children to school with only biscuits and gravy for their breakfast and to feed them the same thing again for supper, but chicken was a dinner of the past, and the cow was nowhere to be found. Annabelle thought longingly of the old cow, which provided much-needed milk. She knew the cow would eventually wander back—if she didn't lie frozen in some distant ravine.

Annabelle sighed, shuffled into the bedroom where her sister wives were fast asleep, and shook the bed. "You'uns get up an' help get th' youngins off to school."

Daisy pulled the quilt over her head and moaned.

Daisy was the third wife. Annabelle was the first, and Rose, who was asleep beside Daisy, in spite of the sudden shake of the bed, was the fourth. The second wife had died while giving birth to Patty, who was like Annabelle's own now.

The women usually slept, all three, in the large four-poster bed. But when their husband was home, he slept in the bed with the wife of his choice, leaving two of the women to make their beds on the floor with their quilts and mats.

Daisy was reluctant to climb out of the warm bed onto the rough, splintery floor boards. They weren't fitted together well enough to keep the cold air out. Annabelle left the room as the women scrambled out of bed. Getting out from under the quilts in the unheated room was miserable and the women dressed quickly, anxious to warm themselves by the potbelly stove.

Rose pulled her feedsack dress over her head. Like Annabelle's, the hem of her dress was uneven and fell to her ankles. She grabbed a sweater from a nail, pushed her hands through the arm openings and buttoned it, not realizing she had started the top button in the second buttonhole. Daisy was dressed much the same, but unlike the others, she took time wanting to look neat and pretty. She peered into a mirror. Its finish was unevenly worn, distorting her reflection as she moved it from side to side.

After they dressed, Daisy and Rose hurried into the children's room to wake them for school. "Get yourselves up, so you'uns can get breakfast an' get off to school," Daisy ordered.

She and Rose helped the twins dress while Joe, Sara, and Patty dressed themselves.

The four-room cabin allowed for no privacy. One interior door in the kitchen led to the living room. The door to the right in the living room led to the women's bedroom. From the women's room a door to the right led to the children's room and through that door to the right led back to the kitchen, making a tight circle. The cabin was a square log building, divided into four smaller, equal squares, with a doorway on each of the four inside walls. There were no hallways. Dusty, tattered curtains hung at each of the doorways, a vain attempt at privacy.

The three older children dressed as quickly as possible, scurried into the kitchen, and sat at the rough wood table. A bench was attached to each side. The unfinished wood often left a splinter or two in the children's legs. The twins were dressed in overalls that belonged to Joe, who was now wearing old overalls that had once been his father's. Sara and Patty wore dresses handed down from the older women. Each of them had a sweater and jacket.

The trip to the outhouse each morning was uncomfortable. Annabelle tired of hearing the children complain about putting on layers of clothing only to reach the unheated structure and take them off again. The building was fifty yards from the back door and stood upon an embankment. The twins were not potty trained and too young to make the trip, so they were being trained to use the slop jar.

The twins had their father's dusky brown eyes and rich brown hair. Curls framed Tammie Sue's pretty face. Jimmie Bob had straight hair like his mother, Daisy.

They sat in their rough, homemade high chairs with gravy smeared over their faces. Jimmie Bob grabbed for his sister's food and managed to stretch far enough to knock her tin plate to the floor.

A scream of displeasure issued from Tammie Sue's wide-open mouth.

"Ya have to learn not to waste food," Daisy scolded. "Food ain't to play with, it's to eat."

"Ain't goin' to school," Joe announced into the confusion of Daisy cleaning up the mess Jimmie Bob had made. "Ya girls go on," Joe said. "I'll go huntin' an' we can have meat for supper."

"I knowed ya hate to miss school and all, but I'll be glad ya did. I've no meat a'tall to cook for supper," Annabelle declared.

After the children had gone, the women began their daily chores. Annabelle and Daisy drew water from the well to heat in the tub. The big tub also served as a bathtub, a kettle for cooking, and a canning pot.

"That good-for-nothin' Jeb don't care if we starve. You'uns knowed it's don't bother him to stay away for weeks at a time, while we wait an' work to keep food on th' table," Annabelle complained, dragging the washboard from under the woodburner. "He's hangin' round th' bar in Windin' Ridge while we go without."

"If you'uns wouldn't nag him all th' time I reckon he would wanna stay home more," Daisy defended him.

"I ain't th' one naggin' him," Rose said. "I like for him to be here an' take me in th' bed with him."

"Quit quarreling an' get th' chores done," Annabelle demanded. "I just made my observation 'bout him not carin' an' don't need no yak-a-d-yak back from ya all.

Joe walked to a place he'd had luck before when hunting, and sat on a log whittling on a small branch. After an hour or so the limb began to look like a slingshot. His real attention was tuned to listening for a rabbit, squirrel, wild turkey, or any small game they could eat.

Standing, Joe stretched, put the partially formed weapon in his hip pocket, and moved on to a better hunting place. To his left he heard a loud crunching noise, and something moved rapidly in his direction. He turned at once and aimed his gun. Out of the brush came Tommy Lee Hillberry.

"Damn you, Tommy Lee, you're too dumb to knowed not to crash out of th' woods that a way. Ya tryin' to get yourself kilt."

"Didn't knowed ya was here. You're supposed to be in school."

"And I guess ya ain't," Joe said. "Get lost, Tommy Lee, I'm huntin' supper for my family an' ya just scaring everythin' away."

"Why don't we go hang out?" Tommy Lee asked. "We can go hide behind th' school an' scare th' girls when they come out for recess."

"Since when do I hang out with ya?"

"Ya think you're too good to hang out with me, don'cha?" Tommy Lee accused.

"I told ya to get outta here," Joe said. "Your foolishness is wastin' my time. And ya knowed damn well I want ya to stay away from my sisters. Ya just up to no good with them."

"You're uppity like ya pa. Them's your sisters, not your girlfriends. I'll go by myself," Tommy Lee said and ran back the way he came.

"Ya betta stay away from my sisters or ya goin' to be sorry," Joe called after Tommy Lee.

Joe continued his hunting, mumbling, "I'd like to go after Tommy Lee an' convince him with a few blows to the stomach that my sisters are off limits to trash like him. But I got to get a catch to put on the table."

"It's gettin' late. It's high time we started supper for th' youngins. Joe ain't goin' to get back in time for me to fix th' meat," Annabelle said in her bossy way.

"What are we goin' to eat if we don't wait for Joe to bring in th' meat?" Daisy fussed

"Don't have nary a thing to fix to eat. Meat an' stuff's 'bout gone. Nothin' hardly left a'tall," Rose complained.

"Hush your complainin'," Annabelle said. "There's taters to eat, there's beans an' peas to make th' soup an' dried fruit enough."

"I'll run out to th' cellar an' fetch th' beans an' peas to fix," Rose offered.

"I sure would like to have some meat for supper," Daisy complained.

"Well wasn't ya th' one sayin' how good Jeb cared for us an' how we was th' ones ungrateful?" Annabelle asked.

"Ain't what I said a'tall an' ya knowed it," Daisy spat.

Ignoring Daisy, Annabelle went out back to draw water from the hand pump that stood just outside the back door. She primed it as always, using hot water in winter, for between uses it tended to freeze. She carried the bucket inside, her huge bulk straining under its weight, and lifted it onto the woodburner alongside a large kettle of water ready for the pump and for their coffee, despite the fact that they'd been out of coffee for the past two days.

The back door jerked open and there stood Joe holding a wild turkey by its legs. Blood dripped from its neck where the head had been. He shooed the sleeping cat off the table and threw the bloody turkey in its place.

## 2

*T*HE MAN DRAGGED THE BOY, INDIFFERENT TO HIS futile screams and thrashing legs, across the road to the truck. Opening the passenger door, he threw him inside. Todd sobbed and pitifully called for his mother.

The truck roared along Interstate 70, putting miles between Todd and his home, as the sun slowly disappeared behind the rapidly approaching mountains. To avoid attention, the man kept the truck at the sixty-five-mile-per-hour speed limit. As the man thought of the money the boy would bring, small flakes of snow appeared. White ice clung to the window, and he flipped the wipers on. An annoying, grating, sound—slap, slap—filled the cab. The snowflakes grew larger and heavier as they fell rapidly from the dusky sky. The surface of the road swiftly turned white, and suddenly the road felt as though it were made of grease instead of pavement.

The snow continued falling relentlessly, obscuring the man's vision and forcing him to reduce his speed drastically. Likewise, the other scarce unfortunates who found themselves out on such a miserable night slowed to under twenty-five miles per hour. He looked into his rearview mirror and saw the rows of headlights following behind him. The lights, one set directly behind another, created a picture in his mind of an army of coal miners with their headlamps lighting their way.

Years before, he'd been a coal miner, before he'd found an easier way to earn his living—working for George Cunningham—and before half of the men in his hometown of Winding Ridge, West Virginia, met their death in an explosion. Ten years ago, in the early eighties, he'd called in sick after having consumed a fifth of moonshine. Late that night he was awakened by the earsplitting wail of the siren. The roar came from the mine; it was the messenger of death.

Cold air rushed in, jerking him from his thoughts of a time gone by. To his dismay and before he could react, the boy's denim bottom slid over the edge of the seat and disappeared from sight. He had jumped!

Oblivious to the spectacle of downtown Wheeling's business community hurrying home for the night playing out below her tenth-story window, Tuesday had the radio turned on hoping for a weather report when the breaking news caught her attention. A boy had been kidnapped less than an hour earlier. The incident troubled her deeply, for two years ago her dearest friend's daughter had been abducted.

Tina, one of the department's secretaries, stepped in. "Got a minute, Tuesday?"

"Sure." Tuesday smiled, showing even, white teeth. She abandoned the design that she would not finish on schedule. "Just so you're not going to tell me that Mr. Broadwater wants to see me." She rolled her eyes, "I want to get home. It's already dark out."

Tina shook her head. "No, it's not our oversexed boss. Did you hear the news story just now? A six-year-old boy jumped from a truck that was traveling along I-70."

"Yes. It's dreadful."

"He told the police that a man grabbed him and put him in a big black truck, after spraying something into his mother's face—they think it was probably Mace—and kicking her unconscious."

"I hope they find out who the man was and hang him by his crotch with a meat hook," Tuesday said. "It's a good thing the roads were icy and the traffic was moving slowly; otherwise, the boy would have been killed."

"I was wondering—could there have been a black Ford truck, with lights on the mud flaps and a red '4 x 4' on the side, involved in the kidnapping of Cora's daughter? You know, maybe the man's the same one."

Tuesday shrugged her shoulders. "The kidnapper took Linda from the streets as she and her mother were out shopping. He sprayed Mace into Cora's face and ran away with the child. Could have used a truck to get away from the scene of the crime. I'll mention this to Cora."

"Do you think Linda will ever be found?"

"I'm afraid she's dead. It's been two years now."

"It's so unfair; the whole, ugly situation. . ."

"It's frightening," Tuesday said compassionately. "You're shopping with your child, a man bumps into you and sprays Mace into your face. The next thing you know, the child's gone!"

"Trauma city," Tina sighed.

"Cora feels responsible. Having her daughter abducted from under her nose messes with her mother's protective instinct."

Tuesday glanced out the window. "See you tomorrow, Tina. The weather's bad, and I want to get home." She put on her coat and freed her silky, blond hair from under the collar as she headed toward the door.

When Tuesday pressed the accelerator and went into a skid, she realized that she had no choice but to reduce her speed. In the eerie darkness of winter, the falling snow covered the windshield as fast as the wipers cleared it away. The headlights pierced the snow and she imagined that she drove through a swaying white lace curtain.

Suddenly her car sputtered and jerked. Alarmed that the temperature light had come on, Tuesday pulled over to the emergency lane. When she opened the door, the icy wind and snow hit her with gale force. She shivered as she stepped out and raised the hood, allowing a wet cloud of hot steam to surge into her face.

"Damn, what luck. Now what am I going to do?"

The wind chill factor was twelve below zero and the wind blew viciously, whipping her coat and hair away from her body. The snow felt like tiny grains of sand, stinging her face as it whistled and swirled around her, finding her only exposed skin. As she stood at the side of the Interstate wondering what to do next, a black truck pulled behind her car. It had come from the long line of slow-moving traffic that continued to move toward unknown destinations. She could see a red glow shimmering beneath the rear-end, a ghostly flame caused by the crimson lights on the mud flaps. A man stepped from the truck and moved toward her. She could see the muscles in his legs straining against his jeans as he walked closer. The beams shimmering from the headlights silhouetted his large form and high-lighted his dark hair waving untamed in the fierce, gusting wind.

"Looks like you've got trouble," he said.

Her heart plummeted. She was apprehensive about being stranded on this dark night if she didn't accept his help. *I don't seem to have a choice,* she decided, *unless I want to freeze to death right here on the side of the interstate.*

The steady stream of funnel-like beams of light from the traffic sent shadows dancing back and forth across his muscular form.

"Jacob McCallister at your service," he introduced himself with a friendly smile.

"Thanks." She made tiny marching steps and crossed her arms over her chest, rubbing her hands up and down her arms to keep her blood circulating.

"What happened?"

"It overheated. It jerked and sputtered and the temp light came on. When I opened the hood, steam gushed out."

"Sounds like a leak," he frowned. "Hold on, I'll be right back." He dug a can from under the snow that had piled up in the truck bed. "This should do it," he strode back toward the somber figure march-ing in place beside her car.

The car had cooled, allowing him to remove the radiator cap. He poured the antifreeze in. "Start the car." She got in on the driver's side. She turned the key, but the engine wouldn't start. She tried again and it wouldn't turn over; she got only a clicking sound for her trouble. It was useless. Her feet were so numb, she could barely tell if they touched the ground when she stepped from the car.

He shone his flashlight under the hood. Anti-freeze dripped onto the snow-covered ground. "That didn't work. You're going to need a new hose. All I can do is offer to drive you home." He slammed the hood shut.

She was uneasy about getting into this handsome stranger's truck, but she knew that under the circumstances she had to trust him. If she sent him to call for help it would take too long. She knew from her friend and neighbor who was a nurse that in this cold weather frostbite was common and dangerous. She had no choice.

She climbed into the truck and was immediately surrounded by warm air. She was grateful he'd had the foresight to leave the engine and heater running.

Jacob climbed into the driver's seat and drove into the line of slow-moving traffic. "Where do you live?"

She smiled tensely and said, "Turn off at the next exit ramp. Lee Street's four blocks up. By the way, my name's Tuesday Summers."

They left the interstate, passing a few abandoned cars that had slid against the guardrails. Apparently the drivers had tried unsuccessfully to maneuver the snow-covered, sharp turn in the off ramp.

When they turned into her driveway, Tuesday exhaled as if she'd been holding her breath. Only then did she realize how tense she had been. "You're welcome to come in for coffee. I know you're wet and cold." Although she was fearful about asking a stranger into her house, her desire to get to know him outweighed her fear.

They climbed from the truck, slipping on the snow-covered pavement, feeling as if they walked on wooden feet. The house was a majestic two-story brick surrounded by weeping willow trees, hedges and a tall fence that hid the building from the street. Inside, they hung their wet coats on a hall tree. The heat, blowing from the humming furnace, melted the snow, and puddles of water formed on the slate floor in the entryway. Needles of pain shot through their feet and hands as heat enveloped them.

"I was getting worried. You're not usually this late." Sandy came out of the kitchen, carrying a plate filled with snacks.

"Jacob, this is my dear friend Sandy," Tuesday said.

"Nice to meet you," Jacob said.

"Sandy, this is Jacob McCallister. He rescued me from becoming a frozen statue alongside the interstate."

"Translated, I guess that means that your car broke down. Nice to meet you too, Jacob. Well, you two, there's an extra plate of snacks and hot coffee ready for you in the kitchen. I knew Tuesday would come home cold and hungry. I'll get it for you," Sandy offered.

"No, Sandy. Entertain Jacob while I do it," Tuesday said.

Tuesday moved toward the kitchen, leaving them to warm beside the fire Sandy had built earlier. The window above the sink provided a view of a large backyard. In the center of the yard was a worn swing set, a relic from her childhood that no one had seen fit to remove. In her mind's eye she could see herself as a small child sitting in the swing, her legs extended, calling to her mother to push her higher.

She poured the coffee and set the cups on a tray with the snacks Sandy had prepared.

"Thank you," Jacob said as Tuesday placed the tray on the coffee table in front of him. "The fire feels wonderful. And coffee's just the thing after being out in the nasty weather."

"It was nice to talk to you, Jacob," Sandy said, "but I'll have to leave you two alone now. I brought work home and need to get to it."

"Sure. Nice to meet you," Jacob stood up.

"I'll see you later," Tuesday said. She sipped her coffee, her thoughts spinning inside her head. *This man helped me out of a bad situation and now I find myself attracted to him. This is definitely not like me.* She shrugged off the thoughts, tired of being so predictable all the time. Actually, she was not. Her friends saw her as witty, unpredictable, and adventurous, but Tuesday saw her late mother as her role model, believing herself to be just like her mom. Her mother had been a person who liked keeping her life on a schedule, and she strongly resisted change. Not wishing to try new things, she didn't modify her wardrobe or her hairstyle as trends altered.

Jacob sat next to Tuesday and startled her out of her thoughts. "You and Sandy roommates?" His question made Tuesday feel apprehensive, but on the other hand, he'd had his chance if he had sinister intentions. "Yes, we are," Tuesday hedged. Sandy was actually visiting and Tuesday was hesitant to tell him she lived alone—or that her parents had died two years ago in a plane crash, leaving her devastated, since she had no grandparents or other family members left living.

"No wedding ring, I see."

"No, I'm not married."

"A beautiful woman like you single. It's a wonder some man hasn't come along and laid claim on you."

"That's an odd statement, Jacob, 'laid claim.' Like I'm a piece of property. Maybe someone will drive a stake in my front yard like in the gold rush days."

"I'm sorry, I didn't mean anything by it. It's just a cliche."

She shrugged it off. His remarks did bring back memories. She was to be married once, but it hadn't happened. An out-of-control truck had hit her fiancé, Mike, and he had died instantly. Thinking of Mike's death, and her parents', brought back her pain, her feeling of aloneness and vulnerability.

"I'm glad you're single," Jacob interrupted her thoughts once again. "Otherwise, I couldn't ask you out to dinner. Will you join me tonight? I detest eating alone."

*After the help he gave me this evening, it would be rude to refuse*, Tuesday thought. Aloud, she said "I would love to. But, first, let me call a tow truck. My car's probably buried under a ton of snow by now."

While Tuesday dressed for dinner, Jacob waited in the living room that was done in exceptionally good taste. The dark green velvet sofa, love seat, and matching chair sat on a plush cream carpet. A large bay window looked out over the front lawn. Another wall gave way to a sliding glass door leading to the outside. The formal dining room extended beyond the graceful French doors that stood open. Plants, paintings, and family photographs decorated the rooms.

"Very nice," he said aloud.

Tuesday chose a periwinkle blue dress with a portrait neckline. It circled around her shoulders, framing her face and hair and making her look bewitching. The dress brought out the color in her eyes and deepened them to a startling blue. Tuesday knocked at Sandy's door.

"Come in."

Tuesday walked in and spun around. "How do I look? Jacob and I are going out to dinner."

"You look simply stunning. I must say I'm surprised, though."

"What do you mean?"

"You don't go out much. I would've never guessed you'd go out with a man you've just met."

"So what? In every case there's the first time," Tuesday threw Sandy a kiss and walked down the hallway.

Jacob stood as she came down the stairs. "You look ravishing. Is there a particular restaurant you care for?"

"Yes, one about four miles from here. It's small and quiet and they have excellent food."

After dinner they drove back to Tuesday's house, laughing about the way the waitress had flirted with Jacob, ignoring Tuesday.

As the truck idled in the driveway, Jacob said, "I'll be away for a few days on business. May I call when I get back in town?"

"Sure." She reached into her purse and handed him her business card.

"Interior decorator," Jacob read from the card. "It shows," he said, nodding toward the house.

"Thanks. I'm glad you approve," she laughed.

Jacob walked her to the door and they said good night.

# *3*

*T*HE WOMEN WERE CUDDLED TOGETHER IN THE four-poster. The bed was a haven of warmth and solace in the cold cabin after a long day filled with many chores.

Rose was the first to awake at the sound of a motor as it slowly moved nearer the cabin. "Jeb's here," she announced.

Annabelle lifted her head from her pillow; she too heard the sound of a motor. As badly as they needed the food he would bring, she hated to leave the warmth of the quilts. She knew, however, he would expect them to greet him at the door. Rose and Daisy had already vaulted from the bed. One of the pleasures in life for each of them was to sleep with her husband, to be the chosen one and have his attention all to herself for the night.

As they scrambled out of the bedroom, he crossed the kitchen carrying a bag in each arm. Snow and cold followed him through the open door, causing dust balls to dance in his wake.

"Thank th' Lord there'll be food for a'spell." Annabelle sighed.

They were so happy to see him that they acted like children. He sometimes told them interesting stories—if he was in a good mood, which was not often—of the world off the mountain. The tales were of a way of life they never expected to see.

The women put the food away and in one bag found warm wool sweaters for each of them. He did not usually bother with their personal needs. But worse yet, he never considered the needs of his children.

*It's just like Jeb, when winter 'twas most over he'd brung warm clothing,* Annabelle decided. But she was thankful just the same; they could have another six or eight weeks of cold weather ahead of them. The thin, loosely woven feedsack material they used to make their clothes did not do much to keep them warm. Annabelle did not remember how long it had been since he had bought them any personal items, for she'd never been one to keep track of time, nor did she have the means. After a long day of wrangling for his attention and cooking the tasty food he'd brought, filling the cabin with appetizing aromas, they finally retired to the bedroom. Each of the women hoped that he'd pick her to share his bed.

"Annabelle, I want you in my bed tonight," he declared. "It's about time you gave me another baby."

Annabelle climbed into the four-poster bed beside her husband. Rose and Daisy made their beds on the floor. They snuggled close together and shared their body warmth in the unheated room. The bed springs began to creak. Rose cried silently. He would scold her if he heard her cry. The women never grew accustomed to sharing their husband with the others; they had each harbored foolish dreams of love, children, and a home of their own.

As it turned out, their life with Jeb was no better than their life before. Rose had left her home eight months ago. Her family—herself, her parents, and her brothers and sisters—had lived like sardines in a two-story cabin. Her life here was not much different, except she had a husband to love. When he chose her to share his bed, her life became, for that short time, what she had hoped for. She knew of no better life.

In the beginning, Annabelle was his only wife, and she had known that the mountain men often took more than one wife for financial reasons. She didn't know polygamy was against the law, but it didn't matter in the remote mountains. The law was ignored, for the sheriff scorned the mountain folks. No one, especially the bigoted Sheriff Moats, cared what they did.

As the sounds of lovemaking grew louder in the bed, Daisy covered her ears. Daisy was known to think that she was his favorite. "After all," she bragged when anyone would listen, "I gave Jeb th' twins." The bed springs creaked as the rhythm of lovemaking increased, then there were sighs of pleasure. Then quiet. "Now," Daisy said under her breath, "we can get some sleep." But as she drifted off, the creaking of the bed springs awakened her.

The next morning Annabelle felt as exhausted as she had when she retired the night before; he had kept her awake most of the night, using her to quiet his sexual desires. Just the same, she got out of the bed, loathing to leave the warmth and touch of his strong body, and started the fires as was her custom.

Waiting for Annabelle's direction, Daisy combed her hair with a comb that had more than half of its teeth missing. She was the only woman in the cabin who spent any time at all on her looks. Looking pretty was her way of getting his attention. Annabelle's was cooking his favorite food. Quiet, shy Rose was not a match for either of them.

Annabelle, having finished with the stoves, handed a broom to Daisy. "Take it, Daisy, an' quit fussin' with yourself an' get out of here 'for ya wake Jeb. I knowed ya eager to be in Jeb's bed th' way ya fussin' with yourself. Ain't no time for that foolishness. Get some of th' mud cleaned off th' floor. Ya knowed there's work to be done."

Satisfied that Daisy would attend to her chores, Annabelle went to the kitchen to prepare breakfast, her slippers slap-slapping as she went. Soon the aroma of eggs, bacon, and potatoes filled the cabin as they sizzled in the skillet, and the smell of food made her mouth water. It had been days since they'd had anything to eat except biscuits, gravy, and the meager turkey. The children ate like animals. They never cared if their father was home or not, except that he always brought food for them to eat.

After the women sent the children off to school, they put the twins back on their mats in the corner of the children's room. The twins played and made cooing sounds to each other. Occasionally they got too rough, and there would be cries of pain until one of the women disciplined them. Tiring of each other's company, the youngsters were soon underfoot.

Annabelle prepared her husband's breakfast while he lay in bed. He refused to eat with the children, preferring to wait until they had left the cabin.

After breakfast, Jeb made his dreaded announcement. "I sold the twins. We can't afford to feed them and buy clothing for school when they're old enough to go."

Daisy began to cry.

He slapped her. "Daisy, shut up your blubbering. I want all of you to go to church Sunday morning. Leave the twins here."

They normally loved to attend church, only not this way, knowing the children would be gone when they came home again. Not one of the women would dare disobey their provider and protector, though. The women were captivated by his macho good looks, and his charisma kept them in love with him. They knew only the mountain way and, although it wasn't easy, selling children when there wasn't enough to go around was the way of life. The neighboring mountain men, though, restricted the exchange to their own kind.

At daybreak on Sunday morning, Annabelle had buckets and pots of hot water ready for the washtub where they took turns bathing.

They bathed the younger children first; Patty, Sara, and Joe had their turns next. By the time the women were ready to bathe, the water was cold and dirty. Only the first to bathe ever felt fresh.

They bundled up and headed down the mountain toward the church. Daisy cried as she stumbled along with the other women trying to comfort her. In many ways they were like sisters; except for the husband they shared, they had only each other to depend upon.

"You're goin' to get used to it," Annabelle soothed. "Ain't th' first time Jeb's sold our youngins. They're probably betta off'n we are."

Daisy could not be comforted. Annabelle knew all too well that Daisy would miss the children all her life. Every day of her life, Annabelle missed the children Jeb had sold in the past, but she knew she could not do a thing about it.

They made their way doggedly down the mountain, with Joe in the lead, picking their way carefully. It was difficult to stay on the path, as the snow camouflaged it, denying its existence.

While the women walked to church with the children, their husband waited for the couple who would come to pick up the twins and deliver them to their new home. He never dealt directly with the people who bought the children. He dealt with the ones who specialized in providing childless couples with children. The children were not always sold to loving couples. Jeb had no conscience concerning what happened to them, nor did he have paternal feelings for them. His feelings were for himself, money, and women. As he sat in the rocking chair on the front porch, waiting to hear a car motor, his children played at his feet. They wore clothes that were too light for the freezing weather, but they did not complain. The novelty of being outside the cabin was a diversion for them.

From the time he was a small boy, Jeb had prepared himself to leave the mountain and live in the city. He'd become the teacher's finest student in the one-room school he had attended in Winding Ridge—the same school he allowed Joe, Sara, and Patty to attend. At the age of sixteen, he began hitchhiking to Wheeling. On one of those occasions he had met George Cunningham in a bar that they both liked to frequent. They had become friendly. Over the next few years, he'd learned that George ran his own law firm and arranged adoptions for large fees. That was when dreams of wealth came knocking at his door.

He stood at the distant whine of an engine that was growing louder as it traveled up the dirt road.

The couple that was coming to pick up the twins and take them to their new home had been there before. It was not the first time they had seen the old cabin that was surrounded by cats, dogs, and trash.

They walked toward the porch, barely avoiding trip-ping over the rubbish that protruded from the snow.

"We're here for the kids," the man said as he and the woman climbed the two steps to the porch. "Here's your money." He produced an envelope from his inside pocket. "You want to count it?"

"There's no need. Take the kids and go."

The children, shrieking and kicking, were strapped into the back seat of the Bronco. After they were gone, the children's screams seemed to linger in the air.

He stood looking at the envelope containing the balance of money he had made on the sale of his children: twenty thousand dollars. He had been paid ten thousand in advance.

That night, to pacify Daisy—he was leaving at first light—he allowed her in the four-poster with him. Happy for his attention, she pushed her babies from her mind. The other women left to sleep on their mats endured the same jealous thoughts as Daisy had the night before. Daisy was more vocal than Annabelle was and that provoked the others to grumble. Rose pulled the quilt over her head to muffle the hated sounds coming from the bed.

"Can't get no sleep a'tall 'round here, with such goin's on," Annabelle enviously mumbled, inviting Jeb's wrath.

In the next room Patty was asleep, but Joe and Sara were listening to the familiar sounds.

"Joe, what do ya think th' folk's are doin' in th' big bed when Pa's in it?"

"You're too young to knowed what's goin' on in th' big bed."

"Am not," Sara protested. "Bet ya it's th' same thing th' animals do when they go sniffin' around one'n other."

"Ya wantin' me to show ya, Sara? If ya do, ya can't tell our maws."

In the tranquillity of early morning, Annabelle plodded about fixing her husband's breakfast by the glimmering light of the oil lamp. The others would still be asleep long after he'd eaten and left for his moonshine stills. *Hogwash*, Annabelle thought. *He ain't goin' to check his moonshinin' stills.* She didn't believe for a minute that he spent his time at any still making booze. She'd heard rumors about Rosily, the town whore, and her man. He liked a good time and had an aversion to hard work, and she suspected he kept himself in big money with the sale of their youngins.

"Get a move on, woman."

Annabelle jumped and turned from the woodburner, startled at the command that shattered the morning silence. Obviously pleased with himself and fully dressed, Jeb sat at the table. Annabelle scooped the food she had prepared onto his plate and set it in front of him.

"I don't want to hear any more whining about the twins when I come back," he talked all the while shoving food into his mouth. "It's a done deal. You make sure the others stay off my back. It gets tiresome putting up with the nagging and complaining every time I walk in the house."

Displeased, Annabelle nodded. There was no need setting him off by telling him she couldn't control what the others did. If he spent any time at all around here he could see that she had a hard enough time getting them to step and fetch it when she needed chores done. No way was she going to tempt fate and open her mouth when anger had control of her voice.

"I know you're biting your tongue to keep quiet.

I can see you're trying your best not to piss me off.
You've done well to keep your mouth shut." He
picked up his expensive coat, pulled on his snow
boots, and left.

Steaming mad, Annabelle vented her anger at the
others. "Don'cha no-goods think you're goin' to
sleep all day. It's time ya got up." Annabelle gave
the bed a vigorous shake.

"Ya don't have to be so mean 'bout it," Daisy said.
"We're goin' to get up. Don't have to scare us outta
our skins shakin' th' bed that a'way."

"I don't want to hear any cryin' about th' twins
neither. Jeb'll not put up with it a'tall, he'll not."
Annabelle knew the household would be unhappy
for a long time to come without the cheerful voices
of the twins. Wasn't anything could be done about
it, though. They'd have to cope.

Everyone's spirits were lifted for a while as
Annabelle's cooking sent an uncommon aroma of
sizzling bacon and eggs throughout the cabin.

*4*

"HOW WAS YOUR BUSINESS TRIP?" TUESDAY asked sipping her after-dinner drink.

"Very profitable."

"Jacob, you're so damn vague about everything I ask you. It's getting really tiresome."

"Sorry, but like I told you before, there's not much to tell. I travel a lot. I sell liquor for a distributor located here in West Virginia. I have no family."

"Those are precisely the same things you told me before, aside from the fact that you have no family. I'm sorry to hear that, because I know firsthand what it's like not having a family. But tell me something different, like, where do you live?"

"I live here in Wheeling. My apartment is across town from you. I'll have you over for dinner if you'll come."

"You can cook?"

"Damn, guess I'm busted," Jacob's dark eyes twinkled behind his mischievous grin.

"Why are you asking me to dinner in your apartment if you can't cook?" she asked, charmed by his smile.

He leaned closer and took her hand in his. "We'll manage together. The atmosphere we create will be the real feast."

"Why, you're a male chauvinist. I don't cook."

"You're being modest. I'll take the gamble."

"Whoa, I didn't say I can't cook, I said I don't. But you're on. The evening sounds intriguing."

The room was done in pink and cream colors. A queen-size bed, placed in front of a large bay window, dominated the room. She had chosen the arrangement because she enjoyed watching the sky as she drifted off to sleep.

Lying in bed, Tuesday thought about the couple Jacob had introduced to her at dinner earlier in the evening as his business associates, George Cunningham and Molly Anderson. He had been obvious about not wanting the couple to join them. After some small talk, they'd left, telling Jacob they would meet with him the next day. They had seemed intensely interested in learning details about the delivery Jacob planned to make. Tuesday had sensed that Jacob had not wanted to talk about the trip, nor about his business, in her company.

After the couple had left Tuesday questioned him. "I'd rather spend time alone with you," he'd insisted putting her off.

At the time, Tuesday believed him. Since she'd had time to think it over, she felt it was odd that he'd cold-shouldered his business associates. She had been right in the first place; he didn't want her to know his business. Oh, she told herself, I'm just being silly. He just wanted to be alone with me, just like he said. I'm making mountains out of molehills. Why is it that I often seem to be defending him to myself? Maybe I'm afraid I'm going to lose him like all the others I've lost. Maybe I'm looking for excuses not to fall in love with him. She fell asleep as a cloud of confusing thoughts spun around in her head.

Tuesday picked up the phone and dialed Cora's number.

"Hello," Cora answered.

"Hi, how about lunch today?"

"You name the place."

They agreed to meet at noon at a restaurant around the corner from Tuesday's office building. It was a favorite place for them to meet. The food was superb, the service was excellent, and they could sit and talk as long as they liked. Tuesday arrived at the restaurant first; she could hardly wait to tell Cora about Jacob. Cora was constantly pushing her to get out and date. "Otherwise," Cora was fond of saying, "how are you going to marry and have children?"

Tuesday was also anxious to find out if the truck that was used in the kidnapping of the boy had brought to light any new leads concerning the investigation into Cora's daughter's case. Tuesday's mood saddened as she visualized Cora's attempts to assist the detective who was in charge of the case. She often called him regarding any information she could get her hands on, determined the child would be found. Two years had passed, though, since the girl had been taken.

Cora came through the door. When she caught sight of Tuesday, she walked briskly toward the table. Cora could only be described as cute, with her dimples and short, curly, red hair. She had a wonderful, bubbly personality.

"Hi, Tuesday. Am I late?"

"Hi. You're always late." Tuesday teased.

Cora took a seat. "Don't just sit there with your mouth open. You told me that you actually met someone you like. Tell me about him," Cora demanded with a crafty grin on her face.

"Well." Tuesday began to tell her story and her mood brightened once again. "It's the first time

I've been attracted to any man since Mike. Anyway, my car broke down on I-70, a little over a week ago. It was the day the newspaper printed the story of the boy who jumped from the truck. Do you remember?"

Cora nodded.

"Anyway, I was terrified when my car quit running. It was early evening and dark already. It hadn't been long since I had read the story and was reminded how cruel some people can be. When the stranger came to my rescue, I was anxious about finding myself in such a vulnerable position, but I was more afraid of freezing along the side of the interstate. By the way, the stranger was handsome."

Tuesday enjoyed telling her story so much that she didn't notice that Cora's mood had changed. "He couldn't fix my car, so he offered to drive me home where I could call a—"

Cora interrupted her. "You didn't! You were taking an unnecessary chance with your life. You know, if you'd locked your car and waited, a policeman or a highway patrolman, or someone who could be trusted, would've stopped."

"Cora! Will you be quiet for a minute and let me tell you what happened?"

"Yes, go on and I'll be quiet, but you were in a dangerous situation," Cora admonished. "Just because a man is handsome does not exclude him from being a murderer or a rapist. He could have knocked you on the head and robbed you and left you along the side of the road to freeze."

"I couldn't just sit there! My car overheated and wouldn't run. It was too cold without a heater and like you just said I would have frozen. Anyway, he couldn't fix my car, so there was nothing to do but let him drive me home. I asked him in for coffee. He needed to dry off and get warm."

"Tuesday, that was stupid and you know it."

"Yes," Tuesday made a dismissive gesture, "but it turned out okay. It's not like I picked him up in a bar. I enjoy his company. And he's handsome and charming."

"Okay," Cora conceded. "I understand, but I don't want you to take a chance like that again." Cora surprised Tuesday when she laughed, her stern look replaced by a smile. "Okay, the lecture's over now. Tell me more."

"I know nothing of him. I want you and Bill to meet him. I want your opinions of him. I was thinking we could play cards one evening. What do you think?"

"I'm anxious to meet him. I'll talk to Bill."

"Let's make it soon. Jacob's on another sales trip, but he'll be back in a few days."

"No problem. Let's order lunch. I'm absolutely starving."

"Somehow, I'm not surprised." Tuesday laughed.

"By the way," Tuesday changed the subject, "did you talk to Cliff about the truck used in the kidnapping of the boy? Maybe it has something in common with Linda's kidnapping."

"Yes, I did talk to him, but there was no truck involved in my daughter's abduction that I saw. He just sprayed Mace in my face and ran with her. I couldn't see after that, so I have no idea what means he used to get away."

"Cora, I'm sorry. I always hate myself when I bring up the subject of Linda and see the pained look on your face."

"Don't feel that way, Tuesday. I know you love Linda. Sure, it causes me pain when someone brings up the subject of her kidnapping, but it would bring me much more pain if they didn't remember her at all."

OME ON OUT, AIN'T YA GOIN' TO SCHOOL TODAY, or ya scared th' sheriff's goin' to come after you?" Tommy Lee Hillberry taunted.

"I'm goin' to break Tommy Lee's neck." Joe gobbled down the rest of his food and bolted from the table pushing past Annabelle. She saw he was even more furious because he didn't get to enjoy the treat of having the bacon and eggs she had fixed for him. "He's botherin' me when I'm huntin', an' when I'm eatin', an' maybe next he'll bother me when I'm in th' outhouse."

"Now don't go gettin' in a fight, Joe," Annabelle rung her hands. "Ya knowed your pa don't want no trouble around here."

Ignoring his mother, Joe tore out the back door, not bothering with his jacket. Tommy Lee hid behind the outhouse. "Look at you rubber-neckin' round that crapper like a scaredy-cat. Ya ain't so brave when I come at'cha. I knowed you're just wantin' to torment Patty or Sara." Joe picked up an old muddy boot standing outside the door waiting for it's next trip to the outhouse. He threw it directly at Tommy Lee's head and missed by a couple feet.

"My pa's gettin' fired up mad at your pa," Tommy Lee jeered. "He don't like it that your pa's sellin' his own flesh an' blood."

"Way I see it, it ain't none of his business what my pa's doin'. Lot's of mountain men sell their kids if they can't feed 'em. Ain't nothin' else to do."

"Pa says it ain't th' same thin'. Your pa's sendin' his kids to those city folk just for th' money cause he's too lazy to work. It's okay to sell to mountain folk so's they'll stay on th' mountain with their own kind."

"Ya don't knowed what you're talkin' 'bout. And your pa's always fired up, Tommy Lee. Don't mean nothin', no how. Ain't no big deal, stayin' on th' lousy ole mountain. I'm gettin' tired of ya runnin' after me tryin' to stir up trouble all th' time."

"Don't be so sure it don't mean nothin'. He says he's fixin' to talk to th' sheriff down in Windin' Ridge."

Joe laughed. "Ya gutless piece of dog turd. Don'cha get tired of makin' them same threats time an' again. I knowed I'm gettin' powerful tired of hearin' it."

"Just wait an' see, Joe, my pa's goin' to talk to th' sheriff. He seen strangers go off th' mountain past our cabin with little babies in their car yesterday. Didn't have 'em when they went up th' road."

Tommy Lee lived in a shack just a mile below Joe's cabin, with his father, Andy Hillberry, his mother, and his five sisters. Andy watched all the comings and goings to and from the cabin above him. He was jealous of what his neighbor had. Andy barely scratched his livelihood from the ground where he grew his meager garden. He managed to keep two cows and a few chickens and sold eggs and milk to The Company Store in town. The Company Store was owned and operated by the local coal-mining outfit.

Andy Hillberry had in fact spoken to Sheriff Ozzie Moats on many occasions about his neighbor's selling children. The sheriff never listened to Andy Hillberry. It was an irritation to the sheriff that Andy constantly tried to stir up trouble. The sheriff didn't really care what was going on with the mountain folk, except that they stay on the mountain where they belonged. The town was his domain. He collected his paycheck and in return monitored the entire town from his office window. If anything had to be done outside those four walls he sent his Deputy, Jess Willis.

"Got anymore eggs an' bacon?" Joe was still hungry after his encounter with Tommy Lee.

"Yeah," Annabelle answered, "I saved ya some. I knowed ya'd be wantin' to eat again after ya'd gone an' hogged your food down in two bites."

"Well I knowed who's goin' to be waitin' for us down over th' hill this mornin'," Patty said, moving over to let Joe sit by her.

"Don't take a brain to figure that out," Joe said. "He's takin' a likin' to ya an' we'll never be shed of him."

"I got news for him," Patty said, "except for ya, Joe, I ain't goin' to have no business with no mountain men. Don't intend to be here that long."

"That's big talk. Just where ya think you're goin'?" Joe said not taking her serious.

"Don't start tellin' your stories 'bout th' dreams what come true," Annabelle said. "I don't hold with such nonsense."

"I don't knowed why ya don't believe me. In my dreams—an' they ain't really dreams—everythin' gets dark in my head an' I see things happenin'. Yesterday I was comin' from th' outhouse an' seen Missy and Mindy. I seen them sittin' in high chairs, gittin' kisses an' hugs. They're laughin' an' happy livin' in a nice house."

"I told ya I don't want that crazy talk in this house. I won't hear it."

"Jo-ooe, there's more. Please listen. Something bad's goin' to happen. There's goin' to be strangers comin' around an' everythin's goin' to be different." Patty looked to him for his support.

"Ya heard ma, Patty, cut it out," Joe said. "You're givin' ever'body th' creeps."

"I don't knowed what to make of my dreams, but I need someone to understand me. I've been havin' dreams of strange men comin' to th' cabin. And I knowed they're visions of what's goin' to happen. They always come true. And in my dreams, ya all are afraid of th' strangers. And Aggie is stayin' here. There's a new woman livin' here too. I'm scared." Patty stalked out of the room.

*D*ETECTIVE SERGEANT CLIFFORD MORAN WAS assigned to the Bureau of Missing Children with the Wheeling Police Department. It was apparent, to those who came in daily contact with him, that he was committed to putting a stop to the widespread trafficking of children by seeking out the men at the top of the organized ring of kidnappers.

Lieutenant Hal Brooks hurried into Cliff's office. "How's it going? Anything new?"

"You bet there is," Cliff dropped the fistful of papers he was holding onto the desk. "I've had word that the Walker girl may have been found and is living in Los Angeles. I'm waiting to hear from the FBI."

"Tell me . . ."

The phone rang, interrupting Hal's comment.

"Sergeant Moran here." Cliff's face broke into a grin. "All-ll right!" His fist like a vise, he extended his arm upward in a short quick jab. "I'll be on the next flight."

Cliff replaced the phone in its cradle. "I'm on my way out west. When I'm sure it's our girl, I'll let you know. You can have the great pleasure of telling her parents we've found their daughter. The agent in Los Angeles said that she's fine, no physical or sexual abuse. She's been living with a couple who were raising her as if she were their own daughter."

"You can bet your shirt that Johnson and Cunningham are behind this." Hal said.

"My gut says this is the break we've been looking for," Cliff said. "Pray that someone out there can give us something to help pin this one on them."

"It amazes me that anyone would resort to buying a child." Hal walked back across the room and made himself comfortable in Cliff's chair, putting his feet up on his desk. "Where do they think the children come from. The tooth fairy?"

"The Wrights were told that the mother signed the child over for adoption. She didn't want her identity known. They said the money was for legal and medical fees," Cliff continued. "I don't believe them though. No one would swallow that story. Fifty thousand dollars for legal and medical fees?"

"Tough for them too," Hal observed, "but they can only blame themselves for losing a daughter they had grown to love. It's a little difficult to feel sorry for them. I'll see you when you get back tomorrow."

Hal picked up his jacket and left for home to enjoy dinner with his wife. He would wait for the call from Cliff telling him to notify the Walkers that their daughter had been found in Los Angeles.

Cliff picked up the phone and dialed the airline reservation number.

Uniting Cora and Bill Walker with their daughter would be a highlight of Cliff's career. The three had grown fond of one another during the past two years. Over that time Cora's undying belief that her child would eventually be found, along with her dedication to help in any way she could, had kept the case alive.

So many parents in these cases were accusing and demanding. Accusing that not enough was being done to find their child. Demanding that the child be found at once, as if there was secret knowledge available and the police refused to use it.

Cliff packed a small suitcase. He'd be staying overnight; his flight back home was not scheduled until the next day. With half an hour to kill before he would leave for the airport, he picked up the scrapbook he kept of the children his department had found in recent years. It was filled with newspaper clippings picturing the children and telling of their abductions. He kept in touch with several of the children's parents. The children he kept in touch with were those who had suffered most at the hands of their captors. The progress that had been made by some of the children was good, but the less fortunate ones were having difficulty going on with their lives despite many hours of therapy.

Cliff's obsession to find children who had been kidnapped, and to catch the ones responsible had begun when he was seven years old and his twin brother, Martin, had become a kidnap victim. Apparently, he had not been taken for ransom as there was never a note or demand for money. As young as Cliff had been at the time, he had vowed that when he grew up he would do something to stop crime against children. Martin had had a kidney disease and lived with routine dialysis treatments that kept him alive until he could undergo a kidney transplant. Knowing Martin would die without treatment, his parents made a plea on nationwide television, asking those responsible to bring their child back, begging people to report to the authorities if they had seen the boy or had knowledge of his whereabouts. They revealed the fact that the boy would die without treatment. The plea had been fruitless. Cliff's brother's body had been discovered weeks later in a wooded area just fifty miles from his home. The kidnappers were never found.

It was time to go to the airport. Cliff put the scrapbook away, along with his painful memories.

The warm breeze blew the leaves as Cliff walked from the airport with the FBI agent who had come to take him to Linda. After the cold, snowy weather back east, the warm sunshine was a bonus.

On the drive to the hospital where Linda waited, her physical check-up completed, Cliff asked Brownie about the child. She would have grown devoted to Lea and Norman Wright in the two years she had lived with them. She had been sold to them at the age of one, she could only have vague memories of her real parents, Cora and Bill Walker. Perhaps there would be no memories at all of the parents she had once loved and depended upon.

The large hospital loomed ahead.

"Are the Wrights waiting with the child?" Cliff asked Agent Brownie.

"No. We haven't allowed them to see her," Brownie answered. "It's up to her natural parents to make the decision as to whether or not they want the child to see them." Brownie was as big as a bear and just as dangerous. He loathed those who broke the law and went after them with a vengeance; otherwise, he was as kind as a puppy.

"You're right, but I suspect that the child will experience less trauma in the transition if she's with people she knows."

"Here we are," Brownie announced. He parked in front of the main entrance. "I'll take you to see

Linda and if you can spend some time with her today, she should be more comfortable leaving with you tomorrow. We've arranged for you to stay in a room here at the hospital. There's a cafeteria where you can eat."

"Thanks." Cliff got his suitcase from the trunk and Brownie closed it again.

"Let's go. I'm expected back at the office as soon as I get you settled. I'll introduce you to Linda and show you the room you'll be staying in."

They walked down a long hallway toward the elevators at the end. They passed a few nurses along the way.

"Wow, what a specimen," one attractive nurse gushed and winked at Cliff.

"Guess the California girls like detectives from back east," Brownie commented good-naturedly.

Cliff walked backward getting a second look at the nurse. "Nice," he laughed.

"Humph," Brownie grunted.

Linda sat at a child-size table, coloring in a book. She looked up as the two men came into the room.

"Hi, Linda." Brownie greeted the child. "Remember me?"

"Uh-huh. Told you, I'm Karen." She had been too young to let her abductors know her name. The Wrights were told that her name was Karen.

"I want to introduce you to Cliff. He's going to take you home tomorrow."

"I want to go home now." Linda got up from the chair and took Cliff's hand. "I want my mommy."

Cliff got a lump in his throat; it was obvious that the child referred to Lea Wright. The child naturally, after living with her for the past two years, thought of the woman as her mother. "I can't take you today, honey. We have to wait until tomorrow. I need to speak to you, though. Brownie's going to show me to my room, and then I'll come back and we'll talk."

Linda looked up at them, appearing small and defenseless standing between the large men. She nodded her head to indicate her willingness to talk to Cliff. Tears had formed in her eyes, ready to spill over. She was much too young to understand what was happening.

While in his room, Cliff called Hal and informed him that the girl was Linda Walker. Hal had fallen asleep in his chair anticipating the call that would bring happiness back into the lives of Cora and Bill.

"We'll arrive at the airport tomorrow at 5:00 P.M. your time. Tell her parents that I've seen her and she's happy and well. I know that it's late back there, but Cora made me promise her that when I got any information at all, I would call, no matter what time it was. See you at the airport."

## 7

*I CAN'T CONCENTRATE ON THIS ASSIGNMENT."* TUESDAY sighed and threw the design she had been working on at the pile of projects awaiting her attention.

Taking her coat from the cloakroom, she pushed her arms through the sleeves. She walked into the reception area. "Good night, Tina. I'm leaving early today."

"Since you started dating that good-looking hunk I hear so much about," Tina teased, "you've quit burying yourself in your work. It's about time. Are you going out with him tonight?"

"Yes. We're going out to dinner. I'd like for you and Wayne to meet him. Let's get together for dinner sometime. We'll ask Cora and Bill, too."

Tina nodded yes as the phone rang. "Broadwater's Interior Design. May I help you?" Tina asked in her sing-song voice.

The call was for Tuesday. Tina pushed the hold button. "You want to take this call?" she asked, arching her eyebrows, knowing full well that Tuesday was anxious to leave and prepare for her date.

"Who is it? I don't have time to talk to a client. If it is, tell them to call back tomorrow."

"Sorry, Ms. Summers has left for the day."

"See you tomorrow," Tuesday called as she opened the door leading to the hallway.

After dinner the couple Jacob had previously introduced to Tuesday as his business associates found their way to Tuesday and Jacob's table once again. Jacob asked them to sit down and have a drink, but Tuesday sensed, as before, that Jacob did not want the couple to join them. She thought he evidently felt he must play the social game for her benefit. She could detect displeasure in his eyes. Apparently the couple didn't notice Jacob's mood, or maybe they didn't care. They sat down and the waiter took their order for drinks.

Their names had escaped Tuesday, and the woman reintroduced them. "I'm Molly Anderson and this is George Cunningham. If you're anything like me, you haven't remembered from our last brief meeting. I'm a nurse in a clinic and George is a lawyer. He has his own law firm."

There was a long pause while Tuesday digested the contradictory information. They were Jacob's business associates. Why would he be associated with a clinic and law firm when he sold liquor for a distributor?

"How are you associated with Jacob? Do you give your patients, or clients, a drink to calm them?" She laughed nervously.

"No," Jacob said before either one could answer. "I sell medical supplies to the clinic. As for George, he is my attorney and longtime friend."

The couple looked at each other with an odd expression. "I didn't mention it before because I've just gone into medical supplies lately," Jacob explained. "I need the added income and it fits in with my current territory."

Tuesday looked at the couple and saw they looked amused. *You didn't mention it now either,* she thought, feeling uneasy. Music filled the room as the band played "My Girl."

"May I have this dance?" Obviously, believing he looked gallant, George held his hand out to Tuesday.

Charmed, she accepted, not noticing that Jacob glared at George with thunder in his eyes.

George led her to the dance floor and took her in his arms. "How did you happen to meet Jacob?"

"Oh, just luck," she teased. "My car broke down on the interstate. He came to my rescue. One thing led to another. Jacob says you and he are friends as well as associates," she arched her brows.

"I suppose you could say we're friends."

"Oh. I sense some tension between the two of you."

The music stopped before George could respond, and she allowed him to lead her back to the table.

Before she could take her seat, Jacob asked her to dance and led her back onto the floor. "Let's go back to your house and have a drink," he whispered into her ear, holding her more closely than she liked.

"I don't want to go home." She pushed against his chest. He had pulled her hips against his groin, a move much too suggestive for her taste.

"I must leave tonight on business. I won't be back for a few days. You said yourself we need to get to know each other."

"We can get to know each other here with your friends."

She had no idea that his blooming obsession with her was partly due to the fact that she held him at bay.

The loud ringing of the phone awakened Cora and Bill from a sound sleep. Both of them bolted upright in bed with their hearts hammering inside their chests, signaling their sleepy minds it was bad news. Bad news never waited until morning and a decent hour.

"Hello," Cora answered the phone.

"Cora, Hal here. I'm sorry to call in the middle of the night. I realize that night calls are frightening, but I have such good news. And you made Cliff promise to let you know of any news about your daughter no matter what time it was. He insisted I call you immediately."

"What is it?" Cora trembled, clutching the phone.

"Cliff is bringing Linda home tomorrow. She's been found in Los Angeles—"

"How is sh-ee?" Cora whispered into the phone, her hands quivering so badly she could hardly hold on.

Bill had gone into the living room to listen in on the other phone after he had turned the bedside light on and seen how white his wife's face had become. He picked up the phone as his wife asked, "How is sh-ee?" It must be news of their daughter.

"Please, God, make it good news," he prayed out loud. He collapsed in the nearby chair.

"She's fine. She's been living with a couple who took very good care of her. Cliff's very words were, 'She looks marvelous.' They'll arrive at the airport at 5:00 P.M. tomorrow."

Cora was crying so hard she could not respond, so Bill took over. "Thank you for calling, Hal. Thank you and Cliff for not giving up on finding her. And most of all thank God."

Bill made coffee, and they sat up all night talking, crying, and laughing. They both were too

excited to sleep. Soon they would have their
beloved daughter back.

It was the glorious moment they had waited for
since the time her daughter had gone missing.
"There they are!" Cora cried. Cliff and Linda
walked, hand in hand, down the ramp from the
plane. The child had changed from a chubby baby
to a slender little girl. Cora ran to Linda and pulled
her tightly to her breast. "Oh, my beautiful baby.
Mommy's missed you so." Tears ran freely down
her face.

"Where's my mommy?" Linda cried, once again.
Cora flinched. Linda looked so small with her red
curls, so like Cora's own, framing her dimpled
cheeks. Linda's tears continued to fall as she looked
around for a familiar face.

"I'm your mother, honey. Don't you remember
me?"

Cora turned to Bill and said, "My heart aches
with sadness and joy at the same time."

"I know," Bill said, "we tried to prepare ourselves
for this, but the reality is difficult to bear."

"We must focus on the fact that our family's back
together, Bill. We'll overcome this hurdle. The worst
is behind us."

Over Linda's head, Cora smiled through her tears
at Cliff and Hal as they watched the reunion. They
all knew the real happy ending was still a bit in the
future when Linda had had enough time to accus-
tom herself to being home again.

## 8

*T*HE LUMP UNDER THE QUILT MOVED UP AND DOWN in a familiar way.

Daisy stopped dead in her tracks, speechless. She had entered the children's room to wake them for school; their mats were pulled together and Joe was on top of Sara under their quilts. Daisy, too shocked to move, stood there and watched. Patty had also been watching from her mat in the corner until Daisy came into the room. Patty smiled, got up from her mat, slipped her gown over her head, and threw it on the floor in the corner. Boldly she stared at Daisy as she shivered in her nakedness. They owned no underwear. Her father held that underwear was a luxury that they could do without, even though he kept several changes for himself. Patty pulled her dress over her head and walked out without a word. She was on her way to the outhouse. Joe rolled on his back. Sara pulled the quilt tighter around her.

"What do ya youngins think your doin' under there?"

"Guess th' same thing ya doin' with Pa in th' middle of th' night," Joe said, defending himself.

"Ya get dressed an get in to breakfast. Your pa came home late last night an' I'm goin' to talk to him about this," Daisy hissed. She left the room.

"Ya think Pa's goin' to thrash us?" Sara asked. "He's doin' th' same thing we're doin'."

"I don't knowed," Joe answered. "We'd betta be more careful th' next time."

"Patty was watchin', ya knowed we gotta watch 'bout her," Sara warned.

"Don't knowed why ya worry 'bout Patty watchin'. Don't make no never mind what she's doin'. We're goin' to keep doin' it 'cause I like to do it," Joe said.

"Yeah." Sara beamed, wanting to please Joe.

"We'd betta get to breakfast 'fore we get another scoldin' for bein' late," Joe said.

In the kitchen, Daisy described to Annabelle and Rose the scene she had witnessed in the children's room. "They weren't carin' I'm standin' there. They don't even knowed they're doin' anythin' wrong."

"Not surprised," Annabelle said. "Them two don't have no one but their selves. They sleep together, play together, an' don't have no friends. They don't get along with Patty 'cause of her crazy talk 'bout her dreams. Can't call that hateful Tommy Lee, what lives just down below us, a friend, goin' 'round an' tormentin' th' girls 'bout their pa sellin' his youngins an' say'n his pa, old man Hillberry's, goin' to have it stopped. Tommy Lee's scared of Joe; he don't torment him, no he don't. Not surprised Sara an' Joe doin' it on their mat, no I'm not."

"What're we goin' to tell Jeb? Can't keep nothin' from their father in this place. If he'd find out an' knowed we didn't tell him he'd be powerful mad. Ya knowed what he'd do then," Daisy predicted.

"I guess you're right," Annabelle agreed. "Don't want him mad, I don't. Don't think he's goin' to be mad no way. He's just goin' to have more babies to sell."

"You're probably right." Daisy said, "Don't make no never mind. He don't care what they're doin'."

"That ain't why," Annabelle scolded Daisy. "Jeb likes th' money he's gettin' for th' babies. Don't make no difference if it'd be our'n or their'n. I always been wonder'n why he didn't sell Joe an' Sara, an' now I knowed. I just didn't think of it.

"Let's get th' youngins off to school," Annabelle continued. "We'll tell Jeb after he's ate his breakfast."

"What was all the fuss in here this morning?" Jeb demanded as he sat at the table. "I could hardly sleep with all the noise."

"Well if ya stayed 'round here more often an' didn't run back an' forth every whipstitch ya'd knowed what's goin' on 'round here," Annabelle said, knowing she could be going too far.

She was.

He got up, almost knocking the heavy table over, and grabbed her by her hair, causing her careless hairdo to pull free, and slapped her. The skillet hit the floor with a clang and grease splattered everywhere; luckily the heavy pan missed her feet by inches. "You clean up that mess and I don't want to hear you speak to me in that tone ever again. I asked you what the fuss was about and that is all I want to hear from you."

Annabelle hurriedly fixed his plate and put it in front of him. She cleaned up the mess and told him what Daisy had witnessed that morning. "She'd gone in to th' youngins room and they're havin' sex, right there in front of Patty, not carin' who saw them."

He laughed, almost choking on his food. "Let them go at it if that's what they want. That's no reason for all the noise this morning. You all knew that I was sleeping. In the future, you remember to keep it down when I'm sleeping. Understand?"

Annabelle nodded that she understood, too furious to speak. There would be no hiding the anger in her voice.

"I'm leaving as soon as I eat. I should be back in a day or two. While I'm gone I want you to think about how you're to speak to me. Allow the children to have all the sex they want; it won't hurt them." He laughed again.

He had reacted just as Annabelle had predicted he would. Now she knew for sure that he wanted the children to have babies so he could sell them. That was why he had allowed Joe, Sara, and Patty to attend school; he had never intended to sell them. The children had been born in the cabin and had no birth certificates. No one off the mountain knew of the existence of any of his children, except for Joe, Sara, and Patty. They were known because they attended school. The school was run on an extremely low budget and many formalities, such as shots, birth certificates, and hot lunches, were dispensed with.

Annabelle, Daisy, and Rose had not been allowed to get an education, and as a result they had no idea how to go out into the world and take care of themselves. Annabelle did not want that for the children. She prayed that her children would not have to live their adult lives on the mountain, even if they only lived in the town at the foothills. Of course, she did not realize that the townspeople would not accept anyone from the mountain, even if he or she had an education.

Halfway down the mountain, camouflaged by over-hanging pine trees and large rocks, was a huge cave where the children played from time to time. They arranged to meet again at the cave when school let out. Joe sent Patty on alone. Joe and Sara had picked the cave for a good place to experiment with their new-found pleasure. They had no friends, nor were there organized activities to occupy their fertile minds and energetic young bodies. They skipped school and spent the day in the cave. Patty walked on to school, mumbling to herself, "I'm goin' to find a way to be alone with Joe. I'll just wait, it's sure to happen. I knowed Sara has to help Aunt Aggie. Pa always sends Sara to help Aunt Aggie 'stead of me."

# 9

"TUESDAY, I HAVE CORA ON LINE TWO." TUESDAY said, "thanks," and then pushed the button that flickered with light. "Hi, Cora. What's happening with Linda? I still can't believe you actually have her back. Is it really true?"

"She's here on my lap. Still, I'm afraid that if I blink, I'll wake up to find it's only a dream."

"I can't tell you how happy I am for you. When you called to tell me that you and Bill were going to meet Cliff at the airport to pick Linda up, I just couldn't believe my ears."

"It's a miracle that Linda, as young as she was when she was taken, didn't totally forget us. At first, when she got off the airplane, she was frightened and wouldn't have anything to do with me. But at the house it wasn't long until she clung to me as if she sensed she was safe with me. I think on some level maybe she remembered the house, and it calmed her. She still asks for Mommy. Although she calls me Mommy too, she misses the parents she learned to love."

"Cora, everything will be fine, I know it will. Just give it time."

"I know, Tuesday. I'm just thankful to have her back."

"Maybe we should cancel our card game so you can spend the time alone with Linda and Bill. It's not every day that you get your daughter back."

"No, she has an early bedtime. She'll be turning in soon after you get here."

"It'll be fun for Jacob to finally meet you and Bill. We'll be there at eight."

"Great. I can't wait to meet Jacob. I hope my cooking doesn't scare him away," Cora laughed.

"It hasn't scared me away," Tuesday teased. "See you tonight."

Jacob had been out of town on business. Tuesday was looking forward to seeing him again and showing him off to her best friends.

"You look great, Tuesday," Jacob commented as they drove to the Walkers'. "I like those jeans."

"Thank you," Tuesday smiled with pleasure. "Hope you enjoy meeting my friends."

"I'm sure I will," he said without conviction. "Whatever makes you happy."

"Since you've been gone, I haven't had the opportunity to tell you the wonderful news. Cora and Bill's daughter's been found. Remember, I told you that she'd been kidnapped. They're so happy to have her back."

She pointed out up ahead. "There it is, Jacob, the next house on the right, the one with the porch light on."

They pulled into the driveway and got out of the truck. The house looked warm and friendly, tucked back from the street with a neatly trimmed hedge running around the snow-covered yard. Cora and

Bill were standing at the door by the time Tuesday and Jacob reached it.

"Hi," Cora said. "You're just in time, dinner is almost ready. I kept Linda up a little later than I usually would. I wanted you to see her before I put her to bed for the night."

Tuesday could see a big difference in Cora and Bill; they looked years younger now that Linda was back home. Linda hid behind her mother's skirt, poking her head around Cora's leg as Tuesday and Jacob walked into the house.

"Jacob, this is Cora, Bill, and their daughter, Linda Walker."

Linda looked up at Jacob with huge hazel eyes.

"Good to meet you," Jacob said as he shook Bill's hand. Tuesday coaxed Linda out from behind Cora and picked her up, happy to see that the child was safely settled back in her home. "Remember me, honey?"

The child reached for her mother. Lately there had been too many strangers in her life.

"Let's say goodnight to Linda," Bill said. "It's past her bedtime."

Cora carried Linda upstairs to her bed. As they climbed the stairs, Tuesday could hear the child's voice echoing down the stairway. "I want my mommy."

Bill fixed each of them a drink. When Cora returned, with tears in her eyes, Bill went up to kiss his daughter good night and tuck her in.

"It breaks my heart when Linda asks for her mommy when she's with me," Cora said. "I know she was taught the woman who mothered her for the past two years was really her mother. That's two thirds of her life. It's hard for me to take, though, and I know it hurts Bill."

Cora continued, "I guess you know that the Wrights are in town to help Cliff in the investigation. I never believed that I would be capable of killing, but I know I could kill the people who are responsible for taking my daughter."

Jacob was complimenting Cora on her cooking when the doorbell rang.

"Hi, Cliff, it's good to see you again. Come in. I'm glad you stopped by. I've wanted you to meet my dear friend, Tuesday Summers. I've mentioned her to you many times. And this is her friend, Jacob McCallister."

Cliff shook hands with Jacob. "Nice to meet you."

"Likewise," Jacob said cordially.

"I'm glad to finally meet you." Cliff smiled down at Tuesday. "Cora has told me so much about you."

"I'm sure she has. She's had nothing but good to say about you, and I'm delighted to meet you. You can never be thanked enough for finding Linda and bringing her home where she belongs."

Tuesday noticed that Cliff had a boyish grin. When his face broke into a smile, a dimple appeared on his left cheek and his eyes twinkled with humor.

"Will you have cake and coffee?" Cora asked. "I just made fresh."

"No, thank you. I don't want to spoil your evening, but this won't take long. I wouldn't have come by without calling, but I'm going to be talking to the Wrights, and I want you to refresh my mind about the day your daughter was kidnapped."

"I told you everything I could remember when it happened two years ago—and many times since," Cora said. "What else can I tell you?"

"Just go over everything again. Refresh my memory for my meeting with Norman and Lea

Wright. You never know, we might come up with
something."

Cora began telling Cliff about the day Linda had
been kidnapped, starting from the time she and
Linda had left the house. She described the man
who had grabbed her daughter and sprayed Mace
into her face. Everything had happened so fast, she
didn't get a good look at him and couldn't tell Cliff
much about him.

Cliff had not seen Jacob's black truck sitting in the
driveway, with the bold "4 x 4" on the side and the
red reflector lights on the mud flaps. Cliff had
parked in the street. The tall hedge along the driveway had prevented him from seeing the truck.

"I don't like that big-feeling detective or the way he
looked at you," Jacob remarked to Tuesday as they
walked to her front door.

Tuesday was surprised at his remark. She had
liked Cliff Moran. "Jacob, that's not fair. You don't
even know him. I'm sure that without him, Cora
and Bill would not have Linda back now. And it's
none of your business how he looks at me."

"Let's go in, have a drink, and forget about everyone else," Jacob said, shrugging his shoulders indif-
ferently. "I've missed you while I was away, and
I've been looking forward to being alone with you
all evening."

Tuesday was more than a little put out by Jacob's
attitude. "Jacob, I'm tired," she sighed as she
unlocked the door. "Hope you don't mind if I don't
ask you in tonight, but I just want to get some
sleep."

Jacob suppressed his anger with great difficulty.
"Okay, I'll call you when I get back in town."

"Fine, Jacob. Good night."

CHAPTER

# *10*

APPINESS LIKE WE JUST WITNESSED, WATCHING Cora and Bill as they were reunited with their daughter after two years of hell, makes our work worthwhile," Hal said, referring to the happy reunion.

"By the way," Cliff said, "the Wrights are due in an hour. I'd give my next paycheck if they could tell me something about the man who drove the truck in this latest kidnapping. I feel he was taking the boy to Johnson or Cunningham. If we can tie Linda to Cunningham or Johnson, we'll be able to prove they're in the baby brokerage business."

Cliff and Hal stood by while Lea and Norman Wright looked through a mug book. So far they had not identified the man or woman who delivered the child to them. When the Wrights finished, without success, Cliff placed a small collection of snapshots on the table. They were shots of the people who frequently came and went from the clinic and the law office. Cliff arranged the snapshots in three rows. First, the five people who worked at the clinic. Next, the lawyer and the two women who worked in his office. Last, the shots of the people who visited both places. The photos had been taken with a high-powered lens from a window in a nearby building.

The Wrights recognized the lawyer, his two employees, the doctor, his nurse, and receptionist as the ones who arranged the adoption. They did not recognize the others.

"Why did you go to these people for a child?" Cliff asked.

"We went to the clinic for medical help," Norman answered. "We wanted to have children, but were told that we couldn't conceive. The doctor—his name's Johnson—referred us to the law firm. He told us that the attorney, George Cunningham, had been successful in placing children in homes without the delays and the usual red tape one goes through with adoption agencies. As it turned out, George Cunningham had a little girl, one year old, to place in a home. He told us the mother had not been able to keep her for reasons she would not disclose and did not want her identity revealed. George Cunningham told us that for payment of the medical and legal fees the child was ours."

"Why didn't you go through legal channels?" Hal asked.

"We tried in the beginning, but we were turned down. They said that we were too old. We were only in our late thirties at that time. How the hell could they say that we were too old?"

There were other considerations that the adoption agency had taken into advisement, but neither Lea nor Norman revealed those. The agency had come up with less than shining character and credit reports.

"We believed that we were using private services when we went to Cunningham to get a child. Believe me, we thought it was legal."

"Why did you come all the way to Wheeling from Los Angeles to get medical help?" Cliff asked. "I'm sure that there are many clinics in Los Angeles."

"We lived here at that time," Norman answered. "I was transferred about six months after we got Karen."

"You know we call Linda, Karen. That's what we were told her name was." Lea Wright sobbed into her now damp handkerchief.

Her husband put his arm around her to comfort her. "I don't know how we're going to live through this. I'm beginning to understand how the Walkers felt. At least we know our little girl is going to be all right. They didn't even know if she was still alive."

"That's true," Cliff agreed. "You should have considered that when you decided to get a child outside the legal channels. As it turns out, you are luckier than you deserve. The Walkers have agreed that it would be a good idea if you aren't cut completely out of the girl's life. It would only confuse her."

"Oh, thank God for that." Lea Wright sobbed and clung even tighter to her husband's arm.

"Have you seen a black truck fitting the description of the one in this story?" Cliff slapped a newspaper on the table that featured the story of the boy who had jumped from the truck on Interstate 70. "Read this," he said, pointing to the article, "and try to remember if you ever saw that truck."

"Okay," Norman sighed. "We want to help prevent this from happening to others, but this is really hard on my wife."

"I realize that. But you knew that buying a child was wrong. By doing so, you aided and abetted a crime against a child. These people would not be kidnapping children if they had no one ready and eager to buy them." Cliff rapped his knuckles on the newspaper.

Lea jumped. There was a look of anguish in her eyes. Defeated by the events that had overtaken their lives, she and Norman carefully read the story about the boy. It had no meaning for them.

Cliff was not finished. "How about the couple you referred to the clinic? Tell me everything you can about them."

"I can tell you where they lived at the time, and where Phil Yost works," Norman said, "but I think they moved across town after they got the child."

## 11

*A*FTER LEAVING TUESDAY AT HER DOOR, JACOB
drove toward his apartment. He was in a dark
mood. "I would not have run into the detective if
not for George Cunningham and his stupidity,"
Jacob said to himself. Suddenly he made a U-turn
and headed straight for George Cunningham's
apartment. Jumping from the truck, he bolted to
Cunningham's door and leaned on the doorbell,
allowing the constant chime to invade the night
quiet of George's apartment.

George scrambled from his bed and opened the
door. He'd been awakened from a sound sleep.
"Jacob, what the hell?" George composed himself
and made a visible effort to calm down. "I'm surprised. I didn't think that you liked my company
well enough to come for a visit."

"Cut the crap, George. I'm worried." Jacob
pushed past George. "I took Tuesday to her friends'
house for a card game. They have a daughter who
had been kidnapped two years ago and she was
found living in Los Angeles. The detective responsible for reuniting her with her parents stopped by

tonight while I was there. Her kidnapping has been connected to a law firm. The detective mentioned a law firm and a clinic; he didn't mention any names. My bet is he's going to come after you."

"How the hell can they involve me? I just place the children in good homes," George said, defending himself. "I wouldn't think of kidnapping a child. The children are simply brought to me by parents who cannot keep them, usually for financial reasons."

"That's crap and you know it, and you sure as hell know that I know it," Jacob said, rage controlling his speech. "Listen, George, you had better not mention you know me if you get caught. Most important of all, as of now, you don't know me. You would play hell trying to involve me. What's between us has nothing to do with kidnapping children."

"Don't you think that I'm smart enough to cover my tracks? They can't have anything on me."

George had taken great pains to make his adoption activities appear legal, using fake birth certificates for each child he matched up with a parent. He also had the adoption papers signed with the forged signatures of the parents named on the birth certificate. Everything appeared to be in order in each case. Anyone would believe that the adoptions had been on the up and up from his standpoint.

Jacob grabbed George by the collar, lifting his feet off the carpet, and said, "Well, I hope so for your sake, but to me it looks like they're on your trail. Just remember to keep your mouth shut about me. And quit hanging around when I'm with Tuesday. Understand?" Jacob let George loose with a shove.

George fell backward, landing in his chair. It tipped and George desperately tried to keep his balance, but to no avail. He and the chair fell back to the floor with a crash. Jacob looked at him with disgust and slammed out of the apartment. George was left on his back with his legs and arms flailing wildly as he tried to get back on his feet. The force of air created by the slamming door caused George's papers to fly off his desk and slowly float around the room. Some eventually settled in the fallen chair with George.

Tuesday hurried home from work, thinking about the evening before and Jacob's behavior, calling Cliff "a big-feeling detective." She particularly resented Jacob's remark about not liking the way that Cliff looked at her. She now realized the entire evening was tense. Why did Jacob dislike Cliff? She could not figure it out. Jacob was fun to be with, and she was attracted to him, but their relationship seemed to be going nowhere.

She stopped at the cleaners to pick up her dry cleaning. She reached for the door just as a man was coming out. There was a brief standoff.

"We meet again," Cliff smiled.

"Hi, Cliff."

"You look distracted. Something wrong?"

"No. Just woolgathering," Tuesday said at a loss for words for once in her life.

"It's great to see you again."

Cliff got in his car and watched her walk into the cleaners. "I'll make it a point to get to know her. All in good time," he said under his breath.

She smiled as he started his car, thinking about how she and Jacob saw Cliff so differently. It bothered her, but she managed to shrug it off. She would not allow Jacob's unfounded opinions of Cliff to be of concern to her.

"What's my surprise?" Tuesday asked, never one to be kept in suspense. She was still a little put out by

Jacob, but had decided to reserve judgment. She remained captivated by his charm and flattered by his obvious attraction to her.

"My secret. You will find out soon enough," he answered. "Get your coat. It's time to go."

They were dining in a restaurant that she had never been in. The dining room was charming, with each table partitioned off for privacy, and hundreds of candles lighted the room. The effect of the candlelight was romantic and intimate, an atmosphere Jacob chose for a purpose: to recover the easy enjoyment in each other's company that he believed they'd had in the beginning.

"Oh, Jacob, this is lovely!"

After they were seated, a waiter brought their menus and Jacob ordered their drinks. Tuesday's eyes sparkled with the reflection of the candlelight as she looked around the enchanting room. She could wait no longer. "Jacob, what is the surprise? This is such a lovely place. Is it the surprise?" She could not help being pleased to be with him; she never failed to notice how women invariably turned to stare at his striking good looks.

"No, just a good setting to give you the surprise. If you want, I'll give it to you before dinner."

"I want," She smiled mischievously.

Jacob reached into his pocket, revealing a small, black box. "Give me your left hand."

She saw a beautiful diamond ring, surrounded by red velvet, emerge when he opened the heart-shaped box.

"Jacob, you can't be serious, I can't accept an engagement ring. It's out of the question. We don't even know each other well. You sure believe in moving fast." She hid her hands in her lap.

"I love you. I'm asking you to marry me."

"Jacob, I have a good time going out with you, but marriage is not in my plans."

"Don't be offended. I just wanted you to know how I feel. I won't press the issue, but it's not unheard-of for a couple to marry after knowing each other for only a few weeks. I can wait, but in the meantime, I want you to know how I feel and what my intentions are. You're a beautiful woman, you have a wonderful sense of humor, and you're a joy to be with."

"That's a lovely thing to say, but let's not talk of marriage. I'm willing to get to know you better and see what develops."

"I can wait."

"You're taking a chance on wasting your time. I have a career that I'm committed to, and it takes a great deal of my time," she said.

"I can wait," he repeated.

"We definitely need to get better acquainted," she said, "and you'll have to admit you haven't told me much about yourself. You've been secretive and mysterious."

"I really haven't meant to be that way. We'll have dinner at my apartment. I'll show you pictures of my family. You can see how I live. They say you can tell a lot about a man by the way he lives. We'll prepare dinner together and we can talk about anything you wish."

"Sounds like a good idea, but remember you've been warned, I don't cook." She was curious about how he lived and about his family. "Since we are going to cook together, we need to decide what the two of us can't ruin too badly."

She had softened her attitude toward him. The marriage proposal had the desired effect. She was flattered.

"You're on." Jacob laughed, relieved. "Give me your suggestions, but make it something easy."

"Well, I'm sure we can't ruin a salad. I have a cookbook that has a recipe for spaghetti sauce that I've always wanted to try."

"Sounds good to me. Just give me a list of what to buy."

"Great." Tuesday smiled. "We'll choose an evening after you return from your business trip."

"Sounds like a plan to me," Jacob smiled.

CHAPTER

## 12

*I*T WAS HIS CUSTOM TO VISIT HIS AUNT BEFORE GOING on to his own cabin when he came back to the mountain after one of his trips. They sat side by side in rocking chairs, which were placed near the old potbelly stove.

"You're so alone here. Why don't you move into my cabin?" He always asked her this question and he invariably got the same answer.

"No sireee, Jeb, ya think your old aunt gettin' to old to live alone, so ya do. I like it by m'self, so I do. Too crowded in th' cabin of your'n anyways, so it is. Ya knowed I don't approve all th' wives ya got, so I don't. Don't approve of ya sellin' your youngins, so I don't." She picked up her can and spat into it. Brown spittle dripped down her chin.

"Have a mind to tell ya what I hear'd 'bout that old man Hillberry, so I do. He's powerful mad 'bout ya selling your own flesh an' blood. He's goin' to make trouble, so he is. One day ya goin' to get ya reckoning, so ya are. Some day th' law goin' to catch up with ya and goin' to lock ya up an' throw away th' key, so they are."

67

"I'm not worried about old man Hillberry; he's not as smart as that mangy cat there." He pointed to the cat at Aggie's feet. The cat rubbed against Aggie's legs, walking left then right. "All that old man's good for is running his mouth, and you know he can't do anything about what I do. He's been running his mouth for years. One day it's about me, the next day about someone else."

Aunt Aggie invariably predicted doom when it came to the way her sister's child lived his life. She was the only person Jeb claimed to love. She had raised her sister's child from a small boy; his parents had died when he was two years old. They had always lived in her family's cabin, except for her brief marriage. Aggie and her sister were born and raised in the cabin, the youngest of ten children. Two brothers were killed in World War II. The others had left to find prosperity in the city and never came back; no one ever knew what had become of them. Before Aggie's father died, he had sold Aggie and her sister to various mountain men. In Aggie's father's mind this was for the girl's own protection; he believed women had no way of caring for themselves and had not wanted to leave them on their own when he was gone. Aggie was sold to Ham Conrad, an older man who had a wife and ten children.

The man's wife had been bedridden, and soon after he had taken Aunt Aggie to live in his cabin, the woman died in her sleep. Aunt Aggie had to work from daylight to dark; she hated her life and she swore that she would do something about it. She longed to return to the cabin where she had been raised.

Aunt Aggie often spoke of how Ham Conrad had died and left her with his ten children. (The man and woman were not nearly as old as they had appeared, but mountain life aged people rapidly, long before their time.) Her nephew was old enough when the man died to remember that Aunt Aggie had sold the children off one by one. The girls were sold to mountain men who wanted wives and the boys to work their land. She had truly believed that it was the only way; otherwise, they would have starved. She'd had no resources to care for them. After they were sold, Aunt Aggie had moved back to her cabin and had taken her nephew with her.

"Aggie, I'm thinking of taking another woman. Annabelle's getting older and doesn't have many more babies in her. I might go to town and see if I can get a town woman, one of those pretty ones," he jested.

"Ya should be satisfied with what ya got, Jeb. I knowed you're goin' to do what ya have a mind to do, so ya are. Ya got three women, so ya do. How many women ya wantin'? It's not goin' to work, mark my word. It's not goin' to work, so it ain't. Your other wives came from life such as this, so they did. Maybe this woman goin' to have more spunk, so she might. You're not goin' to get away with this forever, so you're not. What ya goin' to do when she runs off an' tells what's goin' on up here? What ya goin' to do 'bout that? Ya goin' to jail that's what, so ya are.

"I've tol' ya 'bout old man Hillberry, so I did. He's goin' 'round talkin' 'bout ya' an' what you're doin', so he is. He's a'stirrin' up trouble. Ya just mark my word. You're goin' to have to answer to it, so ya are."

"I'm not worried about that old goat. He doesn't know what he's talking about."

"Don't suppose I can stop you, so I can't." Aggie picked up her can and spit into it. "Got your mind set on it, so ya do. Ya knowed your aunt'll help ya out, if'n ya want, even if I don't approve, so I will. Suppose you're set on this, same as ya set yourself on learnin' when ya was just a boy, so ya did. I remember there was no stoppin' you, so there wasn't. Couldn't get nary a bit of work out of ya a'tall, so I couldn't," Aggie rambled on.

"Hope I got all of the supplies you'll need, Aunt Aggie," Jacob said, getting up to leave. "Got you plenty of snuff this time, know you hate it when you run out. I'll see you when I get back next trip."

"Ya tired of hearin' me go on, so ya are. Can't help myself, so I can't. Hate to see ya leave so soon, though, so I do."

"You wouldn't get lonesome if you'd listen to me and move to my cabin," he said. "See you next time." He got in his truck and left Aggie to her own thoughts.

Aunt Aggie sat in her rocking chair long after her nephew had gone. "This new woman Jeb's taken a fancy to could be a mistake, so she could," Aggie told herself. "I knowed he runs with a girl in town, she must be th' one he plans to bring to his cabin to live, so it is. Don't matter none what I think. I'll help 'im in any way I can, so I will. After all, he's all I've got in th' world."

It was late when he reached his own cabin. He had gone from Aunt Aggie's cabin directly to the town bar for a few drinks, and for Rosily. She was the woman he sought out when he was in town. A few drinks had turned out to be many. Rosily spent time with him, encouraging him to take her to the city, where she told him, time and again, she wanted to live. He was the only person she knew who had knowledge of the city she coveted. She was a beauty and knew it. She used every female trick there was to get him to take her away from the mountain town. So far, all she could get from him was a promise of city life. First, she must prove her devotion to him by moving to his mountain cabin. That was the standoff: she wanted to improve upon her life, not live in worse conditions than she now had.

The women were in bed when they heard the clamor of the truck outside. They hurried out of bed and scrambled to the front door.

He came in, carrying a bag in each arm. The women began putting the food away as quickly as he brought it.

"Daisy, you and Rose go to your mats. Annabelle, you bring Patty in here. I want to see her. After you bring her to me, I want you to get in bed."

Annabelle was worried about his wanting to see Patty, especially this time of night. He never bothered with the children unless it was to scold them. Annabelle shook Patty awake and told her that her father wanted to see her. Patty got up from her mat and went into where her father sat. She had dreamed that her father defiled her body, and the dreams had been frightening. Her dreams were previews of the future that often became reality. When she spoke to the others about her dreams, they became angry. The anger was truly fear: fear that she was like the old woman who lived at the edge of the thick forest, whom most of the mountain dwellers believed was a witch. Of course, no one believed in witches, but if they did exist, the old woman surely was one.

Patty stood quietly in front of him, waiting for him to tell her what he wanted.

"Patty, we're going to the hayloft."

Patty turned and walked toward the back door just like in her dreams. It was cold, but if she snuggled in the hay it would keep her warm. Tears ran down her face as she obeyed her father. He entered the hayloft just behind her and demanded she undress. Patty did as he told her. Fear turned to anger, and disgust burned in her eyes.

Much later, Patty ran, like a frightened doe, back to the cabin. Blood streamed down her thighs, staining her dress and running between her toes.

"Someday, no man'll ever tell me what to do," Patty resolved to Sara and Joe, "not even Pa. I'll not grow up to be like my mas. Someway, somehow, I'm goin' to get off this horrible mountain, and I'm goin' to live even betta than th' town folk. You'ns can accept life here. I see how the kids in town live. I look at th' people in th' catalogs. There's more to life than this stinkin' mountain top."

Annabelle had seen Patty's pale white skin stained with blood, in the flickering light of the oil lamp, as she had stumbled back into the cabin. She now realized what her husband had wanted Patty for and knew that it was wrong for him to have sex with a child, a child who was his own daughter. She felt sadness for Patty, but could not step in to protect her. She knew very well that she could not control what he chose to do to the children.

In the children's room, Patty awakened from a fitful dream. Joe and Sara were not asleep yet. Patty crawled to their mat. "I knowed ya don't want to hear about my dreams, but I've been havin' them more an' more often. Something's goin' to happen," Patty warned. "Things are goin' to change. It started tonight."

Except for complaining earlier about her wish to leave the mountain, Patty did not share with Joe and Sara the horror, of what their father had just put her through. She filed the memory of what had happened in the darkest part of her mind. Only a sense of unpleasantness lingered. Forgetfulness: a safety valve that victims of abuse widely share.

"Go away, Patty," Joe said. "We don't want to hear it."

"Oh, ya take heed, goin' to be changes. Don't knowed why ya won't listen to me, I saw it in my dream an' I knowed it."

"Patty, ya sound like th' old, crazy woman when ya goin' on like that, an' ya betta stop it cause maybe Pa's goin' to send ya to live with her so ya goin' to be close to th' forest where all th' witches live. They live there so's they can get their bats, feathers, and frog's legs to make their magic potions." Joe laughed, making up the absurd tale, his defense to Patty's dream stories was to taunt her.

"There's no need to make fun of me 'cause I have dreams 'bout things goin' to happen," Patty complained and crawled back to her mat. "Ya don't understand, an' ya can't do nothin' to help if ya don't. Still, I'm glad ya and Sara are here. I'm scared."

Patty awoke often during the night, suffering with the pain her father had caused.

The next morning she relaxed a little upon learning that her father had left again. Facing him after her dreadful experience at his hands the night before would have been too much for her. The encounter only served to strengthen her resolve to leave the mountain one day. She was much too young to do anything about her lot in life just yet. She would endure until she reached the age when she could finally leave the mountain, never to return.

*13*

ORMAN HAD TOLD ALL HE COULD RECALL ABOUT
the couple he sent to George Cunningham to
adopt a child. Then it registered in his mind what
had been nagging at him while he read the story in
the newspaper. In the recent kidnapping, the boy
said his kidnapper talked funny. It jarred a memory
of an overheard conversation that was filed as
unimportant in the cobwebs of his mind.

"I just remembered something from an interview
with Cunningham. I was waiting to see him when I
heard an argument down the hall. The voice was
speaking in brogue, like people who live in the out-
back. I remember hearing the man say, 'I'm wantin'
bigger money for th' kids I bring. If ya don't I'm
goin' to call Lloyd an' work for him from now on.'
Another voice, George's I think, said, 'Get the hell
out of here, Aubry. This is neither the time nor the
place to discuss the matter.'"

"Didn't you think that conversation was
bizarre?" Hal asked.

"Yes," Norman hung his head.

"Now we're getting somewhere," Cliff said. "The voice as you describe it is so distinct we have a good chance of identifying it when the opportunity presents itself. Go on back to your motel now. We'll be in touch."

"If you remember anything more, call immediately and let us know," Hal said.

The Wrights left.

"Could the man named Lloyd in Norman's remembered conversation be Steven Lloyd, owner of B A Parent Adoption Agency?" Cliff asked.

"Why're you making that connection?" Hal was surprised.

"I've had conversations with Judy Grear who works at that agency and she has reason to suspect that Steven Lloyd is involved in illegal dealings for profit." Cliff leafed through his note pad that he kept in his breast pocket, and found notes on the subject. "She suspects he deals with disappointed applicants after they are officially turned down by the agency."

"Not very careful about covering his tracks."

"He's not worried about Judy talking. She doesn't have proof, yet. And I sure as hell haven't found anything on him."

"Keep on it. Sounds like you're on to something," Hal said.

"Talk to you later, Hal. I got to go. It's important I talk to the Yosts right away. I'll make arrangements to fly to Los Angeles," Cliff said.

"Get to it," Hal slapped Cliff on the back. "Keep me posted."

Cliff sat in the back-row window seat of a 727 jet. His mind kept returning to Tuesday. "I like her eyes," he said to himself and grinned, "but I don't like her boyfriend for some reason, and I'm a good judge of . . ." He dozed off.

"We are now making our descent to the Los Angeles International Airport." He jerked awake at the announcement. "The captain has turned on the fasten-your-seat-belt light. Please remain in your seats until the aircraft has come to a complete stop at the gate."

Cliff left the plane, found the car rental booth, and rented a car. Afterward, he located a pay phone and called Phil Yost's employer.

"Good afternoon," a female voice answered. "Mr. Kendrick's office."

"Hello. I'm Cliff Moran. May I speak to Mr. Kendrick?"

Just a little while later, in an upper-middle-class neighborhood, Cliff sat in front of the house where Phil Yost and his wife lived. The child the Yosts had bought would be about four years old. He saw a little girl and little boy playing in a sandbox; they looked about a year or maybe even two years old. As he watched, a young girl came running from the house, crying. She was about four and probably was the child the Yosts had bought in Wheeling.

"Where did the two toddlers come from?" he said out loud in surprise. "The couple can't have children of their own. Could they be the neighbor's children? They appear to be the same age. Maybe they're twins."

A woman came out shortly thereafter and sternly slapped the girl, sending her back into the house. She roughly yanked each toddler by the arm and dragged the frightened youngsters into the house, scolding them all the way. Their cries rang in Cliff's ears until the door was slammed shut. The woman matched the description the Wrights had given of the woman whom they had referred to the clinic.

At the station Cliff found the detective whom he had talked with on the phone earlier that day.

"Hi, Sergeant Moran. I'm Sergeant Detective John Martin. Just call me John.

"Well, John, I just saw the children outside the Yosts house. There are three children there. By the way, call me Cliff."

"Sure, Cliff, let's get things rolling."

"We need to identify the two children I saw with the girl. I have photographs and data on the missing children reported in the three-four-and five-year age group. I didn't know they had the younger children. They got the girl illegally, so we'll assume that's how they got the other two," Cliff said.

"How fast can you get data on the one- and two-year-olds?" John asked."

"This phone okay?"

"Be my guest."

Cliff dialed Hal's number.

"Lieutenant Brooks speaking."

"Hal, I need facts on the one- and two-year-old missing children. I found the Yosts, and besides the girl we already knew about, they have two other children, a boy and a girl. The two children appear to be twins. They look to be between one and two years of age."

"As good as done. I'll fax the information to you."

Forensic experts used photographs of children that were taken before their abduction and created a likeness of what they would look like as time went on. The photos were updated each year.

# 14

THE BUILDING WAS EERIE WITH THE ABSENCE OF people. There was no constant clicking sound of typewriters, no voices, or footsteps in the halls. Tuesday was anxious to get out of the building; she hated to be the only person left on the floor that was occupied by the interior decorating offices. But with her work load, she had to work late occasionally to stay caught up. Cora had invited Tuesday to her house for dinner, as she often did when Bill was out of town on business. Tuesday planned to go straight to Cora's house from the office. She put her sketch book away and locked her desk.

Tuesday headed for the elevator, thinking about Jacob. *Cora will be surprised when I tell her that Jacob proposed marriage. I'm still not sure of my feelings for him. We have a great time together and he can be quite charming, but sometimes I don't like his disposition, especially his attitude about Cliff. He has no apparent reason to dislike him, though maybe it's simple jealousy. I guess I'll find out if I give it time. He was sweet when he proposed to me.* She shrugged it off. Time would tell.

As she neared the elevators, she saw that above the door one of the digits was lit up on the panel that indicated which floor the elevator was on. Four, five, six, the elevator moved up. She pushed the down button. She knew whoever was on the elevator was most likely someone who had business in the building; still she did not want to be in the hall if the elevator stopped on this floor. There were three other elevators and she kept pushing the button, hoping that one of the doors would open. But before that happened, the number ten light lit up. She stiffened. The tenth floor was hers.

The door opened. "Jacob!" She was relieved that it was not some night stalker. "What on earth are you doing here?" Her knees had grown weak from fright.

"I wanted to see you, and your car was in the parking lot. Have you had dinner yet?"

"No, but I've been invited to Cora's. I was just on my way over there."

"Tomorrow night then?"

"Sure, Jacob. Seven o'clock okay with you?" She could not see the anger that he fought; nor did she have a clue that he was an expert at concealing his feelings. What she saw were his good looks and charming smile.

"Seven's okay. Let me walk you to your car; you shouldn't be leaving the building alone this late."

Cora had dinner ready when Tuesday arrived. She had prepared lamb chops and salad and had cheesecake for desert, Tuesday's favorite. They talked while they had dinner and purposely included Linda in their conversation. Tuesday noticed that Linda answered to her own name, apparently no longer possessing the need to hold on to the name of Karen.

After dinner they played with Linda until it was her bedtime. When Tuesday put her to bed, she told her a bedtime story while Cora set up the card table. Tuesday made up a story about a little girl who had been taken from her parents and how life became good once again when she was finally returned to them. Linda fell asleep to the comforting sound of Tuesday's voice.

"I think Linda's adjusting very well to being back home after two years. We have a few ups and downs, but overall, things are great," Cora commented.

"She will forget her experience in time." Tuesday predicted. "You'll see."

"I know she will. I sense that she remembered Bill and me somewhere deep inside her mind, while she was with the Wrights. As each day goes by, she's more at home here."

"I prayed every day while she was gone that she would be found. I prayed that no harm would come to her. But I must admit that I was beginning to have a hard time believing she would ever be returned to you and Bill."

"I will never, not in a million years, be able to thank Cliff enough for finding her. I really believe that he went beyond the call of duty to find her. Not only her, but the other children he still searches for."

"He's nice, isn't he?," Tuesday responded. "I liked him right away. Jacob didn't like him, though, and I can't imagine why."

"I can. He looked jealous to me."

"He did say that he didn't like the way that Cliff looked at me." Tuesday laughed.

"I think that Cliff liked you and would have liked to get to know you better if you had not been with Jacob."

"Jacob and I have no commitment. I think that I would like to get to know Cliff."

"For heaven's sake, I've tried many times to get you to meet Cliff and all you would say was that you didn't want to be fixed up with anyone, that if you wanted to meet a man you were capable of finding one yourself."

"Yes, I did," Tuesday smiled, "but I didn't know that he was so handsome, or what an exceptionally nice man he is."

"Tuesday, you're hopeless, you're—"

The phone rang and interrupted Cora's insight into Tuesday's personality. It was Cliff.

"Come on over, I happen to have fresh coffee and a slice of cheesecake with your name on it."

As Cora hung up, she could barely keep the broad smile off her face. "Speak of the devil, that was Cliff. He just got back from a trip to Los Angeles. He's found three more children."

"Wonderful. And it will be nice to see him again," Tuesday remarked.

"Of the two, I vote for Cliff," Cora said with a knowing smile on her face.

"I didn't tell you that Jacob proposed to me. Did I?"

"Are you serious? After only three weeks! He actually proposed?"

"Yes, it was a surprise to me, but he was very sweet. I told him that I would not consider marriage now. I have no idea how I feel about him. I have mixed feelings."

"That must be Cliff," Cora guessed correctly when the doorbell rang. She hurried to let him in. "Come in, I'm sure you remember meeting Tuesday."

"I certainly do."

Cora left them to get the cake and coffee.

Cliff sat on the sofa next to Tuesday.

"It's nice to see you again, Cliff. Making any progress in the investigation?"

"Bit by bit," Cliff shrugged. "I found three more children in Los Angeles. I traced one back to the same people who sold Linda. I'm building a strong case against the doctor and lawyer I've suspected for some time now as being behind the kidnappings."

He's a good-hearted man, Tuesday realized. "You do a great deal for children who can't protect themselves."

"It's my job." Cliff shrugged.

Cora returned and placed a tray in front of Tuesday and Cliff. Quietly, she took a seat across from them. Cliff began telling Cora and Tuesday about the three children he had found in Los Angeles. "I was delighted to reunite the four-year-old, who had been taken from her home a year ago, with her parents. We can't trace the two younger children, a girl and boy who look like twins. There are no reports of missing children who match their description.

"It's a long shot, but I wanted you to look at some photographs of the couple. I really don't think they're involved in baby brokerage," he explained to Cora. "But I want to cover all bases."

Cora looked at the pictures. "No, I don't recognize them."

"I'm not surprised." Cliff returned the photos to his breast pocket.

"We haven't found the man who drove the black truck in Todd's kidnapping. When we do, I bet he'll be involved in these illegal adoptions," Cliff added.

"I hope you don't get upset when I say this, Tuesday. But, Cliff, have you seen Jacob's truck? It closely fits the description of the truck you're looking for."

"No, I haven't." He looked at Tuesday, and she wore a frown on her usually happy face.

"Cora, it's not the same truck. I can't believe that Jacob would kidnap a child."

"I'm sorry, Tuesday. If it's not his truck what's the harm? Suppose it is him?"

"Where does he live, Tuesday?" Cliff asked.

"I don't have an exact address." Tuesday shrugged. "But when he asked me to have dinner at his apartment, he said that he lived in Wheeling—across town from me."

"I can find his license number and address through a name check at the DMV. I'll check it against the number a witness remembered at the scene. He only remembered the first three numbers. If the trucks are identical and if the first three numbers are the same, it would be too much of a coincidence. I would have to take him in for questioning. And he would become a prime suspect."

Cliff hurried back to the office with the information he had on Jacob and his truck.

"Hal, I'm glad that you're still here," he said as he rushed into Hal's office. "I just found out that Jacob McCallister drives a black truck with a red '4 x 4' on the side, and it has red reflector lights on the mud flaps. I think I've got something this time. It's unfortunate for Tuesday if Jacob is the man who kidnapped the boy. I don't want to see her hurt, but I have a hunch that Jacob just might be the one. I don't like or trust the too handsome, roughly polished man."

"Is that the man who's been seeing Cora's friend?" Hal asked.

"Yeah, he's the one. If he's our man, it explains why he was uncomfortable when I stopped in to speak to Cora about the kidnappings."

"Let's check it out." Hal got the file on Todd's case and put Jacob's name in the computer for his license data. When the information came up, the first three digits in the license number registered to Jacob were not even close to the ones that the witness had reported.

"Look at this," Cliff pointed at the screen.

"McCallister's address, General Delivery, Winding Ridge, West Virginia. He told Tuesday he lived in Wheeling just across town from her. I would think that he was telling the truth about that; she said that he invited her to dinner. He couldn't do that if he didn't actually have an apartment in Wheeling."

"Maybe this is not the same Jacob McCallister." Hal pointed at the computer "Or he could have moved to the city recently and hasn't changed his address with the DMV. We'll need to get his license number from his truck to make sure."

"I'll get Tuesday's address from Cora," Cliff said. "I'll call her now. She'll give me an idea of when to send a patrol car to watch for him."

"We need to get a picture of Jacob, too," Hal said. "We'll show it to Todd. Have the officer take a camera. It's worth a try."

*A*FTER SCHOOL, PATTY WALKED UP THE MOUNTAIN alone while Joe and Sara lingered at the cave waiting to walk home with her. They would be questioned if they were not together when they arrived at the cabin.

Patty stopped and sat on a rock, her thoughts consumed with the dream she'd had the night before. In her dream she saw Tammie Sue and Jimmie Bob playing in a nice house with a sweet-looking woman. The dream frightened her as her dreams invariably did. They made her feel different somehow. The dream also made her miss the twins. She stood and began walking.

"Hey, Patty, wait up."

Patty turned and saw Tommy Lee Hillberry hurrying to catch up with her.

"What ya wantin', Tommy Lee? Don't want to talk to you."

They came within sight of the cave and Patty could see Joe and Sara waiting for her. "Tommy Lee, ya had betta get out of here cause Joe's goin' to be mad if he sees ya talkin' to me."

Tommy Lee saw Sara and Joe. He acted brave around Patty, but he made a habit of taunting Joe without getting too close. Joe was much bigger and more powerful than Tommy Lee was, and Joe was a lot meaner, too.

"Just remember what I tol' ya. Ya betta tell your pa, he's goin' to be in trouble if he don't stop sellin' his own flesh and blood." Tommy Lee walked past Patty and took the path that led to his cabin. The path branched off a few yards below where Joe and Sara waited.

"What's Tommy Lee a'wantin'?" Joe asked Patty.

"He's jus' stirrin' up trouble, just like his pa. Ain't nothin'."

"I want ya to stay away from 'im. Ya understand?" Joe demanded. "He's sweet on ya an' just a'wantin' to talk to ya an' don't knowed how."

"I dreamed about Tammie Sue and Jimmie Bob again last night," Patty changed the subject as she walked closer to Joe and Sara. "I think they're in a different place from where they was 'fore, when they had a big house an' was always playin' in a sandbox with a bigger girl."

"Patty, stop that nonsense," Joe said. "Ya can't knowed anythin' from your stupid dreams."

"Ya knowed she can. She dreams somethin' an' it happens, ya knowed that," Sara said.

They walked toward home, not daring to be late. "There's pa's truck. He's home from his trip," Joe said.

"Ya look like ya seen a ghost, Patty," Sara whispered as the three scrambled into the kitchen where their pa sat at his meal.

"Get them noisy kids out of here." Jeb glared at Annabelle.

"Ya youngin's can eat after ya finish your chores." Annabelle let them know they weren't welcome to eat with their pa. "Hurry and get your work done. I knowed you're hungry. Ya ain't ate since noon."

As hungry as they were, the children tended to their chores without complaint. Sara and Patty carried wood into the cabin, and Joe chopped it, swinging his powerful arms high in the air and bringing the axe down on the logs with skillful blows. Sara stepped inside with a load of wood and her father told her to stay home from school the next day to help Aunt Aggie. Now Patty would get her chance, she thought. She would get Joe in the cave with her. He would not need much coaxing into spending the time with her. Patty was sure it was Sara, not Joe, who was afraid of her because of her dreams. Joe was not tolerant about what he considered her silly, girlish dreams, at least that was what he portrayed as the way he felt. Living with Patty, hearing about her dreams, and seeing them happen was astounding.

When Jeb had finished his dinner and stood up, a cat, enticed by the leftover food, jumped up on the table and earnestly lapped up the scraps. Jeb caught sight of the cat out of the corner of his eye, just as he was turning his back, and reaching out with his powerful arm, viciously threw the cat across the room. It landed on its feet and scrambled toward the door, terrified of the man.

"Can't you women keep the damn cats out of this place? I'm not going to put up with this mess, or the damn cats taking over."

Annabelle looked at him with fire in her eyes. "How ya expect a body to clean this place up with all th' people crowded in it?"

He slapped her. "Do as I say, woman, and don't talk back. Let this be the last time I have to tell you. You're getting to be a little uppity lately, and I don't want to hear it! A couple of days locked in the cellar might do you a world of good. Think about that the next time you feel like talking back to me."

Using foul language the women had never heard,

he barged out the back door and slammed it, tripping over the cat he had just thrown off the table.

Annabelle watched him through the cabin window. Can't please Jeb a'tall no more, she thought. Ain't ever seen 'im so edgy. I just open my mouth, an' no matter what comes out, it makes 'im mad. She turned from the window and saw that the cat had slithered back inside and was on the table again.

Grabbing the mangy cat by the scruff of its neck, she threw it out the door. "Can't figure how ya vermin get in th' cabin all th' time." She was going to have to find a way to keep them out. There was no other way but to do as her husband wanted.

"Rose, ya and Daisy get some cleanin' done," Annabelle ordered, taking her pent-up anger out on them. She guessed they would not be able to find their way around the cabin if she were not there to tell them. At the same time, she wondered why her husband was so interested in having the cabin clean. He had never been concerned about it before.

Hours before dawn, the women were awakened by his resounding voice. "Get up and do your chores. I want to rest and I don't want to listen to your snoring. And I want the animals out of the cabin."

He was dumbfounded that the cats slept by the potbelly stove after his direct orders earlier to the contrary. He had gone into town when he had stormed out earlier and had had a little too much to drink with Rosily. She had been insistent that he take her to the city to live. He was too out of it to deal with the women and cats now. All he wanted to do was to climb into the warm bed and sleep it off.

At the sound of his slurred voice the women scurried out from under their warm quilts and got dressed. It was still dark. He fell onto the bed and was soon sound asleep.

Later, Patty and Joe left for school and Sara

walked up the mountain, alone, to take care of Aunt Aggie's chores. Sara could see Aunt Aggie's cabin through the trees and ran the rest of the way, anxious to get the work done.

"There ya are youngin, thought ya neve' goin' to come back to help ya old aunt, so I did," Aggie gushed over the girl. "I sure missed ya visitin' with me, so I did."

"Ya knowed I can't come till Pa says." Sara put the water on to heat and they rocked to and fro in their chairs and talked. Sara talked about her mothers and how everyone was doing, and Aggie told Sara a few stories that Sara always loved to hear.

"Don't ya be a big baby. Take me in th' cave. Ya goin' to like me betta'n Sara."

Joe stopped walking and stared at Patty. "I want to do it to ya. It's in'm future plans anyways," he said.

"What ya mean by that?" Patty asked.

"Never mind. I'm goin' to take ya to th' cave."

"Okay, let's go. Its goin' to be warmer in th' cave."

Sara finished the chores for Aunt Aggie and made her way back to the cabin. Since she and Joe had started having sex, this was the first time they had been apart. Aunt Aggie's cabin was the only place Sara went without Joe. When she came in sight of the cabin, she ran. When she reached the back door, she rushed in, slamming it behind her.

Her father sat at the table, eating. "What the hell you running from, girl? Did you do everything Aunt Aggie needed doing?"

"Yeah, Pa. I did everythin' she wanted me to do."

Sara hurried into the bedroom to look for Joe. He was not there; it was past time for him to be home from school. She threw herself on her mat.

Annabelle came into the room. "What ya doin' lyin' on your mat? Ya got chores to do," she scolded. "Joe an' Patty goin' to get a good thrashin'. They're late." Annabelle only knew they were late because it was getting dark. The children usually were home from school this time of the year by the time the sun began to disappear behind the top of mountain that towered above them.

She left the room and Sara followed.

"I'm going to be gone for a longer time this trip," her husband said. "I have something special to do; you'll have to make do with what you have. I'll bring food when I come back. I don't know how long, only that it could be longer than usual. I can't be running back and forth when I have business to take care of."

Annabelle knew that they would go hungry for sure. They barely got by the way it was; their food supply dropped dangerously low between her husband's visits. Perhaps they would have no food left at all by the time he decided to come back.

She could barely hold her tongue.

"I don't want to hear any complaining about it. And you can wipe the defiant look off your face. I have business to take care of. It may or may not take longer than usual. I don't have it worked out just yet. I want this cabin to look presentable when I come back and I don't want to hear excuses as to why you can't do it. It's not as if you have something to do or somewhere to go."

This made Annabelle furious. She and the others worked from dawn to dark the way it was, and it was impossible to keep the crowded cabin in any semblance of order, but she did not dare to voice her opinion after the dark anger she had aroused in Jeb earlier.

ORA SAT DOWN AT THE TABLE IN TUESDAY'S kitchen with a groan. She watched Tuesday's face closely, wanting to study her reaction to the latest news. "I guess you'll be glad to know that Cliff compared the license number registered in the name of Jacob McCallister to the numbers that the witness memorized. The numbers were not the same, but he could have used a stolen license plate and removed it after he had committed his crime. Of course, that's speculation; they can't prove that the license plate was stolen."

"I'm glad it didn't turn out to be Jacob. I like him. I would not like to think that I was such a poor judge of character, either.

"Todd, the boy who was kidnapped, was shown a photo of Jacob along with photos of five other men." Cora said. "He only cried and said he couldn't remember what the man looked like. He was too scared. All he remembered was that the man had whiskers and a floppy hat. He couldn't see his eyes or his face clearly."

"That doesn't sound like Jacob," Tuesday said relieved.

"Come on, Tuesday, any man can have whiskers and wear a floppy hat."

"So?"

"Tuesday, this doesn't eliminate Jacob as a suspect! When they entered his name in the computer, his address came up as an out-of-town address. Either someone has the same name or Jacob could have lied."

"I think that's strange. If Jacob lives in Wheeling as he said, why wouldn't that information come up on the computer?"

"Cliff said he could have recently moved here and not changed his address. That's not unusual. Licenses expire every four years, and that's the most convenient time to make changes. Many people wait until it's time to renew them before changing their address. The out-of-town address could very well be his old one, and in that case Jacob did not lie."

"I would bet that's the case." Tuesday was relieved; she had not made a decision to stop seeing him.

"Maybe you shouldn't see him until we know for sure he's not involved," Cora suggested.

"Cora, I've been out with him several times. I really don't believe he's involved. He's not the kind of man who would be involved in kidnapping a child. I just don't believe it, and I really believe I should give him the benefit of the doubt. Anyway, I'm not a child, he's not going to kidnap me."

"Fine, you're a big girl. You know him better than I."

"It's fun going out with him. We're becoming good friends. That's all I want right now. Just someone to be with, whom I enjoy, and someone who enjoys being with me."

"By the way, Cliff is having your house watched so they can get Jacob's license number. He wants to verify what name is registered to his license number. The address they got by starting with his name could be of some other man with the same name, or Jacob could be using an alias."

"I'm having dinner with Jacob tonight. Cliff will get the license number tonight, then. My bet is that Jacob's not the man they're looking for."

"I hope you're right. Look at the time. We need to go. You're probably wanting to get ready for your date, anyway. Thanks for the hot chocolate."

Cora put Linda in her wrap. "Call me tomorrow, Tuesday, and I'll let you know if I hear from Cliff."

"Okay, Cora, I will. Tell Bill hello for me. Good night, Linda." Tuesday gave her a hug.

After they left, Tuesday hurried to get ready for her date with Jacob. She had considered canceling the date before Cora had told her that the truck in the kidnapping had not been tied to Jacob at this point. Now she felt safe again, but there were questions that needed to be answered.

"Something on your mind? You're unusually quiet."

They were enjoying after-dinner drinks. Tuesday had been thinking about her conversation with Cora and debating on whether or not to ask Jacob how long he had lived in Wheeling. She had considered waiting until she heard from Cora about the cross check on Jacob's license, but decided to go ahead.

"I was wondering how long you've lived in Wheeling. Were you raised here or just relocated here for your job?"

"No, I wasn't raised in Wheeling. I have a second house here because of my job. I like the convenience of having a place when I'm in town. I stay with my aunt when I travel to northern West Virginia for the company."

Tuesday was relieved. If he had said he had lived in Wheeling all of his life, she would have had to consider that he had probably lied to her all along about everything. She did not want to mention Winding Ridge. She knew that if she revealed that he was being investigated, it would only lead to many questions. He would want to know how she got that information. And if, by some remote chance, he was actually the man who had driven the truck, she did not want to alert him to the fact that he was being investigated.

The next morning, Cora called Tuesday at her office.

"Cliff got Jacob's license number last night," Cora said. "The address and license number Cliff got for Jacob turned out to be the same address and number they already had, which did not match the one the witness remembered. That probably means he recently moved to Wheeling and hasn't taken the time to change his address on his vehicle registration."

"Good. He didn't lie, Cora. Yesterday evening I asked him how long he's lived in Wheeling and he told me that he has a second house here. He'd rather not stay in a motel when he's in town on business. I really didn't believe that Jacob would turn out to be the man who drove the truck in the kidnapping."

"Cliff said that Jacob was not off the hook yet, and he hasn't been dropped as a suspect. The truck used in the kidnapping fits so closely to Jacob's that Cliff won't discount it as the one used in the crime. Remember, the kidnapper could have used a stolen license plate. Also, the boy did not confirm that Jacob was not the man who kidnapped him."

"Cora, the boy did not say any of the six men in the photos was or was not the man. I feel that I should give Jacob the benefit of the doubt, and I'm having dinner at his apartment one evening soon. We have agreed to tell each other about our lives, and I'll bet that he's led an interesting one. I can't say why, but I'm curious about him and his past. He has such a great sense of humor, but sometimes I sense something . . . I just can't put my finger on it."

"What do you mean? I don't understand. If you have suspicions about him, for heaven's sake, don't date him."

"No. Not suspicions. He's just so complex, he's hard to figure out. Maybe he has a dark side." She liked to tease Cora and get a reaction from her. Cora was quick-tempered.

# 17

ROSE HAD BECOME UNCOMFORTABLE AND clumsy as her time grew nearer; the child she carried would be born soon. "I'm goin' to burst if I don't have this baby soon," Rose complained. "Goin' to have to wrap a quilt 'round me, cause I'm too big for my clothes."

"I'm goin' to have another baby, too," Daisy bragged. "It's been past two moons since I'd got my time."

"He'll just sell it," Annabelle warned. "Sold some of mine at two months. Don't knowed why he kept th' twins so long 'fore he sold 'em."

"I knowed," Daisy bragged. "It's cause he loves me betta than you. He wanted to keep 'em, he did. But he needed th' money to feed all of you'ns an' buy your clothes." Tears filled Daisy's eyes at the mention of her twins.

"Don't be stupid, Daisy," Annabelle said. "He don't spend very much of that money on us. Ya knowed right well he don't buy us any clothes. Don't spend much of that money on food neither. If he did, we wouldn't be cold an' hungry all th' time. Ya don't knowed anythin' 'bout money or how much things cost. He uses th' money to have a good time. He ain't workin' when he's gone. Don't ya notice th' fancy clothes he's warin' when he comes home?"

In the children's room, Sara and Joe lay on their mats. "I didn't like it knowin' ya was with Patty today. What was ya an' her doin'? She was wantin' ya to take her to th' cave, I knowed it."

"Sara, I'm gettin' tired of hearin' ya complainin' 'bout Patty an' what I'm doin' with her. I'm goin' to do what I'm wantin' an' I don't want to hear no more 'bout it from ya. It's time ya stopped questionin' me 'bout what I do. Ya need to learn not to talk back to th' menfolk."

As Joe got older he became more like their father, developing into the typical mountain man. More and more each day, Sara and Joe lost their childhood closeness. Using his father as his role model, Joe had learned to treat women as inferior people.

"Come here, Sara," Joe said.

In the other room, the women heard them. Annabelle worried about allowing brother and sister to have sex, but she could do nothing about it since their father approved of it. It made her angry to think about the reason that he allowed it. *More babies to sell, that's why he don't care,* she thought. *Th' children do seem happier, though. Lord knowed they don't have much to be happy 'bout.*

Rose's cry of pain rang in Annabelle's ear, startling Annabelle and interrupting her thoughts.

"What's th' matter, Rose?" Annabelle turned toward Rose, who lay between Daisy and herself in the four-poster bed. "Is it th' baby?"

"I've been a'havin' pains all evenin'," Rose panted. "They're gettin' closer an' stronger now. I guess I'll be able to see my feet again. Was beginnin' to think wasn't never goin' to get shed of this baby."

"Get up, Daisy," Annabelle ordered. "Boil some water an' get th' baby things out of th' old trunk in th' corner. Go on. Step an' fetch it!"

Daisy got up and pulled her sweater on and groggily stumbled out back to pump the water, complaining as she went. "I knowed where th' baby clothes are. I had his babies, too."

Joe and Sara were told to go and bring Aunt Aggie to care for Rose. No one would get much sleep that night. The children reluctantly got up and began to dress. It would take them half an hour to get there, but an hour or more to get back. Aunt Aggie could not climb down the steep grade of the shortcut that Joe and Sara would take to go for her. Joe and Sara went to visit Aunt Aggie as often as they could get away with it. She told them stories that were partly true and partly made up. She told the stories in great detail, changing her facial expressions and voice to fit the tale. She loved to get a reaction from the children when she told her stories, especially one of fear.

When the children returned with Aunt Aggie, Rose's pains were just one minute apart. She twisted and turned in her pain. Even in the cool cabin air, she was sweating. Her hair and gown were wet clear through. Aunt Aggie tossed her coat aside and hurried to Rose.

"Her water broke just a few minutes ago. It shouldn't be long now," Annabelle predicted, hovering over Rose.

Aggie saw that Rose fought the pain instead of helping the baby along. "Don't push yet, Rose," Aggie said. "Ya fightin' it, so ya are."

Aggie instinctively knew how to deliver a child, although she had never given birth herself. Aggie began massaging Rose's stomach and pushing down with each contraction. Aggie's massaging quieted Rose, and she did as Aunt Aggie bid her to do, calmer with the older woman by her side. Rose was in trouble; her water had broken. If the child did not soon follow, Rose would have a dry and painful delivery. Eventually, Rose screamed with each pain. Aggie checked and saw that Rose bled much too heavily. There was nothing she could do until the baby started moving down the birth canal except to push down on Rose's stomach.

Much later, and after much blood loss, the top of the baby's head appeared. Suffering a dry delivery and being so small, Rose had torn as her body pushed the baby out. Soon after the baby's head slipped out, revealing a tiny face topped with dark hair, the shoulders appeared. Aggie ordered Rose to push as she felt each contraction. After a few minutes had passed, the baby suddenly popped out into Aggie's capable hands. The baby was a girl.

Annabelle took the baby from Aggie and began to clean the blood from her. Aggie attended to the afterbirth. Rose was so tired and weak she could barely speak. She had lost a great deal of blood and, at best, would have to spend a few weeks in bed to regain her strength. Annabelle was afraid Rose would not even live, though, to see the next day. Aggie packed old rags between Rose's legs, hoping to stop the blood flow. They could not call a doctor to stitch her up. They could only wait, hope, and pray that the bleeding would stop before it was too late.

After Rose and the baby had been cleaned up and were both sleeping peacefully, the women gathered around the rough wooden table.

"I'm tired, bein' up most all night an' all," Annabelle complained. "Jeb's goin' to be gone for a long time so's I'm not goin' to worry about th' cabin now. Goin' to lay down for a'while an' rest my weary bones. Don't knowed why he's a'care'n 'bout th' cabin no how, he neve' did 'fore. You'ns can fix yourself somethin' to eat."

Aunt Aggie sipped her coffee. "Maybe he's goin' to bring a new woman to live here," Aggie taunted. Her nephew had mentioned in their last conversation about taking a new wife.

"Don't be so hateful Aggie," Annabelle spat.

"Joe, ya an' Sara walk Aunt Aggie back to her cabin and get straight back here and do your chores. Don't be late to go to school now," Annabelle ordered.

Annabelle worked in the kitchen preparing food; first she made one mess, then cleaned up another. As if stalking its prey, the cat jumped onto the table, once again tempted by the food Annabelle had put there. She grabbed the cat by its tail and threw it viciously out the back door. She looked up, as the cat miraculously landed on its feet, and saw Joe walking toward the back door. She could not believe her eyes. The old cow followed leisurely behind him.

"Thank th' Lord." Annabelle said to no one in particular. "Thank th' Lord. We're goin' to have milk now." Her mouth watered as she waited on the back porch for Joe. While she waited the cat crept back into the cabin, unnoticed by Annabelle.

"Look, I found th' old cow," Joe proudly informed Annabelle.

They entered the cabin just in time to catch the cat on the table, busily eating Annabelle's preparations for breakfast. Annabelle grabbed the cat and threw it out into the backyard, feeling defeated. "I just don't knowed what we're goin' to do 'bout th' cats an' th' dogs comin' in th' cabin. Your pa just don't like it no how. Don't knowed how to keep them varmints out, though. They make him powerful mad creepin' in th' cabin, they do."

# *18*

*H*IS SHOPPING TRIP COMPLETED, JACOB PUT THE food away. He had added a new item to Tuesday's list, just to ensure everything would go as planned. He put the sleeping pills on the top shelf behind his cans of food.

"Old George is good for something," Jacob bragged to himself as he worked. "He's afraid not to do what I tell him. He made sure Doc Johnson got me the strongest sleeping pills there were."

Jacob kept a large supply of food in his apartment. During his childhood, he had known hunger much of the time. Although he seldom ate in, he always made sure there was plenty to eat in his kitchen.

He had stopped at several thrift stores and found a few old picture frames offered for sale. The frames still contained old photos, and the old photos were what he had really wanted. He hung a few of them on the wall. The few that still had the support on the back, he stood on various side tables around the apartment.

"There, Tuesday, meet my dead family that I miss so much," He said out loud as he practiced telling

Tuesday about his pain of having no family left. Only their pictures remained to remind him of his loneliness.

He had finalized his plan, which meant getting her to set a date for their dinner at his apartment. "It's time. She wants and desires me. I'll teach her her place in life."

Cliff and Hal discussed their next move in the investigation into the kidnapping of Todd.

"All we know now is that McCallister moved here from Winding Ridge. Cora said that he has a house here in town. I'll check with the utility companies for the address. Even though his license plate number is not the same as the one the witness gave, he could still be our man. I believe that he had a stolen plate on the truck. He bears watching."

"I agree, Cliff. I want to bring him in for questioning, but let's see if we can get something more on him before we do that."

"Too bad Todd couldn't identify his kidnapper from the photos," Cliff said.

"Tough luck," Hal agreed.

"I think it's a good idea to have something on McCallister before we bring him in, if we don't wait too long. If he's the one we're looking for, Tuesday just might be asking for trouble spending time with him. There's just something about him I can't put a finger on. I don't believe even Tuesday completely trusts him. Cora says that Tuesday doesn't believe he's involved in the kidnapping, but I'm worried that her friendship with him can only lead to trouble."

"Yes, but we can't arrest him just because his truck happens to fit the description of a truck involved in a crime. There must be hundreds of trucks that meet the description. If it's him, he'll make a mistake. We just have to keep our eyes open."

"Cliff asked me if you and Jacob were serious. I took the liberty of telling him that you were just friends," Cora said as she sat a cup of coffee in front of Tuesday.

"That's true enough, but why would he be interested in my relationship with Jacob?"

"He wants to ask you out for dinner and didn't want to make a fool of himself by asking you out if you were committed to Jacob." Cora poured herself a cup of coffee. "I told him that you thought he was a nice person and would like to get to know him."

"He is nice, not to mention handsome," Tuesday commented.

"He asked me to ask if it's okay for me to give him your phone number. Is it?"

"Sure."

"You are not committed to Jacob, so there's no reason that you can't go to dinner with Cliff. Frankly, I like him better than I do Jacob."

"Okay already, you've convinced me. I said give Cliff my number. Anyway, your judgment of Jacob could be clouded by the investigation," Tuesday observed.

"Possibly. I admit that I don't know him very well."

*A*FTER A FEW MOMENTS, THE ROCK SHE HAD thrown hit the water below. A splash disturbed the ever-foaming water that rushed down the mountain. Patty sat on the edge of a cliff about a mile from the cabin. It was her place to be alone and think. She had dreamed the night before about Tammie Sue and Jimmie Bob and longed to tell an adult about the dream. Joe and Sara would not listen. The twins were with a different woman in the dream; she was good to them and they appeared to be contented now. Patty jumped up and ran toward the cabin. She hurried into the cabin and saw that Annabelle was the only one in the kitchen.

"Girl," Annabelle shouted, "what do ya think ya runnin' from, th' devil?"

"I saw th' twins again in my dream last night. I'm just wantin' to tell ya they're with a nice woman now."

"Ya crazy girl, ya knowed I don't want to hear your crazy stories," Annabelle scolded, at odds about how to handle the girl. "Get outta here."

Patty stumbled out the back door, her posture slumped with rejection. "Wish someone would listen and help me understand," she shouted back at Annabelle. "My dreams are goin' to happen. I need to knowed what to do 'bout 'em."

*I don't knowed what to do about that girl,* Annabelle worried. *Goin' to have to do somethin'. She's goin' to spook everyone till they won't have nothin' to do with her. She has dreams 'bout Daisy's first set of twins Jeb sold a couple years ago, now it's the other ones Jeb'd just sold. Now she's always talkin' 'bout th' dreams of trouble comin'.*

Annabelle and Daisy worked, cold-packing a deer that Joe had killed. It was a time-consuming process. The cold-packer held seven jars and they took eight hours of boiling on the woodburner, requiring constant attention. The time was necessary to fully cook the meat. Wood had to be added to keep the fire going and water added to the pot as it boiled away.

After boiling eight hours, the jars were allowed to cool. As they did, they sealed with a loud pop. Before each trip to the cellar, Annabelle pressed down on the lids and knew that the ones that did not make a clicking sound at her touch were sealed. She carried those to the cellar house. The women sugar-cured their meat and hung it in the cellar house when they could. They liked the meat sugar-cured, and it was less time consuming, but their salt supply had run out and they were forced to cold-pack.

The cellar house was directly to the right of the back porch, only thirty feet from the back door. They used it for storing their food supply and it was where they hung the meat for curing. The huge cavern was dug back under a hill where the food would not freeze in the winter. The temperature also stayed cool during spring and summer. The only part of the cellar house visible, year around, was the door. A great bank of snow covered the huge mound. In the spring and summer it was covered entirely by brushy growth and wild flowers. Inside, the storage shelter was a haven for rats.

Patty sat brooding near the outhouse, and Joe climbed up the bank to join her. "You're supposed to be doin' your chores, ain't ya?

"I told Annabelle 'bout th' twins bein' with a nice lady. She told me to go on an' do m'chores. No one want's to listen to me. No one cares 'bout me."

"I care 'bout you. Just don't want to hear 'bout your dreams, ya knowed that. Ya wantin' to go to th' hayloft with me?"

"Yeah," Patty answered, "but we're goin' to get in trouble. I'm supposed to be cleanin' out th' barn. You're supposed to be choppin' wood since ya finished th' milkin'."

"We won't get in trouble. Pa ain't here, an' our mas ain't goin' to pay any attention," Joe coaxed.

"Okay, go on an' take th' milk in, an' I'll meet ya in th' loft."

Joe hurried to the cabin with the bucket of milk. He had just finished the evening milking. No one was in the kitchen, so he put the milk on the table and ran back to the loft where Patty waited.

Annabelle came into the kitchen and let out a squeal loud enough to be heard a mile away. Two cats were standing with their paws clinging to the rim of the milk bucket. The cats were helping themselves, lapping up the milk as fast as they could. Annabelle grabbed the cats by the scruff of the neck and shook them vigorously.

"I just don't knowed what to do with ya cats," she yelled, dangling the cats close to her face, as if making sure that they heard what she said. "It's beyond

me how you'ns keep gettin' in th' cabin. Ya vermin
sneak in every time th' door opens an' closes. No
one ain't wantin' ya vermin in th' cabin. Want me to
shoot you, or ya goin' to stay out where ya belong?"
She threw the cats out and went back inside to
check the milk. Of course, she would not throw it
out; it was needed too badly.

Annabelle had no way of knowing just how
much time had passed since her husband had left.
She knew that many nights had passed; actually it
had been seven days. She remembered that it had
been shortly before Rose had her baby. *Jeb's goin' to
be happy 'bout th' baby an' th' money it'll bring him*, she
thought with antagonism.

Annabelle looked out the window just in time to
see Joe hurry into the barn, and suspected that Patty
waited in the loft for him. Annabelle did not like it;
Sara was jealous of Joe's attention to Patty and she
did not want to see Sara unhappy. Annabelle loved
Patty, but Sara was her daughter, and there was that
special bond one has for a daughter. Annabelle
sighed. *Ain't a thing I kin do 'bout it since Jeb ain't
carin' if they do it.* She went on with her work,
resigned to her fate.

Annabelle tried vainly to keep the cabin in some
semblance of order, but mud had been tracked in.
The pots that were used for canning were scattered
everywhere. The rough wooden table, where they
had cut the deer, was littered with scraps of meat
that dripped with blood. Muddy, wet clothes hung
from the spike nails and littered the floor where they
had fallen. There had been no time to do the wash.

"Daisy, come in here an' help me with th' cookin',"
Annabelle yelled. "Wish we had some taters for supper cause I'm in th' mood for taters, I am."

"Jeb's goin' to sell th' new baby," Daisy predicted.
"Maybe he'll let me keep this baby I'm goin' to

have. I'm goin' to ask him, an' maybe he'll let me keep it."

Annabelle was in no mood to listen to Daisy's foolish dreaming. She went about her work, just wanting to eat and get some rest.

Sheriff Ozzie Moats sat at his desk. There was never much going on in Winding Ridge, except a few brawls at the town bar or maybe a drunk making a nuisance of himself down on Main Street, which happened to be the only street in town. Since the early eighties, when his brother Aubry had left town soon after the mine explosion killed thirty-three of his fellow coal miners, Winding Ridge was minus one serious troublemaker. Ozzie constantly worried his black sheep brother would tarnish the good name of Moats, blissfully unaware that he was doing a pretty good job of tarnishing the name himself.

The problems in town that gave him the most headaches were the domestic ones. There were a few men who, after having too much moonshine, would go home and for some reason feel the need to beat their wives. After the man would pass out, the woman would call the sheriff, insisting that Moats put him in jail. Ozzie Moats could see no reason to put a man in jail after he had passed out and was of no further threat. The man would eventually sober up and go about his business.

"Sheriff," said Deputy Jess Willis as he came into the office, causing the sheriff to quickly sneak his *Playboy* magazine under the newspaper. Ozzie Moats mistakenly thought that no one knew he spent his time reading the sexy magazine, or that he got his kicks watching Rosily strut down the street in her high-heeled shoes with her sexy body straining against her tight sweater and short skirt. He did not bother to hide his disapproval that she, a town girl, was making time with a worthless mountain man.

"What are you doin' here, Jess? I told you to wash the patrol car." The patrol car was actually a Jeep. In bad weather, in the higher elevation, a car was not the best way to get around. Winter brought snowstorms to the mountain town that made them useless.

"I washed it. Don't take all day to wash one car. What you wantin' done now?" Deputy Willis asked the sheriff.

"Has Andy Hillberry been around makin' trouble today?" the sheriff asked.

"He's always makin' trouble. Keeps wantin' me to investigate his neighbor. I have to say, though, Sheriff, I think he's right. We should look into it. If the man's selling his children to city folks, it has to be stopped. One of these days a sheriff from the city's goin' to come here. When it's discovered what's goin' on, he'll want to know why you allow it."

The sheriff laughed. "City people ain't interested in my town. There's never been another officer of the law, except me, near Winding Ridge as far as I know. I don't give a damn what those no-good mountain folks are doin'. It don't concern me as long as it don't affect my town. Now go in the back and clean the cells—had a drunk upchuck in the back one."

"You just remember what I told you," Jess said. "I know you don't want to get involved with Andy Hillberry's complaints. You just wish the man would stay up on the mountain where he belonged, away from the town. You should remember the sheriff's job takes in the entire county."

"Yes, and if you want to keep your job you'd better get in the back and do as I say," the sheriff said as he stood and leaned his huge bulk over his desk. "I say what goes on here, and don't you forget it." The sheriff's meaty fist slammed down on the desk with a resounding blow.

Later, Jess Willis gathered the cleaning supplies. "Worthless sheriff," Willis mumbled. "I could do a better job. Stupid county sheriff thinks he's just in charge of the town. Who the hell does he think takes care of the county? Just too lazy to do anything except sit at his desk and read his trashy magazines."

"Better watch out, Willis," taunted the drunk who had thrown up in the cell. "The sheriff's goin' to hear you, and you're going to be out of a job for sure."

"Just shut your mouth, Harley. What's a drunk like you know anyhow?"

# 20

ANNABELLE AND DAISY BUSILY CUT, CHOPPED, and canned the wild game that Joe had shot on yet another hunting jaunt. Rose, still weak from the blood lost bringing her daughter into the world, rocked in a chair beside the potbelly stove. The kitchen looked like, well, just what it was. A slaughtered animal was scattered over the table and floor. Clumps of bloody meat lay on the table and were smeared on the floor. Trails of blood trickled away from the pieces where they had fallen.

Annabelle heard the sound of a motor in the distance. "Oh, no. It's Jeb comin' home." Annabelle scurried around, picking up scraps of meat from the table. "Daisy help pick up, don't just stand there. He don't knowed how much work an' stuff it takes to keep us in food."

"He ain't supposed to be back this soon." Daisy began picking up muddy sweaters and coats that had fallen from the nails where they had been carelessly hung.

He slammed the front door as he came in and tracked ugly puddles of wet, dirty snow across the floor, oblivious to the mess he left behind. When he got to the kitchen he stopped dead in his tracks. "What the hell! It looks like a slaughterhouse in here. Maybe you women would be more at home locked in the cellar house for a few days."

"Go on ahead," Annabelle said. "Maybe then we're goin' to get to rest."

He reached over and slapped her so hard she fell back against the woodburner and knocked a pot of boiling water to the floor. "Don't talk back to me woman," he yelled as the boiling water just missed her and splashed over the floor, anger flashing in his eyes. "I'm not going to lock you in the cellar house this time, but that doesn't mean that I won't," he threatened. "This is your last chance, Annabelle. I won't tolerate any more back talk from you."

His yelling woke the baby and she started crying, adding to the confusion. "Good," he said. "That's what I came for. I'm selling the baby," he said, and looked at Rose sternly, knowing that she would make a fuss. "I had hoped it would be born by now. This time I'm going to deliver it myself. I don't have time to run back and forth arranging for someone to come after it. There's too much business to attend to in town."

"Is it a boy or girl?" he asked, over Rose's loud, annoying sobs.

"It's a girl," Annabelle answered.

For him to deliver the baby to the clinic himself was dangerous. It was not smart for him to be seen taking a baby to the place where George Cunningham would consummate the deal. The fact that Cunningham had agreed to pay more for a child under a month old, added to the fact that funds were getting seriously low, clouded his normally good judgment.

"Sit down, Rose. You don't look well." He sat beside her and motioned for the other women to sit.

"I want all of you to listen to me. And if you don't obey, I promise you you'll be very sorry. Understand?" He waited for their heads to nod and continued. "I'm bringing a woman to the cabin. I'll be bringing her in the next few days. I want all of you to look presentable. You look like you haven't had a bath or combed your hair for a month. If you don't obey, I promise to lock you all in the cellar for a week. And," he looked pointedly at Annabelle, "you won't like the rats. Is that clear? Remember what I say if you know what's good for you." His reference to the rats was intended to take care of Annabelle's smart-aleck remark about the cellar being a place for needed rest.

Annabelle was shocked. Another woman to share the cabin! Why would he want to bring another woman to the already crowded cabin? But she had known all along that he could decide anytime to get another woman. Why not? He had three. She had heard rumors, when she and the others on occasion attended church, that he spent time with Rosily, a woman who had an undesirable reputation. Could she be the one? Nevertheless, Annabelle knew they had no choice in the matter when it came to what he wanted.

"Tomorrow I leave and take the baby with me. I'm going to sleep for a while. Get that noisy baby out of the bedroom."

Sobbing, Rose obeyed and then rejoined Annabelle and Daisy at the table.

"We've got to do what he's sayin' to do," Annabelle said. "Shet up, Rose, an' listen to me."

Rose could not stifle her sobs.

"I knowed you're unhappy to lose your baby," Annabelle continued, "but Jeb ain't goin' to like it if ya keep a'cryin'. While he's a'sleepin' we'll heat th' water and take a bath. If we don't do what he's sayin' he's goin' to lock us up. We don't want that to happen.

"Daisy, ya step an' fetch th' broom an' start th' sweepin'. I'm goin to clean th' mess we made can-nin'."

Daisy and Annabelle began their work and Rose nursed her baby. Annabelle was sorely disap-pointed. When he had told them to sit down, that he wanted to talk to them, she had thought that he was going to tell them stories about life off the mountain and pay attention to each of them like he sometimes did when he was in a good mood, certainly not that he was going to bring another woman to the cabin. Oh, she knew there was always a likelihood he would take another woman to give him more babies to sell. Yet she had deluded herself that it would not happen, in the already overcrowded cabin.

That night after the children had gone to bed, the women prepared their mats for sleep. The women's activity awakened him after his almost-all-day sleep. "Daisy," he bellowed, "get in the bed with me."

That was fine with Daisy. She abandoned her mat and climbed in beside her husband. She would show him that he did not need another woman. Annabelle turned out the oil lamps and lay on her mat next to Rose. They tried to sleep, knowing it would be impossible with the oh-so-vocal Daisy in his bed.

In the earliest morning hours, Annabelle prepared breakfast, and Daisy cleaned up after her. Daisy did not make much progress. For as quickly as Daisy cleaned, Annabelle made another mess as she cooked. Clothing that Patty and Sara had washed the evening before, while Jeb slept, was hung across a clothesline. The line was strung around the kitchen. The clothes only added to the disorder.

Jeb awoke hungry; he had slept most of the day and night. He came into the kitchen and stopped dead in his tracks. The kitchen looked even worse than it had the day before. "Are you women trying my patience?" he shouted. "I gave you all strict orders last night to get the place cleaned up or you'd be severely punished."

It did not matter that the women had nothing to work with. There was no storage space, no counter area to work on. It was too cold for the clothes to dry outside. Red-faced with unaccountable rage, he violently jerked the clothesline. The line fell across the table, pulling the clothes through the food Annabelle had prepared and put on the table. This new mess was unbelievable. Gravy and other foods stained the clothes as they were strung out across the table.

Jeb sat down on the bench. With a wide motion of his arm he swept everything that was in front of him onto the floor. Annabelle hurried and filled another plate with food. She could not believe that he had wasted the food, knowing they almost never had enough, or that he had made a bigger mess, considering he wanted the cabin neat. She knew she could not show her fury. He was in no mood to hear what she had to say or deal with her anger. She suppressed her feelings and put his food in front of him.

"When I come back this place better be presentable, no matter if you have to stay up night and day," he warned. "After I eat, I'm leaving. Have the baby ready."

Annabelle suppressed a wild giggle. It was absurd that he had made such a horrible mess, then so calmly demanded that the cabin be clean.

He drove along with the crying, hungry baby at his side. "Shut up," he shouted. The child cried louder; she needed her mother for nourishment. The women did not even know there were such things as baby bottles, let alone use them. To quiet the baby, he reached over and covered its face. She screamed louder. He drove faster. For a change, he had no control over the situation. Not only was the infant a nuisance, it was stupid for him to drive over the speed limit and risk a ticket, and unsafe for him to be seen at or near the clinic. Little did he suspect the building was being watched around the clock.

As he drove along, the crimson lights, attached to the mud flaps, caused a red glow in the patches of snow. The robust cries from the hungry infant rang loudly in his ears.

*D*ID YOU KNOW TWO OF THE MEN INVOLVED IN the kidnappings were arrested?" Cora asked Tuesday.

The women were having lunch together, catching up on the events that were swiftly taking place in their lives.

"No. Who where they?"

"I didn't recognize the names, I'm sure you wouldn't have either."

"I'm going to have dinner with Jacob tonight. We're going to cook at his apartment."

"I hope he can cook, then. I know that you sure can't."

"Don't be nasty, Cora." Tuesday laughed. She knew full well that Cora was just telling the truth. "It doesn't suit you. But, seriously, tonight I'm going to tell Jacob that I'm not going to date him anymore. I've realized that I was just infatuated with his extreme good looks. He's shallow, and I don't want a close relationship with someone so superficial.

"Why see him then?"

"Why not? I'm curious about him, and we'll continue to be friends. For a friend, he's okay."

"Just from what I know about Jacob, you're grasping at straws. Friend is not a word he associates with women. He's a male chauvinist if I ever met one. I think, deep down, if you'd admit it, you don't trust the man!"

"Now who's grasping at straws?" Tuesday pointedly raised her eyebrows.

"Hi, Jacob. Just give me a few minutes. I'm running behind." Tuesday left him with his drink and hurried upstairs to finish her make up.

He finished his drink in one swallow and poured another. By the time she came back down the stairs, the drinks had taken the edge off his irritation at her tardiness.

"Sorry to keep you waiting, but my day has not been very organized."

"No problem," he smiled. "We have plenty of time. Are you ready to go now?"

When they arrived at Jacob's house, Tuesday noted that it didn't have a lived-in look. There were pictures on the wall and on several stands, but there were no other possessions that make a house look homelike. "Who are the people in the old photographs? Are they family?" She looked from picture to picture, feeling apprehensive.

"Yes, they are." He pointed to a picture on the stand beside the sofa. "That one's my grandparents. The one hanging above the television is my mother and father."

"You must not spend much time here," Tuesday commented. "The place doesn't look lived in."

"You know I spend most of my time traveling."

George Cunningham sat with a look of disbelief on his face. Hal and Cliff were in the room firing questions at him. "Who was the man driving the truck the night Todd was kidnapped?" Hal asked. George could not involve anyone else. If he did go to jail, his life would not be worth a plug nickel if he were locked up with any one of the depraved men who worked for him. They would know that he had talked and would see that he was punished for doing the unthinkable: ratting on one of his own kind. "I have no knowledge of the kidnapping except for what I read in the newspaper."

"Who is Jacob McCallister?"

The blood drained from George's face.

"Who is he?" Cliff fired the question at George. He had seen the color leave George's face at the mention of McCallister.

"I can assure you that I do not know anyone by that name."

Cliff waited as George tried to compose himself.

"I want the name of the man who drove the truck," Hal took over. He moved his chair up close to where George sat and put his foot on it, leaning up next to George's face. "Again, was the man Jacob McCallister?"

George reared back, farther away from Hal's accusing face. "I tell you, I don't know anything about all this. I swear." Bubbles of sweat were forming around George's hairline.

Cliff and Hal had been questioning George for two hours and he had revealed nothing.

Later, Hal sat in Cliff's chair with his legs propped on Cliff's desk, while Cliff paced back and forth across the room.

"Hal, I know that McCallister's involved in some way with George. I bet he was the man who drove the black truck. The look on George's face when I mentioned his name was one of panic mixed with disbelief. Up until then, he'd been utterly confident we had nothing on him."

"I got the same impression," Hal said.

"Let's have the FBI run a check on McCallister."

With the cookbook open on the counter and the meatballs browning in the oven, Tuesday and Jacob mixed the ingredients for spaghetti sauce. As they worked, they talked about their childhoods. Jacob told her a mixture of truth and fantasy.

"It's time to put the meatballs in the sauce," Tuesday said, opening the oven. "The sauce and meatballs can simmer while we cook the spaghetti, and then we eat."

Tuesday turned around and saw that his ebony eyes were alight with dark desire. The look made Tuesday uneasy, and she realized her decision not to continue seeing Jacob was the right one. She also realized his agenda was sexual and that was what had been nagging at her all along. He had no character, and Cora had been right; he was shallow.

"Good, I'm starving and the sauce smells wonderful."

When they had finished eating, Jacob said, "That was good," as he carried his plate to the sink. "We'll let the dishes go and have a drink in the living room. Go ahead in and find some nice music and I'll join you after I get the drinks."

When Tuesday had left the room, Jacob got two wine glasses and poured some of the wine he had chilled into each of them. He got two of the pills out of his pocket, where he had put them earlier, and crushed them with a spoon. After he had poured the powder into her glass and stirred it well, he carried the glasses into the living room. He handed Tuesday hers and sat beside her.

"I think we did a marvelous job on the spaghetti," Tuesday remarked nervously.

"I'll drink to that." Jacob put his glass to his lips and sipped the wine.

Tuesday smiled and sipped hers. Still curious about him, she said, "Tell me more about yourself, Jacob."

"Like I told you before, I come from a very poor family. We lived miles from the nearest city. My aunt, who raised me, had no money, nor did she have an education. She did a lot of the work I should have done so I could get an education and make something of myself."

"It sounds dreadful compared to my life with parents who provided everything that I could possibly have needed or wanted. I suppose I've never married because they wanted me to have a career so I would be independent. Keeps me busy."

"I'm glad you didn't marry. If you had I wouldn't have had the privilege of getting to know you. Most women your age have already married."

She smiled. She was having a hard time keeping her eyes open. *Why am I falling asleep?* She struggled to keep her eyes open. They only grew heavier.

By the time Jacob had refilled the glasses, she was sound asleep. "Guess I'll finish mine alone," he said to her sleeping form and sat at her feet. Tonight was the final step in his plan. It was time to move. He would not allow anyone to have Tuesday; she belonged to him. He would take her away, to a place where she would do as he bid.

He picked up her purse and found her house keys. Ready to act, he threw a blanket over her and left the apartment. It was no trouble getting into the house, but it took him ten minutes to find her closet. Having never been upstairs, he had searched each room until he found the one he wanted. After he found a suitcase, he packed several sweaters, blue jeans, sneakers, and socks. Her high heels would be useless where she was going. He found a couple of nightgowns that he liked and closed the suitcase. He was ready to take Tuesday to her new home.

Jacob carried the suitcase out to his truck and put it in the back with the supplies he had bought earlier that day. His work finished, he returned to the apartment.

Everything was arranged. Jacob carried Tuesday to the truck while she slept soundly. He left her there and went back to lock the door.

The headlights sliced the darkness as Jacob drove through the night. Tuesday moaned and turned in her seat.

"Damn it. Don't wake up," he whispered.

She lay still and slept on.

"Soon, Tuesday, you'll be in your new home," he laughed softly.

# 22

*M*OVE OVER YOU'NS. YA TRY'N TO PUSH ME OUT of th' bed?" Annabelle complained.

"I can't move 'cept I'll fall on th' floor," Daisy whined.

Rose still had not recovered, either physically or mentally, from her difficult delivery. Beyond that, she had drastically regressed mentally since Jacob had taken her child away. She simply lay there not complaining.

They all heard the truck's motor at the same time.

"Oh, no!" Annabelle said. "Jeb's brung that town girl. I hate to think of it. No good goin' to come of it."

Annabelle and Daisy climbed out of bed as fast as they could. They had to prompt Rose to get her out of bed. They hurried to the front door.

As Jacob came within sight of his destination, Tuesday continued to sleep soundly. Parking the truck close to the front door, he turned the headlights off and then the motor. He moved to the passenger side of truck and, holding the door open with his thigh, he lifted her into his arms. The motion did not awaken her. He carried her across the porch and kicked the front door open.

There in the light cast by the oil lamp stood the three women. They looked as if someone had plucked them from a rag bag. Their gowns were poorly made of feedsack and hung on their bodies in wrinkled messes.

"Get some clothes on. I brought a new wife, and I want you women to be good to her. I don't want her to have to do any hard work. She's not used to hard work. Give her a little time and she can learn to cook and do her share of the chores."

He left them standing with their mouths open and carried Tuesday to the bed and laid her down. Tuesday continued to sleep soundly, blissfully unaware of her predicament.

*C*LIFF HURRIED INTO HAL'S OFFICE. THERE HAD been an extraordinary turn of events.

"Hal, I'm worried about Tuesday Summers. She's come up missing."

"You sure about that? She's a grown woman."

"Tuesday and Cora were to meet for lunch today, and Cora hasn't heard from her all day. Cora called all their friends and they haven't heard from her, either. Cora's sure that McCallister's behind this. She believes that he took Tuesday against her will. The last time Cora talked to her was on Wednesday, just hours before Tuesday's dinner date at McCallister's apartment. Tuesday told Cora that she planned to tell McCallister that she wouldn't date him anymore. Cora thinks that Tuesday told McCallister and that he's done something in revenge. According to her, it's not like Tuesday to be out of touch for so long."

"But why would McCallister take her against her will?" Hal asked.

"Who knows? I don't have another explanation," Cliff said.

"All along, we suspected that McCallister kidnapped Todd. Maybe Tuesday learned something McCallister didn't want her to know," speculated Hal.

"Cora didn't trust McCallister from the beginning and neither did I. Cora told me that Tuesday had made a few strange remarks to her. One remark was that he seemed to have a dark side. Cora also said that Tuesday had told her on several occasions that she didn't like McCallister's attitude but she didn't want to make rash judgments."

Hal patiently listened while Cliff paced back and forth in frustration, telling the morbid news through clenched jaws.

"When I met him, I told you there was something about him that I didn't trust. You know my instincts are usually right. When we found out that McCallister's truck fit the description of the one that was involved in a kidnapping, I should have tried to keep her from seeing him. But at the time, there just didn't seem to be a concrete reason. I'm afraid that I allowed my own feelings to interfere. I found myself becoming interested in her, and I feared my motive for wanting her to stop seeing him was just good old-fashioned jealousy. My ability to see the urgency to intervene in the relationship was clouded."

Hal had a sick feeling in his stomach; he had called the tail off Jacob—and as it turned out, a few days too soon.

Cliff continued, "The man who was spotted carrying a small infant into the clinic, the day before George and Sam were arrested, was identified as Jacob McCallister."

Hal flinched when Cliff pounded his right fist on the side of the wall, emphasizing his frustration.

"When did that happen?"

"About an hour ago," Cliff answered,

"That's enough to get a warrant out on him," Hal said.

"I'd bet my last dollar that he's the man who kidnapped Todd," Cliff said. "The infant, the truck. My instinct was right. Remember George's face when we asked him if he knew Jacob McCallister? The question frightened him. He hadn't known just how strong our case was until we mentioned McCallister."

Hal watched and listened while Cliff paced the room, clenching and unclenching his fists. "Cliff, I'm sorry. I guess that I made a mistake when I told you to call off the tail we had on McCallister."

"Forget it. How could you have known?"

"The clinic has been shut down, pending investigation, and the children placed wherever there was available room," Cliff continued. "The infant Jacob left at the clinic is in the city hospital being checked out. And we're trying to locate her parents. The pieces of the puzzle are beginning to fit together. He's not going to get away with this. McCallister's the ticket to the baby brokers. When we find him, we find the key. I should have talked more to Tuesday about the case. Now that I realize McCallister knows Cunningham and works for him, I know it's possible that McCallister had mentioned Cunningham to her, but that's a long shot. Anyway, it's too late now."

"Can't waste time on what-ifs, Cliff."

"I know. You're right," Cliff said.

"Not to change the subject, but anything on the twins?" Hal asked.

"No, not a thing. It's just like they didn't exist before they were found in Los Angeles. Could they somehow be tied into all this?"

"How do you mean?" Hal asked, having no idea what Cliff was getting at.

"I don't know, I just have a weird feeling that all this ties together somehow. I mean the infant . . ." Cliff shrugged.

"Let me know if anything comes of your weird feeling. In the meantime, I'll put an APB out, covering the tri-state area, on Tuesday and Jacob McCallister," Hal said. "We'll find him and all the loose ends will finally be tied up."

After his discussion with Hal, Cliff went to the record room and looked through the missing-children reports. He sat back and ran his fingers through his hair. Of the many recent reports from the fifty states, none matched the infant or the twins. "This is strange," Cliff said to the clerk. "Why isn't someone looking for these children?"

"The infant must have been unwanted," the clerk suggested.

"Just left somewhere for anyone to pick up?" Cliff said. "No, that doesn't fit. McCallister's not a good Samaritan who would go through the trouble of picking up an abandoned child and take it to a clinic. Nor did McCallister just happen upon an abandoned child just waiting to be sold so he could make some easy money. No, there's something more to this. I don't believe for a moment that the infant was an abandoned child who McCallister just came along and found. He kidnapped it."

"You're probably right there," the clerk said. "From what you've said about McCallister, it doesn't seem he's the type to go to the trouble to help anyone."

"If the infant and the twins aren't missing children, then kidnapping doesn't fit. McCallister can't be the kidnapper if there was no abduction." Cliff was stumped. "What do I do next?" he asked. "I can't mess up. Tuesday's life could be at stake."

"If you find McCallister," the clerk said, "you'll find the answer to the infant."

"We do have proof he brought the infant to the clinic. Maybe the answer to the infant will enlighten us on the twins," Cliff said and grabbed his coat. "Maybe the FBI has found something on McCallister." He had almost nothing else to go on.

"Sergeant," the FBI agent greeted Cliff as he came into his office. "What can I do for you today?"

The agent's name was Mark Myers. Cliff had worked with him many times and they had great respect for each other.

"Well, Mark," Cliff answered him, "I'm hoping you've found something on Jacob McCallister. I know it's not an FBI matter at this point, but I'm desperate."

"Not a thing, Cliff," Mark answered. "He has no record. If I had his prints, I could check to find out if he has an alias."

"That, I don't have." Cliff was disappointed. Another dead end.

# 24

UESDAY LOOKED AROUND THE STRANGE ROOM in dread. *Where am I?*

With disbelief she stared at her surroundings, astonished that the walls were built of logs. Protruding from the logs, spike nails dotted the room, with clothes hanging limply from them. An old-fashioned wooden crib stood in the corner. In yet another corner, old quilts and a few thin mattresses were piled in a tangled mess.

Tuesday was horrified. *Where am I? How did I get here?*

The last thing she could remember was Jacob sitting beside her. They had been drinking wine and talking about his past when she suddenly found herself fighting an unexplainable drowsiness.

Now she heard muffled conversation. One masculine voice mingled with feminine voices. She wanted to call out to him because his voice was the only familiar element in the nightmare that she was living, but she was much too frightened. She could not make her vocal chords work.

She looked around again, unable to accept what she had seen the first time. The room was small, and the bed was the only furniture in the room, except for the crib. There were two doorways, one on each inside wall, with a crude ragged curtain hanging crookedly over each one. She was appalled that the material was badly soiled. There were gaps between the drape and the log door-jambs, but she could not see what was on the other side. Not knowing what else to do, she lay there waiting. *What am I waiting for?* She listened to the voices coming from another room.

In the kitchen, Jacob ate his breakfast. The women scurried around working to please him. They catered to his every need. It was Saturday, so the children had no school. They waited in the barn for him to finish his breakfast so they could have theirs. They lay together on a pile of hay up on the loft.

"Ya knowed," Joe said to his sisters lying next to him, "I'm goin' to live like our father. Ya girls are goin' to live with me when I build my own cabin. Ya can have my children and take care of th' cabin an' fix th' food. I'll keep a house in th' city like Pa does."

"I'm not goin' to live my life on th' mountain," Patty said. "I'm goin' to th' city one day. Ain't goin' to have babies for a man to make money on. There's a betta life than this, and I'm goin' to find it."

"Patty, ya should be more like Sara, here. She's not always dreamin' about things she can't have. Ya knowed ya can't take care of yourself here or in th' city, so quit talkin' nonsense."

"Let's go in and eat. I'm hungry," Sara said. They had yet to learn that their father had brought a new woman home.

Annabelle stood at the kitchen window and saw the children when they walked from the barn. *I ought to thrash th' youngins. Foolin' around in th' loft an' not doin' nary a'bit of th' chores,* she fussed to herself.

Jacob pulled the musty curtain aside and entered the room where Tuesday lay in bed.

"Where am I, Jacob?" she screamed at him. "Why have you brought me here? Take me home. Now! I have never seen such a filthy place."

"This is your home. I'm kind enough to share my home with you, and you had better like it. Now get dressed, and I will introduce you to the rest of the family." He threw her suitcase on the bed.

"My home? Family? Are you crazy? This is not my home. This place is filthy and it smells rotten. Look at this bed. It's disgusting. The sheets and quilts look like they've never been washed. Jacob, you will be arrested for this. You cannot just bring me here against my will. My friends will find me, and you will be locked up, and I will see that it's for life. If you know what's good for you, take me home."

He laughed in a menacing way. "You have no idea how remotely removed you are from your former home. Now, shut up and get dressed!"

Her eyes grew wide with fright. His tone of voice terrified her. She got out of bed and shivered; she was still in her dinner dress with the spaghetti straps. She could not believe how cold it was.

"Jacob, where's the bathroom? I need to go."

"There's no bathroom. Get dressed and the women will show you what you need to know."

"What women?"

"Tuesday, get dressed before you freeze. I will take you to the bathroom if you would rather. It's outside and it's very cold out there."

"Very cold out there," she mimicked. "What do you think it is in here? How could the bathroom be outside?"

"Tuesday, do as I say!" He lost patience with her and walked out of the room, hoping that she would calm down with him out of the room and get dressed.

She stood there in disbelief, horrified.

The children were in the kitchen eating, and to avoid being in the same room with them, Jacob sat on the sofa in the living room. He waited for Tuesday to get dressed and come out of the bedroom. Alone again, Tuesday looked wide-eyed at her surroundings. She stood beside the bed and saw the room from another angle; the quilts and sheets were badly stained and body hair was visible on them. She had never seen anything like it and could not believe she had been forced to sleep in that bed. She looked down at the floor and saw why she felt ice-cold air blowing around her ankles; there were cracks in the wooden-plank floor almost an inch wide between some of the boards. Cobwebs and dust balls blocked out the light and air in many places where they clogged up the cracks. The floor looked as if it had never seen a mop or bucket of water.

Tuesday needed to go to the bathroom badly. She also desperately wanted to take a shower after sleeping in the filthy bed. *What did he mean, "There is no bathroom?"* Having forgotten about dressing, Tuesday went through the curtained doorway as Jacob had. She found herself in a living room that was as primitive as the room she had come from. The sofa where Jacob sat watching her facial expression was old, faded, and threadbare. The stuffing protruded from the worn fabric in many places. At one time, judging from the color in the creases where it had not had as much wear, it had been a wine color.

The room had three doors. One was on the outside wall and opened at the front of the cabin. The others were located on the two inside walls: one she had just walked through, the other one was to her left. The outside door was to her right and the one to her left had a curtain, which hung crookedly just like the one behind her. She could see the curtains were hung from a wire. A spike nail, which had been driven in the corner of the doorway, held each end. As in the bedroom, the floor was bare wood and the walls were made of logs. Large nails were scattered on every wall, with muddy clothing hanging from them.

Jacob watched her reaction and for the first time saw the cabin through another person's eyes. She had a look of stunned disbelief on her face.

"Jacob, I must go. Now!"

He got up and sighed. "If you think this is bad," he mumbled, "what are you going to think of the outhouse?"

"What did you say?"

"Never mind. You didn't get dressed. I'll get your coat; it's cold outside."

He led her through the door to her left, and to her dismay there stood three strange women and three children. Six pairs of eyes stared at her. She fainted.

"Oh, my word she's fainted, she has," Annabelle said.

"Shut up, woman," Jacob ordered. "Don't you think we can see? Get me some water."

Annabelle got a pan of water and a soiled rag and handed it to Jacob. He dipped the rag in the water and wiped Tuesday's face with it. The odor from the mildewed rag brought her out of the faint as effectively as an ammonia capsule would have. She opened her eyes and saw the strange faces looking down at her. The women looked wild: their hair was dry and stringy; their clothes were ill-fitting and stained.

"Who's she?" Patty asked. "What's she doin' here?"

Ignoring Patty, Jacob took Tuesday by the hand and helped her to her feet. He led her to the out-house.

"It's not Rosily he'd brung here," Annabelle said to the others. "When he'd told us he was goin' to bring a woman here, I thought it'd be Rosily. I knowed he's been runnin' 'round with her. Where on earth'd he get that one? I ain't never seen no one with shiny gold hair such as that."

Andy Hillberry left the mountain road and walked up Main Street; he was on his way to speak to the sheriff about Jacob McCallister. Andy saw Albert Towns and called to him, "I'm goin' to see th' sheriff 'bout th' goings-on at Jeb McCallister's cabin. Want to come along?"

"You're crazy man. Why don'cha mind your own business?" Albert said.

"I'm not crazy, on the kon'tra-ri," Hillberry said. "I'm just th' man to stop it. Tired of 'im goin' 'round in his fancy truck actin' like he's betta than other'ns what don't got so much. He won't even give th' other mountain folks th' time of day. Thinks he can do any-thin' he's a mind to. I'm goin' to show 'im he can't fool with th' likes of me. When I'm done with 'im, he'll wish he'd shown some respect to 'is neighbors."

Andy hurried up the brick street. He walked straight down the center as if the sidewalk did not exist. In his envious frame of mind he had a mis-sion.

"Sheriff." Andy Hillberry rushed through the doorway, banging the door against the wall.

"What the hell you want, Andy? You know better than open a door that a'way."

"I'm gettin' fed up. McCallister's sellin' his own flesh an' blood. It's got to stop an' I'm here to com-plain."

"Just what you here to complain about?"

"Told you. Jeb McCallister's sellin' his youngins to city folks."

"How do you know that?"

"Ya knowed, I live just a mile from 'im on th' mountain. I see th' fancy people comin' to take th' babies away. There's always one of them women burstin' with a baby. But there's never no kids around, except for th' three he keeps to do his work for him. He just wants to drive up and down th' mountain in that fancy truck."

"Andy, I can't sit up on the mountain watchin' McCallister, and I've told you time after time I don't want to hear it. I have too many other important things to take care of. You bring me more information and I'll do something about it. As far as I can see he's done nothin' to break the law."

"If that's th' way ya feel about it, Sheriff, I'm goin' to get a petition signed. I knowed the other people goin' to want it stopped. I'll be back."

Andy Hillberry could neither read nor write. The petition was just an idle threat. No one knew why Andy Hillberry ran a personal vendetta against Jacob McCallister. Sheriff Ozzie Moats had yet to act on any of Andy Hillberry's charges. There were rumors involving McCallister's selling his children up and down the mountain. No one but Andy Hillberry seemed to mind.

LIFF PULLED INTO CORA'S DRIVEWAY, PRAYING
that she had heard something from Tuesday
since they had talked that morning.

Cora opened the door just as he was ready to ring
the doorbell.

"Hi, Cliff. I'm so worried about Tuesday. This is a
nightmare. Why would Jacob take her? Where
would he take her? This just doesn't make sense to
me."

"My bet's Winding Ridge. That's where his driver's license was issued, and that's where I'm heading. If I don't find them there, I may find out
something about him that will be useful in my
search. Winding Ridge seems to be the logical place
to start."

"Yes, I'd have to agree with that."

"Have·you heard anything new from any of Tuesday's friends since I last talked to you? Maybe
someone saw her or heard from her?"

"No," Cora answered, "I know she wouldn't
cause me to worry like this if she could help it.
There's just no reason she would go off somewhere
and not tell me, or leave work with no word at all."

"You've had some opportunity to get to know McCallister, and I'm sure you've had conversations with Tuesday about him. Can you think of any reason for him to be taking an infant to the clinic?"

"No, I can't."

"I'd say he's mixed up in Cunningham and Johnson's illegal adoption agency. I'm leaving first thing tomorrow morning for Winding Ridge. If it wasn't so late I'd leave now, but I plan to get a couple hours sleep and leave before daylight. We only have a general delivery address for McCallister in Winding Ridge, but it's a small town. I should have no trouble finding where he lived before he moved here. Maybe he has family there."

"You sound as if you are going alone. Why?"

"I don't want to alert him to the fact that I'm on his tail. One man won't draw as much attention as two. I can always use the local law enforcement agencies when the time comes. Cora, I promise that I'll find Tuesday, and I'll bring her back with me."

"I don't think that the fact that she's missing and Jacob took an infant to the clinic is just a coincidence. I think there's more to all this than we know. When I first met him, I felt that he could not be trusted," Cora said.

"Me, too. Are you sure you've told me everything you know?

"Yes, I'm sure. The time Tuesday brought him here, he didn't have much to say. I really wasn't sure if he was shy or just unfriendly. I got the impression that you didn't think much of him either when you stopped in that night."

"No, I didn't. No reason, just a feeling."

Driving east on Interstate 70, rapidly heading toward 79 South, Cliff cursed the early-morning fog. After driving an hour, he exited at Fairmont. It would take him three and a half hours to get from that point to Winding Ridge traveling along on narrow, twisting country roads.

Up ahead was a sign that was so weather-worn the words "Winding Ridge, 20 miles" could barely be made out. Cliff passed a few farms here and there, and as he drew near the town proper, he saw a few more houses clustered together.

He had followed the dirt road for ten minutes when he came to an intersection and saw another sign with an arrow pointing to the right. Above the arrow, large block letters proclaimed "Winding Ridge, Population 932." Someone had marked over the "2," making it a "3." Apparently there had been a birth since the last census.

Cliff turned to the right and the road wound steadily higher, climbing the foothill leading to the foot of the mountain. Deep ruts and dangerous snow slides cluttered the road. In some places only one car at a time could pass through. If Cliff met a car coming the other way, one of them would have to back up and find a wide place to pull over. As Cliff gained higher elevation, the going became increasingly hazardous. He should have rented a four-wheel drive. Where the snow had drifted halfway over the road, his car spun and slid. He inched forward at a snail's pace. The snow was too deep for his tires to secure the necessary traction.

He finally made it up the foothills to the small town at the foot of the mountain in spite of the snow. Where the road leveled off, he saw a sign with the words "Main Street" painted across it. Actually, it was the only street. On each side of the street for three blocks were buildings of various sizes. A theater, a post office, a boarding house, and a few other business establishments. Cliff parked his car in front of the boarding house, an old three-story structure.

A porch wound around the front and both sides of the picturesque building, and the small yard was surrounded by a white picket fence. A sign nailed to the front of the house read: "Rooms to Let."

Cliff left his car and walked up the steps toward the front door. A banister circled the entire porch. Rocking chairs were scattered here and there in a sociable arrangement. Two old men came from inside the building as Cliff climbed up the front steps. They were in desperate need of shaves. Both wore bib overalls with plaid flannel shirts, heavy plaid jackets, and old floppy hats. Occasionally, as they stood talking just outside the door, one or the other would spit a wad of tobacco juice over the banister, making ugly brown stains in the otherwise brilliant white snow.

"Who do I see to get a room?"

"Go on inside. Jus' holler an' somebody'll come'n help you. Don't cotton to strangers here 'bout's, we don't," one of the old men answered. He spit a large wad of tobacco juice at Cliff's feet.

"Going to be a long haul," Cliff grumbled under his breath as he entered the boarding house.

# *26*

"WHY DO I NEED A HEAVY COAT TO GO TO THE bathroom?" Tuesday exclaimed.

"Don't be difficult, Tuesday. Just come with me," Jacob warned.

"Difficult? Difficult?" Tuesday exclaimed. "Are you crazy? Have I gone crazy? Why did you bring me to this place? None of this makes sense."

He led her out the back door ignoring her outburst.

Tuesday thought that she would faint from the putrid smell just outside the door. But she noticed that Jacob, so accustomed to the odor, did not appear to mind. The women constantly emptied their bath water, cooking water, and cleaning water off to the side of the back porch. They had nowhere else to dispose of it; therefore the ground was constantly wet, and a decaying odor, from the rotting pieces of food, filled the air. The ground was still covered with about a foot of snow, except at the side of the back porch where the water was constantly thrown. Two cleared paths led to the outhouse and the barn, and several trampled-down paths trailed through the snow to places one could not see. Piles of trash protruded out of the snow everywhere. Tuesday looked around with disbelief in her eyes. She could not comprehend that she was indeed standing here.

The back porch, which extended about five feet in length and five feet in width, gave with her weight. It felt to her as though the boards under her feet would give way at any second.

Pulled along by Jacob, she stumbled down the single, bowed step that led from the porch to the ground. He led her up a steep path, holding her arm firmly so she would not slip and fall back down. Approximately fifty yards from the back door of the cabin, they came to a little narrow structure. The building, about six feet tall and four feet wide, was constructed of bare, rough boards.

Jacob pulled the door open. "Go in."

Tuesday had no choice but to do as he said. She had never in her life imagined or seen anything like this. She wondered if she was ever going to smell pleasant odors again; the stench coming out was unbearable. She stood motionless, still not able to make herself go in.

"Go in, Tuesday," Jacob grumbled. "We can't stand out here all day. It's too cold."

Tuesday stood speechless and immobile, until a push from Jacob forced her to step into the small, confining area. The door shut behind her and she found herself in almost total darkness. Somehow she found her voice and screamed, "Jacob, please open the door. It's dark in here."

Jacob opened the door.

"Is there a light switch in here?" she asked, fighting hysteria.

"No! Tuesday, I'll leave the door open. You just do what you have to," Jacob snarled.

"Turn your back and I will," she demanded. She knew she had to pull herself together and not allow her fear to take over.

"I don't intend to stand out in the cold fighting with you about the door," he said and turned his back.

It was not only dark in the rank toilet; she knew from the cobwebs that insects inhabited the repulsive place. Somehow she found the strength to look around. She could reach out and touch any of the four rough wallboards and not move from the spot where she stood. The seat where she would sit was simply a wooden bench with a round hole cut in the center; the nightmare was the filth rotting in the hole. It was piled within two feet of the top. She lifted her coat and the dress that she wore under it, and slid her panties down. She sat on the crude bench, miserably aware of the rotting filth inches below her exposed bottom.

*How did Jacob manage to bring me here without my being aware of it?* she puzzled, fighting back gut-wrenching terror. She was mortified to be relieving herself in this primitive structure, with a madman standing just outside the open door. *My last memory before awaking in the cabin was becoming so sleepy that I could not keep my eyes open. I never fall asleep during the evening; I never fall asleep at such inappropriate times. He drugged me,* she realized in horror. *That's the only answer. But why?* She struggled to deal with her situation one minute at a time. *I must not panic. I'll need all my wits to get out of this nightmare. I will find a way,* she promised herself silently.

She looked around for tissue paper and saw nothing but old catalogs, loose pages scattered on the floor, and cobwebs. "Jacob, there's no tissue in here."

"Tuesday, don't be prissy. That's what the catalogs are for. Just rub a few pages together and that will soften them a little."

With tears of fear and frustration running down her face, Tuesday did as he said.

Jacob led her back to the cabin.

*The hideous little cabin looks even worse from this angle,* she thought.

Weatherbeaten and seeming out of place in the clearing, the unpainted log cabin was an ugly contrast to the beauty of the jade-green pine trees that surrounded the cabin and spotted the rocky mountain face. The peak dominated the background as it reached majestically toward the sky.

The children stared in awe at Tuesday when she and Jacob came back into the cabin. In their eyes, she looked like a storybook princess. Aunt Aggie often told them stories; some were fairy tales, which they loved. To the children, Tuesday was what a princess right out of Aunt Aggie's stories would look like. Her soft, healthy, glowing skin, her even white teeth, and her shiny blond hair were out of place in the primitive cabin. The other women, with the exception of Daisy, who took a little better care of herself, had rough, weatherbeaten skin and dry tangled hair; the contrast in the women was startling.

Jacob led Tuesday to the bench that was attached to the table. Annabelle slid a plate in front of her. Looking down at it, Tuesday saw two overcooked eggs, three strips of bacon, and home fries. It all looked greasy and overcooked. "I can't eat. I feel sick to my stomach."

"Try," Jacob said, putting his hand affectionately on her shoulder.

She shrugged her shoulder so that he would remove his hand. She could not stand his touch; it made her ill.

"Try to eat a little," he insisted. "You haven't had anything since dinner yesterday."

She could see that it irritated him that she had displaced his hand from her shoulder. Tuesday knew she could not eat anything. The horrible odor of this cabin and the food floating in grease was too much. Her throat closed up and her stomach was tied in knots. She sat at the table, her food untouched in front of her, with tears running down her face. She did not understand what had happened to cast her into this horror-filled situation. She thought of her home and the lovely furniture and cozy warmth.

Jacob put two sleeping pills into her coffee and insisted she drink it. She turned pale, wondering what would become of her now. He carried her to the bed and laid her down. She did not protest; she was too sick and frightened. The tranquilizers were swiftly taking effect and she no longer cared that he had put the pills into her coffee.

After finishing their chores, the children met in the barn. The topic of conversation was the new woman their father had brought to live in the cabin.

"What ya thinkin' of th' city woman?" Patty asked. "She's a pretty one, ain't she?"

"Yeah," Joe commented, "she sure is."

"What's she here for?" Sara asked.

"Pa's gone an' got himself 'nother wife," Joe answered, "just like I'm goin' to some day."

"I like her," Patty said, ignoring Joe's remark.

"How'd ya knowed?" Sara asked. "Ya ain't talked to her."

"I knowed," Patty insisted. "I dreamed 'bout her."

HE LADY CLIFF RENTED A ROOM FROM COULD
have been the fat lady from the circus. Rather
than being the typical jolly fat lady, she was uncom-
monly unfriendly. The people in the mountain
region did not trust strangers.

"By the way, can you tell me where Jacob McCallister lives?" Cliff asked as he pocketed the key to
his room.

"Ain't none of my business, an' I suppose it ain't
none of your'n neither. I mind my own business,
an' it ain't my place to knowed some other'ns," she
told him.

It was obvious she wouldn't talk even if she knew
the answers. He gave up the useless questions and
went up to his room, finding it clean but rather old-
fashioned. A large brass bed dominated the room,
with an oak closet standing in one corner and a
chest of drawers in the other. The windows were
covered with sheer curtains. The room seemed like
a morbid replica of the bedroom in Alfred
Hitchcock's movie *Psycho*.

As Cliff walked around town later, he questioned everyone he saw. He got the same reaction that he had gotten from the fat lady, the two old men, and the ten other people he talked to—even worse in some cases. Cliff stood on the sidewalk in front of the old post office building, looking around the coal-mining town. The more substantial homes were on the south side of town. They were well cared for, freshly painted, and surrounded by trees and hedges; each had its own charm. Most had white picket fences with snow piled almost to the fence tops. At that end of town, the street was called "Bosses' Row" by the townspeople. On the north side of town the homes were smaller, look-alike houses, and not as well tended. The coal miners lived there.

Inside the post office, behind the barred window, stood an old man. He did not look as dirty and weatherworn as the folks Cliff had talked to on the street. The man, who was so thin he looked as if he could slip through the bars, appeared to be upper class.

"Can I help you?" the man behind the bars inquired in a unfriendly tone of voice.

"You sure can, sir. My name is Cliff Moran. I'm looking for Jacob McCallister. The address I have for him is General Delivery, Winding Ridge, West Virginia. Can you tell me how to find his house?"

"Nope," the man behind the barred window said.

Again, it would be useless to push for an answer. "Thanks, pal," Cliff said and walked out.

He crossed the street. The sign above the building there simply boasted: "The Company Store." Once again he had no luck with the people inside. He headed for the gas station, where there was a pay phone, and called Hal.

"Hello," Hal answered. "What's up?"

"You wouldn't believe these people here, Hal. They resent strangers. They either don't know McCallister or just don't want to talk. It's almost like an unspoken agreement. 'Don't make strangers welcome. We don't want them.'"

"What are you going to do now, Cliff?"

"I'm going to talk to the sheriff," he answered. "I don't know if it's wise, though. He'll need to keep his mouth shut. I don't need someone to tip McCallister off that I'm here. We'll lose them. You know in these small towns gossip travels like wildfire. I wouldn't be surprised if the sheriff has the same attitude as the townspeople."

"I think you should try talking to him, though," Hal said. "You're going to need him if you're going to get anywhere with those people."

"Remember that conversation Lea and Norman Wright overheard when they were in George Cunningham's law office?" Cliff said. "A voice speaking in a backwoods brogue? They heard the voice say, 'I'm wantin' bigger money for th' kids I bring you. If ya don't I'm goin' to call Lloyd and work for him from now on.' And a man they believed to be George said, 'Get the hell out of here, Aubry. This is not the time nor the place to discuss the matter.'"

"Yes, I do. What's your point?" Hal said.

"The way Lea and Norman described the man's speech is the way these people in Winding Ridge talk. Maybe I'll find the key to the abductions right here in this time-forsaken town."

"That's food for thought. I'm digging for anything I can come up with on McCallister."

"Get anything you can," Cliff said. "Could be, the voice Lea and Norman heard belongs to a man who came from around here. Perhaps he and Jacob work together."

Cliff picked up the phone again to call Cora. "Hi, Cora, Cliff here. Just wanted to check to see if you heard anything from Tuesday."

"No, Cliff, not a word," Cora answered. "There's no doubt that something's wrong."

"I was hoping that you would have heard from her." Fear for Tuesday filled his heart. "I'm staying in a boarding house in the town of Winding Ridge. There's no phone in my room, so you can't call me, but I'll keep in touch with you in case she calls you."

"Please do, Cliff. I'm so worried."

It was time to see the sheriff. When Cliff walked into his office, the sheriff was behind his desk, happily reading *Playboy* magazine. Hearing the door open, the sheriff swiftly hid the magazine under a newspaper, a ritual he went through several times a day.

"Hi, Sheriff. I'm Sergeant Cliff Moran, a detective from Wheeling." Cliff flashed his badge. "I'm looking for Jacob McCallister."

"I'm Sheriff Ozzie Moats. What you wantin' Jeb for?" The sheriff said in irritation. Moats was a big man. His large belly overlapped his belt. He needed a shave, and Cliff could smell the odor of tobacco as he walked closer to the sheriff's desk.

"You call him Jeb?"

"That's what he goes by in these parts." The sheriff spit in the discolored brass spittoon that he kept behind his desk. "We don't need no fancy names around here. Jeb's good enough."

"I suspect that he kidnapped a woman from Wheeling, and I need to know where he lives."

"Well, Mr. Sergeant Detective, do you have a warrant?" The sheriff picked at his tobacco-stained teeth with the end of a ragged toothpick. Hostile beady eyes betrayed his annoyance at being confronted with the city detective's questions.

"No, I don't. I told you that I suspect that he kidnapped a woman. I'm trying to find her."

"What evidence do you have?" Sheriff Moats spit in the spittoon again.

"I don't have any evidence, except he was the last person she was known to be with."

"Can't arrest a man if you don't have evidence." The sheriff's jaw jutted out, swollen with the wad of tobacco.

"I can question him, though," Cliff said. "What's your problem? Seems like you're a sheriff obstructing justice!"

"He lives four or five miles up the mountain. Ain't no mail goes up there. Can't give you a address. I'll check into the matter and you can come back in the morning. If the matter warrants it, I'll send a man up with you."

Obviously, no help would be forthcoming. It would be a waste of time waiting around for the sheriff to check it out. There was no convincing the stubborn sheriff to act immediately. Cliff left to continue checking around on his own. If the sheriff decided to help, Cliff would accept it; if not, no time would be wasted waiting. Cliff walked briskly back to his room to put a sweater on under his heavy jacket. It was colder at this elevation than he was accustomed to. He walked up Main Street as far as the business section went and crossed the street. Then he walked back in the direction he had come. Sitting on the steps of the old courthouse was a young boy.

The boy was not a town boy. He lived higher up on the mountain and was taught to not only to dislike strangers, but also to hate them. As a matter of fact, he had been taught to dislike townspeople, too; regardless, he liked to hang around town.

"Hi, there," Cliff said.

"Hi, yourself. We don't cotton to strangers. Wot ya wantin'? I seen ya walkin' up th' street like you're lookin' for somethin'."

"You're right, boy. I'm looking for someone. If I can find someone to tell me where he lives, I'm going to pay him twenty dollars."

"Who's that ya lookin' for?"

"Jacob McCallister. You may know him as Jeb," Cliff answered.

"Can't tell you. I don't like strangers pokin' their noses around an' askin' questions."

"Okay, but I'm sure I'll find someone who wants twenty bucks." Cliff started to walk away.

"Wait a minute, mister. If ya don't tell I told you, I'm goin' to say."

"I can't tell who told me, boy," Cliff said as he turned back. "I don't even know your name."

"Gimme th' twenty bucks first."

Cliff reached into his pocket, pulled out a twenty-dollar bill, and handed it to the boy.

Tommy Lee stood up, ready to run. "Jeb's livin' up on th' mountain, but I don't knowed how far," he lied. "He doesn't come in to town hardly neve'. When he does, he jus' comes to th' bar or Th' Company Store an' to th' post office. Townspeople don't cotton to th' mountain folks an' they stay away mostly."

"Can't you be a little more specific? How far up and which way?"

"Don't knowed," the boy lied again. "Jus' knowed he's live'n on th' mountain." The boy turned and ran down the street before Cliff could ask any more questions.

Darkness slowly fell over the town. It was only four o'clock in the afternoon. The mountain range above blocked out the sun, and shadows fell across the town as if prehistoric giants walked around the outskirts.

"Jess, get out here," Sheriff Moats ordered. Deputy Willis came out of the back room carrying a dirty mop.

"I want you to see what you can find out about McCallister. Don't arouse anyone's suspicions. I don't want that old fart Hillberry to get wind of what you're doin'. He could mess up a one-car funeral goin' around runnin' his mouth."

"You've never been interested in tryin' to catch McCallister at sellin' his youngins to the city folk before. Why are you so interested in him now?"

Sheriff Moats removed a wad of tobacco from his huge jaw, threw it into his spittoon, and spit. Then he said, "Jess, there's a detective nosin' around town. He thinks McCallister has kidnapped a young woman and brought her here to his cabin. I want you to find out what you can. We don't need a big-feeling city cop nosin' around about our business. We have taken care of this town for years and haven't needed outside help before. I don't want him here, thinkin' we can't handle our own business."

Deputy Willis knew better than to say, "I told you so." The sheriff always feared his brother; Aubry, would get into really serious trouble and ruin the Moat's name. Rumor had it that Aubry got his new fancy truck, almost identical to McCallister's, from profits earned kidnapping children for an adoption agency in the city of Wheeling. "You want me to go to McCallister's place and talk to him? See if there's trouble there? Like maybe a woman who don't belong?"

"Yes, but don't arouse his suspicions. If there's something going on come back and tell me. We'll take it from there."

No one was going to make it easy for him, so there was nothing left to do but make his way up the mountain. Cliff crossed the street and headed toward the company store. He needed supplies.

When Cliff walked into the store for the second time, the same four men sat gathered around the potbelly stove, self-important in their rocking chairs. They all quit talking, and four pairs of eyes watched him as he walked around, gathering the supplies he wanted to purchase. He bought a canteen, a tent, food supplies, warmer clothing, and a few other items that he thought he might need on the mountain. Cliff took his supplies back to his room. He could not do anything tonight. Tomorrow he'd have to go to the nearest car rental; he needed a four-wheel drive vehicle. A car would never make it up the snow-covered mountain trails.

Meanwhile, Deputy Willis put his cleaning supplies away, climbed into the sheriff's Jeep, and drove up the mountain toward Jacob's cabin. Willis knew the way and had the four-wheeler, so the late hour did not concern him. Jess Willis held the belief that if he were the sheriff, Jacob would have been stopped from selling his own children to the city folk. As far as Willis was concerned, the sheriff had no intention of stopping McCallister. To the sheriff, it was all the fewer mountain children invading the town's school. Most of the people living in the town, including the sheriff, had the attitude that what the mountain people did was their business, as long as they stayed where they belonged, up on the mountain. But not Jess Willis. He had dreams of being sheriff someday, and then he would take it upon himself to get to the bottom of the matter.

# 28

*T*UESDAY OPENED HER EYES AND SAW A YOUNG girl standing beside her bed, a pretty child with bright blue eyes framed by long, dark lashes. Her hair was dark brown and fell to her waist in soft waves. She had a pink rosebud mouth. A purple birthmark covered the right side of her face from one eyebrow to the corner of her mouth, extending back to her ear. In spite of this, Tuesday saw that she was a beautiful girl.

"Hi, there," Tuesday said.

"Hi," Patty answered. "I hope you're not mad 'cause I'm in your room. Just want to talk to you. Are ya all right? It scared me when ya fainted."

"Where am I? Who are you?"

"You're on the mountain, and I'm Patty."

"There must be a name of a town," Tuesday said in frustration. "You must know where you live. You do live here, don't you?"

"Yeah, I live here. We're on th' mountain above th' town of Windin' Ridge. I always been here. You're pretty as a fairy princess. Why are ya here?"

"I don't know, Patty. Jacob brought me here against my will. Who is Jacob to you?" Tuesday sat up in bed.

"If ya mean Jeb, he's my pa," Patty answered.

Tuesday felt a cold chill go down her spine at Patty's answer. "Who are those women?"

"They're my mas."

Tuesday stared at Patty. "Patty, it's not possible to have three mothers."

"Yeah, I do. Annabelle, Rose, and Daisy are my mas. I hav' to go now. If they find me here I'll be in trouble. I want to talk to ya again, I dreamed we're goin' to be friends. I've never had a friend." Patty was gone before Tuesday could question her about the odd remark about her dreams.

The children watched from near the barn, where they worked, as the sheriff's Jeep moved up the road to their cabin.

"Let's see what he's a'wantin'." Patty pulled on Joe's hand.

"No. We'll go in th' barn. He'll ask questions, an' it's betta we don't answer. Pa won't like it if we talk to 'im." Joe ushered both girls into the barn.

"Someone's comin' up the road." Daisy stood looking out the window.

Annabelle came up behind Daisy and looked over her shoulder. "It's th' sheriff's Jeep. What's he wantin'?"

They watched as the Jeep drew nearer and stopped behind Jacob's truck. Jacob had walked up the mountain to visit his aunt. Instinctively Annabelle knew Jeb would not want anyone, let alone the sheriff, know that the woman was here. "I'll talk to 'im outdoors," Annabelle said. "Ya get Tuesday out th' front way for a spell."

"It's th' deputy," Daisy declared. "Ain't th' sheriff." Daisy had seen him in church many times. He always wore his uniform wherever he went. "What's he wantin' up here?"

"Folk's been talkin' 'bout Jeb selling our youngins," Annabelle answered. "Maybe that's it. Aunt Aggie swears it's against th' law. Ya knowed that old man Hillberry keeps goin' 'round stirrin' up trouble. His son, Tommy Lee's, always plaguin' Patty. He's scared to plague Joe."

Annabelle opened the back door and stepped out, closing the door behind her. "What ya wantin' here?"

Deputy Willis swaggered toward the cabin. "I want to talk to McCallister."

"He ain't here. He done took off a'walkin'. ' Spect he's gone to visit Aunt Aggie."

"I hear there's a young woman bein' held here against her will." Jess stood at the back porch with his right hand on his holstered gun, trying in vain to look important.

"Are ya crazy? Why would we be wantin' to keep someone here when we can't feed our own selfs most of th' time?" A chill of apprehension ran up Annabelle's spine. How could he possibly know there was someone else here? She was glad that she had told Daisy to get Tuesday out of the cabin when they saw the sheriff's Jeep. Jeb would be furious if the deputy saw her.

While Annabelle talked to the deputy, Daisy led Tuesday from the bedroom and walked her out to the front porch. Tuesday did not know that someone had come looking for her. She could not hear the talk out back. And she was groggy from the sleeping drugs that she had been given in the past two days. She obediently went along with Daisy, praying in vain that Daisy was going to help her out of her ongoing nightmare.

"Come, girl, I'm just wantin' to let ya get some fresh air," Daisy said in explanation of her sudden interest in her. The icy air failed to clear Tuesday's mind. "I think it's much too cold to stand out here without a coat."

"Air's good for you," Daisy answered, detaining Tuesday until the deputy had left.

While Tuesday endured the cold, hoping to win Daisy's confidence, Jess Willis was allowed to walk through the inside of the cabin.

"See, there's no one here." Annabelle noticed that Daisy had thrown Tuesday's quilt off the bed. Luckily it had landed on top of her suitcase where Jess couldn't see it. "Don't knowed why anyone thinkin' there's someone here, except for us," Annabelle, relieved they'd been successful with the deception, escorted the deputy to the back door by his elbow. The weight of her huge arm lifted him to his toes. He looked like a scarecrow accompanying her. "Ya knowed Jeb'll not like town's folk nosing 'round. Ya better just get on back to town."

As Annabelle and Daisy led Tuesday back to bed they agreed not to mention the deputy's visit. If Jacob knew they allowed the man into the cabin, there would be hell to pay. Never mind they'd kept him from seeing Tuesday.

Later in the day the drug Tuesday had been given by Jacob wore off and she sat up in the bed. Since her arrival at the cabin, she had stayed in bed the larger part of the time in a semi-drugged apathy. Now she decided to do something constructive. She threw the quilts to the side and slid her legs over the edge of the bed. When her bare feet touched the floor, she drew in her breath sharply. The ice-cold air blew around her feet as it found its way through the cracks in the floor.

She stood and looked around until she saw her suitcase. Opening it, she found a pair of jeans and a warm sweater. She felt around for warm socks and only managed to make a mess of everything. Jacob had crammed as many of her things into the one bag as he could.

Finally she found warm socks and underclothing. Jacob sure planned well, she observed. He had packed only warm, durable clothing. She wondered how he had managed to bring her here without her knowledge, and why! She shivered, clad only in the dress with spaghetti straps. Getting dressed as fast as she could was the only thing she would allow herself to focus on for now. Thinking about her bizarre situation was just too depressing. She found sneakers in the bag and put them on. She closed the suitcase and put it back where Jacob had placed it beside the old, homemade crib.

Feeling comfortable in the warm clothing, Tuesday moved toward the doorway. She heard the women talking in the kitchen. Taking a deep breath to steady her nerves, she pulled back the musty curtains and walked into the living room. There was no one there. She turned left, parted the curtains, and walked into the kitchen. Three faces stared at her, surprised that she had gotten out of bed without Jacob's permission. Each of the women had their mouths open as if they had been talking all at once and had stopped simultaneously as she appeared. If her situation was not so horribly frightening, their faces might have been funny.

Annabelle recovered first. "Sit yourself down. Annabelle's goin' to make ya some hot coffee." She knew Jeb would not tolerate any abuse of Tuesday.

Not knowing of anything better to do, she sat. "Your name is Annabelle?" Tuesday asked.

"Yeah," Annabelle said.

"Where am I?"

"Ya wantin' to knowed somethin', ask Jeb," Annabelle said. "I don't knowed anythin'."

*So they call Jacob Jeb,* Tuesday thought. *What if what Patty said is true? What would it mean if Jacob was Patty's father and these women posed as her mothers? Why did Jacob bring me to this place? This is unbearable; I must be having a nightmare. This is not reality.* But she knew she was not having a nightmare; she only wished she was.

"Where is Jacob?" Tuesday asked.

"We don't call 'im no fancy name. Jus' call 'im Jeb." Annabelle said.

While Tuesday drank her coffee, having difficulty holding on to the greasy cup, she watched the women. She noticed that the one called Rose just sat and stared, not doing or saying anything. She looked thin and sickly rocking back and forth in her chair, dressed in her ugly, faded dress. Tuesday noticed it was worn in places and was stained. Her hem was crooked and her shoes looked as though they belonged to a man. The primary difference in the women was that Annabelle and Daisy were more active and alert than Rose was.

Sitting at the table in her pink sweater and jeans, Tuesday looked like a rose blooming out of season.

"Daisy, step an' fetch th' water," Annabelle ordered. "I'm fixin' to start th' supper."

Annabelle and Daisy kept glancing at Tuesday as they worked; they had never seen such shiny, blond hair, nor such a soft, pretty, pink sweater.

Daisy lifted a large tub from the floor. It was kept in the corner behind the potbelly stove. There were half rings on each side. To grip them was just about as far as Daisy could extend her arms. She picked it up and with each step she took it bumped against her knees. She carried it out the back door. A short time later, she called for Annabelle to help her bring the tub back into the cabin. Water spilled out on the floor as the tub swayed back and forth with each step they took. They made it to the woodburner and lifted the tub up on the stove.

Annabelle used a poker to stoke the dying fire, and it roared to life when she added kindling wood. She sat an iron skillet on top of the stove and used a wooden spoon to scoop a large portion of lard into the skillet.

Jacob and Aunt Aggie rocked in their rocking chairs as they warmed themselves by the potbelly stove.

"Is th' town woman givin' ya any trouble an' such, Jeb? I knowed she would, so I did."

Aunt Aggie picked up her spit can, an old can that beans had come in. Her teeth were brown from her constantly rubbing snuff, and her bottom lip always protruded on the right side where she put the snuff between her lip and teeth. She invariably had brown stains on her chin where it dribbled when she spit.

"So far, Aunt Aggie, she's just stunned. I don't think she's going to give me any trouble. She wouldn't know how to get away. She can't call a cab. There's no phone. She would freeze if she tried to find her way off the mountain. She would get lost trying. I gave her sleeping pills to keep her unaware while I brought her from the city. I've kept her drugged most of the time since," Jacob explained to his aunt. "She has no idea where she is or how to get back home."

Aggie realized that it was not Rosily whom Jacob had been talking about. It was someone from the city. "It ain't goin' to be winter forever, so it ain't. She can walk, can't she? Ya can't keep her drugged forever, so ya can't. I can't imagine her stayin' in th' cabin an' doin' ya biddin' like th' other women, so I can't. She must be smart enough to know there's a town somewheres, an' she'll walk till she finds it."

"She's like a fish out of water in these surroundings, Aunt Aggie. What can she do? Nothing, except as I say." Jacob answered his own question. "I must go back to the cabin and see if the women are taking care of Tuesday as I ordered. She should be awake now. I'll bring you more supplies in a few weeks, but I'll come to see you again before I leave the mountain."

Jacob left his aunt rocking beside her potbelly stove and walked back down the rocky trail toward his cabin. In addition to his obsession to learn, he was obsessed with his health and strength. In his Wheeling house, he had a set of weights, and he worked out when he stayed there. When on the mountain, he walked often and, along with Joe, chopped wood. That was the only time he spent with his son. Both of them were large and muscular. And as a result of the exercise, both had powerful arms and legs. Another man would think twice before tangling with either of them, even though Joe was only fourteen years old.

Jacob walked inside the cabin, carelessly letting the door bang against the log wall, causing three faces to turn his way. Rose merely sat in the old rocker slowly rocking while she stared at nothing in particular. Annabelle and Daisy were busily preparing supper. Tuesday sat at the table, looking like a ray of sunshine in the midst of a dust storm.

"Hi. How are you feeling now, Tuesday?"

Tuesday did not bother to answer him. She simply looked at him with tears of anger and frustration in her eyes.

Jacob ignored her obvious depression and sat down beside her. "Are you hungry, Tuesday?"

"No," she answered. She did not wish to speak to him, but knew that she must. She could inadvertently learn information that would reveal a way to get back to her own home.

"You can't get away with this, you know. My friends have the police out looking for me." She knew that Cliff had Jacob's address, but she was smart enough not to let Jacob know that.

"Jeb, ya wantin' to eat before th' youngins?" Annabelle interrupted.

"You knowed damn well I don't want to eat with the kids. Fix something for Tuesday and me. After we eat, we're going in the bedroom and rest. Tuesday looks tired. You women sleep on your mats tonight."

Having been drugged much of the time, it had not occurred to Tuesday, until Jacob mentioned sleep, to wonder where everyone in this small cabin slept. She had not looked behind the curtained door into the room that was adjacent to the kitchen and bedroom, but now guessed it was a second bedroom where the women slept. Still, she had no idea where the children slept.

Annabelle put heaping plates of food in front of Jacob and Tuesday. Tuesday was hungry by now and ate a little, not knowing what it was. The food was fried mush, made with cornmeal, milk, and lard. When they had no milk they substituted water. "Wash the sheets and quilts tomorrow," Jacob snarled at Annabelle, who was busy frying mush for the others.

"Can't wash them quilts and sheets," Annabelle said with surprise. "They ain't goin' to dry an' ya will freeze with nothin' to keep ya warm."

"As soon as the weather is warm enough, I want them washed." Jacob backed down.

Annabelle turned her back to hide her smirk.

Tuesday thought she would faint. She had to sleep on those detestable sheets again tonight, but she said nothing. She knew there was nothing she could do about it, just yet.

In the bedroom, Tuesday got her nightgown out of her suitcase. "Get out, Jacob," she ordered.

"No," he said and grabbed the gown from her hand. "Take your clothes off. I'm tired of waiting."

"Not until you get out. I want to take a bath. How do we bathe here?"

"We bathe in the big tub every Sunday. It's too much trouble to heat the water for bathing every day. You've seen the big tub the women use for cooking and cleaning. It's large enough."

Tuesday wanted to laugh and cry at the same time. She did not know what good it would do anyway to take a bath and then sleep in the foul-smelling bed.

"Take your clothes off, or I will take them off for you," Jacob demanded with a depraved look in his eyes. "I've been patient too long."

She cowered back toward the log wall, dreading what she knew was coming. He grabbed her by the arm and pushed her backward onto the bed. With her wrist held in his powerful hand, he used his other hand to unbutton her jeans. She raised her knee to kick him in the groin. He grabbed her leg and with his knee holding her legs down, he unzipped her jeans. She twisted and screamed.

Jacob slapped Tuesday across the face, hard enough for her to stop fighting for a moment. "If

you don't want to be hurt, you had better stop acting like a child. You know that you want this as
much as I do."

He pulled her jeans down while she lay there
stunned. With her jeans down around her ankles,
she desperately tried to twist her legs over the side
of the bed. He held her firmly. Her fruitless exer-
tions were no match for his great strength, and he
pulled her jeans off. She felt his hand tugging at her
panties and struggled to get her hands free to stop
him. She could not. She sobbed as she felt her
panties slide down her legs. He tossed them aside.

She felt exposed as she wept and begged him to
stop.

After he left the room, she lay motionless while pain
throbbed deep inside her soul. She knew that she
must discipline herself and not allow him to break
her spirit if she hoped to get away from him. She
realized that she did not have the luxury of wallow-
ing in self-pity. After the degrading experience she
had just gone through, she knew that she must get
away from him at all costs. She could not bear the
thought of another repulsive rape.

*I can't sit and wait for someone to find me. He's
deranged, she thought. I must have a plan. He defied all
logic to get me here and will not allow me an opportunity
to get away if he can help it. I must think of a way to get
back home, but I don't have the slightest clue as to which
way to go. I will not stay here, she resolved, even if I die
trying to get away. I must find a way.*

*Why did I keep seeing him, ignoring the misgivings I
had about him?*

Knowing she needed her rest to be able to think
clearly, she tried to sleep, loathing the fact that he had
raped her. Sleep was the only way she could think to
escape this living nightmare, even if for a short time.

Sleep was not soon to come, though. Tuesday was kept awake by the activity of the others preparing for bed. It was not until after the children had retired for the night that Tuesday realized the room behind the tattered curtain was where they slept.

A flickering light caused Tuesday to open her eyes in alarm. She was dismayed to see that the source of light was Annabelle, carrying an oil lamp. Rose and Daisy followed her. Tuesday was dumbfounded when they pulled their shapeless dresses over their heads and threw them on the floor. Similar garments replaced the dresses; she supposed they were their nightdresses. Each of the women unrolled a mat. They placed them on the floor at the foot of the bed. After Annabelle turned the oil lamp off, consigning the room to darkness, the women lay on their mats. Tuesday knew that it was frigid on the floor with the winter air blowing through the cracks. Even in her misery, Tuesday felt sorry for the women.

Just as she felt she could not stand her surroundings another minute, Jacob climbed back into bed and reached for her. Now she knew she was not merely having a nightmare and would soon awaken. This was reality. She had fallen into the pits of hell!

# 29

*S*EVERAL ROCKY, SNOW-COVERED DIRT ROADS
wound up the wild mountain terrain. Cliff
chose the one that looked well traveled. He came to
a fork in the road once again. If he followed the left
or right trail each time, he might circle back to the
foot of the mountain instead of winding his way up,
so he alternated right, then left. Cliff had been driving for half an hour when he came to the first
house. It looked like a huge shed; still he thought it
must be a house because there was smoke coming
from the chimney.

The trail widened enough for him to park his
Blazer out of the way of any traffic that might come
by, although he had not passed nor seen another
vehicle since he started up the mountain. A footbridge crossed the raging stream. Built upon stilts, it
was the only way to reach the other side. He
climbed out of the Blazer and walked toward the
bridge. The floor was at least six feet above the sav-
age stream and did not appear to be stable. Frayed
ropes extended from the poles, spanning the length
of the bridge, and were attached to them for hand-

holds. The bed was constructed of narrow boards bolted to rusty cables that extended from the rotting poles at each end.

The bridge swung from side to side as his weight shifted. Through time, this type of construction had earned the name "swinging bridge." As he walked across, Cliff held the ropes tightly each time he grabbed a handhold, keeping a precarious balance.

When he reached the other side, Cliff began to climb down the ladder-like steps. Suddenly the booming sound of a shotgun blast startled him, and he jumped back a step. Fortunately, he caught his balance, preventing a fall into the churning water below.

There, only a few dozen yards away, was a big, burly man standing in the open doorway of the shack. His face was almost hidden by his shaggy, unkempt beard.

The man continued to point the gun at Cliff. "Ya have no call to walk on my property. Jus' turn 'round an' get back to where ya belong. Maybe I won't shoot ya if ya do."

Obviously, the man was in no mood to talk. Cliff moved hastily back across the bridge, causing it to sway precariously back and forth with each step he took. Disturbed by the swinging action, hunks of snow slid over the side into the untamed, frigid stream.

By the time he made it back to the Blazer he was sweating in spite of the cold mountain air.

Half an hour later he came upon a little log cabin nearly hidden among the trees. The forest surrounded the cabin, uniting with it. Smoke rose from the chimney, disappearing as it reached the tree tops. There was no driveway to pull over onto. He drove the Blazer through the brush that grew right up against the cabin, far enough to get the vehicle off the road. Alert for a repeat performance of the menacing shotgun welcome, he walked toward the front door. There was no unstable bridge this time. There was no need to knock on the door, either.

Apparently the old woman who resided in the cabin had heard him drive up. She stood at the door waiting as he walked toward the cabin. She looked like a witch straight from a child's storybook. Framed in the doorway, surrounded by the primitive setting, she was foreboding. Her hair was steel gray and matted in a tangled mess; evidently she took no pains with her appearance. Framed by the wild hair was a face webbed with seemingly endless wrinkles. "Wot ya wantin'?" she demanded in a raspy voice, showing her badly rotted teeth.

"Please don't be afraid. I just want to talk to you for a minute."

"I don't knowed nothin' to talk to ya 'bout. Go away," the old woman said, with obvious fear.

"I beg you, just give me a minute of your time."

She squinted her eyes as if she suddenly recognized him. "Come on in out of th' cold an' visit a spell." She opened the door wider, allowing him to walk inside. The stench almost knocked him over.

Tin plates and iron kettles, stained with dried food, cluttered the sink. The one-room cabin held an incredible assortment of junk. In the center of the room was a square table made of rough wood, and a wooden chair stood at each end. Pots, jars, plates, cups, and items that could only be described as rubbish covered the top of the table. Near the only window was an old-fashioned woodburner stove, the kind commonly used before electricity and gas. In one corner stood a potbelly stove that was used to heat the cabin. Beside it sat a box filled with wood and small branches that the old woman used for fuel. A cot, by the front wall just under the window, was covered with a worn patchwork quilt. Everything was made of splintered, bare wood. The entire cabin needed a good cleaning and coat of paint.

The old woman invited him to sit at the table.

"I'm trying to find Jacob McCallister. Maybe you know him as Jeb." Cliff said. He moved a pile of dirty clothes from the chair so he could sit down. "Will you tell me where he lives?"

"I'm so happy ya came to visit. Gets lonesome here by myself. I'm goin' to make ya some hot coffee," the old woman announced excitedly.

She selected two cups from among the many dirty dishes and moved over to the stove. From a wooden crate nailed to the wall to the left of the window, she reached for a jar of instant coffee. She unscrewed the lid and poured a generous amount in each cup. She did not own a spoon. From a tea kettle steaming on the back of the woodburner she poured hot water into both cups. She sat the cups on the table and took a chair, eager for a visit that until now had only taken place in her vivid imagination.

"Do you know Jeb or Jacob McCallister?"

"Maybe I knowed Jeb McCallister. He ain't come to visit nary a one time. Maybe he gone an' moved away. Or did I heared he passed on," she rambled.

Cliff caught on that she did not know what she was talking about. She lived in her own world of fantasy and could not give him any information, so he got up to leave.

"Ya not goin'?" she complained when he stood. "Ya never' come to visit anymore. Jus' drink ya coffee an' visit a spell."

"I really must go," he said, in a kind voice. "Thank you very much for the coffee and letting me visit with you." He had not been able to drink the appallingly strong coffee; she had put enough coffee in the water to make five cups. He moved toward the door with her trailing close behind.

"Now ya come back to visit, ya hear. Ya don't come to visit 'nough. Now ya come back an' see me tomorrow, ya hear."

"Thanks for the coffee, but I really must go," Cliff said and opened the door. After the obnoxious odor of the stale cabin, the air had never smelled better. He took a deep breath.

Little did Cliff know that he had just visited the woman who the mountain children thought to be a witch. Some of the parents used the children's fear of her to keep the younger ones closer to home.

Cliff continued his journey up the mountain. Soon it would be fully dark. A madman with a gun and a crazy old woman had done nothing to raise his hopes of finding Tuesday.

$\mathcal{J}$OMETHING WARM AND SOFT COVERED TUESDAY'S face. She opened her eyes; a big, mangy cat stared back at her. Pushing it away, she screamed in panic. The women were scurrying around trying to please Jacob with a hearty breakfast when they heard the commotion. He ran into the bedroom. The quilt was on the floor where she'd thrown it. She clung to the post at the head of the four-poster bed.

Jacob looked around the room to see what had brought on her scream of alarm and saw nothing that could cause panic. At her outcry, the cat had scurried out, as frightened as she was. "What happened? Everything's fine. Did something happen? Maybe you had a bad dream."

"You're a bad dream. This whole place is a bad dream!" Tuesday screamed at the sound of Jacob's voice. Jacob tried to take her in his arms to calm her down, but she beat his chest with both her fists. "What frightened you so badly? I want an answer."

"A mangy cat," she finally said, sobbing. "It was in my face when I woke up."

"A cat," he said with deadly calm. He released her and stormed back into the kitchen.

"I told you stupid women to keep the damn animals out of the cabin. Can't you do anything I tell you?"

When Tuesday heard the slap following Jacob's hateful yelling, she put her arm across her face and tried not to think, especially not about the night before. The rapes had been almost too much for her to endure, and the fact that Jacob forced her to have sex while the women were in the same room was unthinkable. She actually wanted to kill him with her bare hands. She could hardly believe he was the same man she had known in Wheeling. His cruelty had become increasingly apparent each hour of her captivity. How could she have seen him as fun-loving, witty, handsome, and charming? In Wheeling he had shown a completely different personality, leading her to believe that he was someone he was not.

She could not stay here to be defiled by him and to be at the mercy of his will. But how was she going to make her escape? Obviously, she knew Jacob would not allow it, but she did not know to what lengths he was willing to go to keep her with him.

*I don't even know where I am,* she worried, *or which way to go. How far am I from home? There is no phone here.* Scattered thoughts ran through her mind, and she was unable to form a plan. *I don't even know if I could get a letter to Cora. I don't think these people have paper and a pencil, even if I knew how to get a letter to her. Cora must be worried sick, not knowing where I am, and wondering why she doesn't hear from me.*

She didn't know that the mountain people had to go into town for their mail. And she didn't know which was worse: lying in the defiled bed to keep warm or getting up and freezing while she dressed. She had to go to the bathroom badly, so she had no choice. She found her suitcase, put it on the bed, and opened it. She chose a pair of jeans, a heavy sweater, and underclothing.

Annabelle came into the room just as Tuesday finished dressing. "Jeb said ya worried 'bout a bath. He told me to fix a bath an' ya can bath first. He says we all have to bath 'cause ya want a bath. It's 'most ready."

"I have to go to the bathroom," Tuesday said.

"Go on an' go, an' when ya get back ya can have your bath," Annabelle said.

Tuesday went into the kitchen, where Jacob sat at the table eating. The women had the washtub filled with hot water. It sat on the floor in front of the pot-belly stove. Jacob stood up as she came through the shabby curtain.

"Come with me. I'll help you to the outhouse."

She said nothing and followed him out the back door.

Once again, Tuesday was made aware of how beautiful it was beyond the cabin walls, if she looked past the trash and ugly outhouse to the snow-covered mountain ranges that loomed above them. The deep green pine set off the brightness of the sparkling white snow. Shadows filled the valleys that were formed by the towering mountain ranges, creating a sharp contrast to the awesome ridges that were brilliantly lit by the winter sun.

They stepped down the one step to the ground. When Jacob took her arm to steady her, she wanted to scream and jerk it away. But she needed Jacob's help to manage the climb up the steep path. Her sneakers were not meant for walking in the snow.

Jacob opened the door of the outhouse. "Hurry, it's freezing cold out here," he ordered. "You're going to have to learn to come out here by yourself. I can't be here all the time to help you."

After Tuesday finished, Jacob helped her back down the steep path. When they returned to the kitchen, the children were busily eating their breakfast. Tuesday sat at the table, next to Patty, and Jacob stood at the back door.

Annabelle put a plate on the table in front of Tuesday. "Ya eat your breakfast an' ya can have your bath," she said.

Tuesday was so hungry by then, it did not matter that the eggs and bacon floated in grease.

"I will be back in a few hours," Jacob announced. "I want everyone to get their bath over with and get this mess out of the way. " He pointed toward the tub. He hurried out the back door without an explanation of where he was going.

Tuesday finished eating and sat staring at the back door, wondering if she was expected to bathe without solitude. Do these people even know or care about privacy? She doubted it.

"Take your bath before th' water gets cold," Annabelle said.

"I can't bathe with everyone watching," Tuesday complained

"Who's goin' to watch," Annabelle said with irritation. "We've got work to do. We ain't goin' to watch. Th' youngins'll go to their room till you're done."

Tuesday undressed for her bath, feeling victimized. She was a modest person and felt extremely uncomfortable bathing in front of the women. And she did not wish to bathe in the same tub that was used for cooking, bathing, cleaning, and who knew what else. She just knew that she needed to take a bath. She was sure she smelled as bad now as these women and Jacob did. She wondered if Jacob ever bathed when he was in the cabin; he hadn't since their arrival. What a contrast to the clean-shaven and well-dressed man she had met in Wheeling.

It felt good sitting in the warm water, even though the tub was too small for her to stretch her legs out. Her knees were bent up to her chin and her toes cramped against the rough inside ridges. "Will you tell me where we are?" she asked.

"I done tol' ya, I don't knowed," Annabelle answered. Annabelle was smart enough to realize that Jacob had brought the city girl to the mountain against her will.

"But," Tuesday urged, "you must know where you are. Don't you ever go anywhere, to movies or out to dinner?"

"Humph," Annabelle grunted.

"We don't go nowhere." Daisy said. "Neve' been anywhere, but to th' church in th' town at th' foot of th' mountain. Don't have no reason to go nowhere."

Tuesday sat in the tub, miserable, with tears running down her face. *At least,* Tuesday thought, *now I know there's a town at the foot of the mountain, but which way?*

"Hurry an' finish your bath, 'fore th' water gets cold," Annabelle said in a kinder voice. "Th' youngins need to bath an' get on to school."

Tuesday finished her bath and went to the bedroom to give the children their privacy. She lay across the unmade bed and began forming a plan to get away from Jacob and the continuing nightmare her life had become. If it were not for the heavy snow cover, she would not hesitate to go. She knew she would eventually find the town that Daisy talked about at the foot of the mountain. If only she knew how far away the town was and on which side of the mountain it was located. She had no idea if the town circled the foot of the mountain or what she would find if she started down the wrong way. She knew it would not take long to freeze to death exposed to the cruel mountain winter. At least in the cabin, although it was cold, the fires in the woodburner and potbelly stove kept the temperature above freezing.

Tuesday felt someone's presence in the room and opened her eyes. It was Patty.

"Hi," Patty said, almost in a whisper.

"Hi," Tuesday answered quietly, knowing the girl would run away if she became frightened.

"Ya don't like it here do you?" Patty asked.

"No, I don't, Patty. Do you ever go to town?"

"Yeah, church and school."

*She knows the way to town,* Tuesday realized. "Patty, how do you go to town? Do you walk, or do you ride a school bus?"

Patty looked surprised. "I walk to school. Don't have a school bus comin' up here. I jus' walk off of th' mountain."

"I know the town is off the mountain," Tuesday prodded, "but which way? I saw more than one dirt road leading from here when I went to the outhouse."

"Well, th' big woods's thick an' ya can get lost if ya go on th' back side of th' mountain. Ya goin' to try to get away from here, ain't you? I knowed ya are. I been havin' dreams. I was in th' dreams with you. My dreams come true, but nobody believes me 'round here. Thinks I'm crazy."

"What dreams? Tell me."

"I dreamed ya was walkin' in th' forest an' I was with you. We was scared pa was followin' us. I have dreams an' then they happen. My mas an' pa an' Joe an' Sara don't like it when I talk 'bout th' dreams. After pa sold th' twins, I seen them in my dreams. Everyone gets mad when I talk 'bout it."

Tuesday was horrified. Terror filled her heart at the mention of Jacob selling twins. She remembered that Cliff had talked about twins he had found, but he could find no record of them as reported missing.

"You're sure, Patty? He sold twins?" Tuesday felt faint. She knew Jacob was coldhearted and dangerous, but selling children?

"Yeah," Patty shrugged, "once when I was little he'd sold twins, and a couple weeks ago sold another set. He sells all the women's kids. Except for me, Sara, and Joe."

Tuesday shrugged off her shock; she needed to think straight if she was to get away from him. "You're telling me you have dreams and they really come true?"

"Yeah," Patty answered.

"I've heard there are people who have the ability to predict the future by dreams, or visions as some call it. You must have it. Patty, tell me about the twins. Who did they belong to?"

"They're from Daisy. Th' baby he sold's from Rose. That's why Rose's so sick an' won't talk. Don't knowed why he don't sell me an' Joe or Sara. He sold all th' otherns."

Tuesday grew more alarmed by the minute. Could what this little girl was saying be true? Patty had said, "all the others." What others? She knew in her heart that it was true. Still, she found it hard to believe that anyone would sell his own children. Jacob's cruelty to her and the others was proof, though, that he would do anything. She now knew the other women were Jacob's wives. If she had not seen for herself, she would never had believed it. She wondered how she could trust her own judgment ever again. She was sure now that he was the man who had kidnapped Todd and left him to die when he jumped from the truck. And she finally knew why Cliff could not find out who the parents of the twins were. No one had looked for the twins because their own father had sold them.

Patty was ready to say something more, but

Annabelle's loud voice interrupted. "Patty, where are ya? Get in here an' bath," she yelled. "Th' water's gettin' cold."

Patty turned to go. Annabelle must not discover that she was talking to Tuesday. Patty would get into big trouble for talking about her pa's business. He expected the women to tend to the cooking and cleaning, never minding the men's business.

"Patty, wait." Tuesday said. "Please come talk to me when you can."

"I will. Ya are my only friend in th' world." Patty parted the curtain and hurried into the other bedroom, then into the kitchen through the connecting door that led from the children's room. Annabelle would think she had come from her own room when she came into the kitchen from that doorway.

*I'm leaving this place,* Tuesday decided. *No matter what I have to do. I cannot allow myself to be held prisoner and raped at his whim. His very touch makes me feel used and defiled. I'll convince Patty to go with me. She can find the way to town. Patty isn't happy here, and she would just grow up to be a carbon copy of these women. She will go with me. It's my only hope.*

Tuesday was terrified of what lay ahead for them when they actually made their move to leave the cabin. But she was more horrified of staying and subjecting herself to Jacob's bizarre behavior. Escaping safely might just depend on Patty and her ability to find their way to town and freedom. Jacob would be caught totally off guard. Clearly, he believed Tuesday would not get help, not from his women or children.

*I will get away from here. I will not allow him to keep me here against my will. I will convince Patty to leave with me. And I will see Jacob rot in jail!*

# *31*

*I*T WAS CLOSE TO DARK WHEN CLIFF STOPPED TO eat. There was a trail to the right that had been taken over by weeds, attesting to the fact that it was seldom used. He drove his Blazer through the weeds and brush and found a small clearing surrounded by pine trees, where he would not be seen. He stepped from the Blazer's warmth, retrieved his basket of food, and sat on a large rock. From a loaf of bread and package of lunch meat he had brought along, he put together a couple of sandwiches, and then he opened a can of soda. After he ate, he put the leftover food back into the basket and walked around to exercise his legs.

The thought of sleeping in the cold mountain air was not appealing; however, to drive to town and back again the next morning would take too much time and was not practical. He would attract attention traveling back and forth. The questions he'd asked the townspeople were more than enough for them to realize he was looking for Jacob. If he kept out of sight, perhaps he'd be out of mind. Time was crucial. He must find Tuesday. He continued on his way.

The Blazer bounced and jerked as it rolled up the steep incline. The snow-covered, rutted dirt road was getting narrower and it became increasingly difficult to maneuver the vehicle. Several times he slid around in a complete circle and found that he faced the way he had come. But he was determined to keep going. Eventually he came upon a huge log cabin, much larger than the others he had visited. The narrow, two-story structure stood in the midst of trash and litter that protruded from the white snow.

He parked the Blazer behind a new Ford pickup truck. Most of the trucks around town, and the few he had seen as he drove up the mountain, were old and beat up. A new truck was unusual in this territory, judging by the vehicles he had seen so far.

To get to the cabin, he would have to cross a footbridge that was a twin to the bridge farther down the mountain. He climbed the ladder like steps. As he walked across the bridge, it swung back and forth with every step. He climbed down on the other side; there was no burly man with a shotgun waiting for him there. No loud shots rang in his ears. Cautiously he walked toward the cabin, through trash that littered the front yard. The snow covered the ground about a foot high in places and hid most of the ugliness.

Cliff reached the door and knocked. Voices, coming from inside, were muffled by the heavy logs that made-up the cabin. Soon the door opened and revealed a girl of about fifteen.

She stared up at him with frightened eyes.

"Is your mother or father here?" Cliff asked the girl.

"Nope," she answered. "Who ya wantin'?"

An older woman came to the door and stood behind the girl. She was enormous; her hair was cut close to her scalp and it stood straight up all around her large head. She resembled a porcupine.

The two were dressed in rags. Their dresses were so worn the colors had long ago faded out.

"What ya wantin?" the porcupine woman asked.

"Is there someone here who can tell me where Jacob McCallister lives?"

"Don't knowed him. Don't knowed nobody, but ones that lives here," the porcupine woman said.

"Is there anyone here that might know?" Cliff asked. "Maybe your father or husband?"

"My father don't live here," the woman said. "My husband ain't goin' to like ya comin' here. Ya betta go on now."

Cliff was witness once again to the mountain code. He was clearly not going to get answers from these women. He thanked the women and turned to leave with the angry cries of a baby ringing in the background. As Cliff turned, a man walked from around the corner of the cabin. There was no time for a run-in with a cantankerous husband who might have a gun. The man wore bib overalls and a heavy jacket that flapped open as he swaggered closer to where Cliff stood. His jaw was swollen with a wad of tobacco, and he looked as if he had not shaved for days. The man stopped about five feet from Cliff and spat a glob of tobacco juice at Cliff's feet.

"What do you want, mister?"

"Can you tell me where Jeb or Jacob McCallister lives?"

"Don't know," Frank answered. "We don't socialize with our neighbors. That's why we choose to live in this remote area. Sorry I can't help you."

Cliff turned to go. The hard, no-nonsense glare in the man's eyes said he would not reveal anything and it would be useless to continue asking questions.

After Cliff left, Frank Dillon considered taking a drive up to Jacob's cabin to tell him that someone was looking for him, but decided it was nothing to him, nothing for him to be concerned about. Frank was not concerned about anyone except himself.

Frank's parents had died when he was sixteen. The two-story cabin was left to him at their death. And he made use of it, although he did not spend any more time there than he had to. Frank hated to work but liked to gamble, travel, eat good food, and maintain comfortable living quarters. With Jacob as a role model, Frank bought a house in Wheeling, using money from the sale of his children, when he was only twenty-four. He spent as much of his time at his house in Wheeling as he could. He could hardly stand the primitive cabin with no electric power, no plumbing, and no phone. He had to spend part of his time at the cabin though, or there would be no babies for him to sell.

His women were easier to control when he paid some attention to them. He slapped them when they disobeyed him to keep them in their places, at least what he considered to be their places. If hitting them did not work, he had another form of punishment that worked well. The punishment was confinement in a cage that he kept in the far corner of the open upper floor. One of his wives had died as a result of that punishment. The knowledge of the cage served well to keep them under control.

# *32*

*I*'M GOING TO LEAVE TONIGHT, SHE RESOLVED. IF I
*can get Patty to come with me, I will have a better
chance. Either, way I'm going. I can't bear being near
that bastard another night. Please, dear God, she prayed,
I hope I can get her to go with me. I can't stand it here
another second.*

Tuesday could not imagine why she had trusted
Jacob and had believed that he was someone
entirely different from what he actually was. It was
difficult to accept that her life had changed so drastically overnight, just because of him. She felt as if
she was walking through the worst nightmare and
could not wake up.

*This isn't a nightmare, she told herself, this is real. I
must do something, even if it's just getting up from this
disgusting bed and talking to the other women. Maybe
just by conversation they will tell me something that will
be useful later.*

"Can I help you with anything? I really would
like something to do," Tuesday asked Annabelle.

"Jeb said ya don't have to do no work. We have to do what he says. Ya sit down an' I'm goin' to give ya some coffee."

Tuesday sat at the table and Annabelle gave her a cup of coffee, a plate of biscuits, and a bowl of gravy. "I really would like to help. I see how hard you and Daisy work."

"He says 'no,' it's no," Annabelle said.

"Well, we wouldn't want to disobey the lord and master," Tuesday said in contempt.

"Here's your lunch. Gravy an' biscuits goes a long way. It warms ya an' fills ya belly," Annabelle said, choosing to ignore Tuesday's sarcasm.

It had not been long; it seemed to Tuesday, since she'd had breakfast and her bizarre bath. She knew she could not eat the greasy food. She knew that when they mixed the dough for the biscuits they did not bother to wash their hands. She realized that they had not been taught about cleanliness.

Just as Tuesday reached for her cup of coffee, the cat jumped from out of nowhere. It came from behind her, leaping onto the bench, then onto the table. The smell of the gravy had tempted it to venture where it knew it was not allowed. It startled Tuesday, causing her to spill her coffee. The cat lapped up the gravy as fast as it could.

Annabelle grabbed the cat by the scruff of its neck and threw it out the back door. "Don't knowed what to do. Jeb's goin' to lock me in th' cellar if I don't keep th' cats out of here."

Hearing Annabelle's defeated statement terrified Tuesday. *What does she mean? Would he really lock Annabelle up? That's barbarous.*

Tuesday couldn't help comparing her home to the cabin, and the contrast was unbelievable. Her interior decorator's mind could not even imagine making this place livable.

A few minutes after Annabelle cleaned up the mess the cat had made, Jacob appeared at the back door. Tuesday felt sorry for Annabelle when she pleaded with her eyes for Tuesday not to mention to Jacob that the cat had been on the table.

Jacob sat beside Tuesday. "You're looking much better," he said. "I hope it means you are becoming more comfortable in your new home."

Tuesday just sat there, not bothering to honor his absurd remark with a reply. *How could he possibly think I would want to live in this filthy hovel with a monster who would bring me here against my will?* she marveled. *What would possibly make him think that he can get away with it?*

"Annabelle, I'm hungry," Jacob growled. "Where's my food?"

Without acknowledging Jacob's nasty attitude, she put a plate of biscuits in front of him and Daisy brought him a bowl of gravy. Tuesday noticed that Annabelle and Daisy tried in every way to please Jacob. And Rose did only what she was told; otherwise, she sat and rocked in her rocking chair beside the potbelly stove. When Jacob was gone the cats used her lap for their bed.

Dumbfounded by his piggishness, Tuesday watched Jacob eat his biscuits and gravy. He dipped his biscuit into the gravy and, while allowing the gravy to drip down his fingers, he stuffed the mess into his mouth. *How did he learn the table manners he practiced when we ate together in Wheeling?* There had been a time that she would never have guessed she would watch him as he ate like a pig.

The children came in from their chores. Shyly, Patty smiled at Tuesday. The other two children paid no attention to Tuesday, except for a curious glance in her direction.

"Ya youngins go to your room an' I'll call ya

when I get your food ready," Annabelle instructed the children.

After Jacob finished eating, he left the cabin again. He had grown restless hanging around the place. Earlier he had gone to visit his aunt Aggie. Now he headed into town for a drink. He was aware that the townspeople were not friendly toward him simply because he lived on the mountain, but he did not care. He had no use for the townspeople either. They did not bother him and he did not bother them.

Tuesday was nervously excited and relieved that he had left. Now she would have a chance to leave without his intervention. Quietly, she went back to the bedroom, hoping Patty would soon follow.

While she waited, she looked through her suitcase for the warmest clothing she could find. She found an extra sweater for Patty. She knew that Patty's clothes were not heavy enough for the extremely cold outside air. The only food she could think to take was a few biscuits. Soon Patty came soundlessly into the room.

"Patty," Tuesday said in a low voice, "I'm leaving while Jacob's gone. I can't live like this. People just don't have to live this way. I want you to come with me. You can live with me. My house is comfortable and there's always food to eat. You would never go hungry or be cold."

"Why ya wantin' to take me with you? I'm too ugly. My pa couldn't even sell me cause I'm so ugly."

"Patty, you're not ugly. You're a pretty girl. That would not matter anyway. You need to get away from here. And I need you to help me find my way to town. I would freeze if I got lost. The life you're living here is not a normal life. There are many things you need to learn. Your life should be happy, not a drudgery to endure. I have no idea which way to go. Jacob knows that and that is why he's so sure I'll stay here. Please, come with me. You'll be happy with me. There's a nice school. I'll buy you clothes and you'll have your own room. I'll even adopt you legally and you'll be my daughter. Jacob can't do anything to us once we get to Wheeling. Selling children is illegal. Kidnapping me is illegal and he will go to jail," she promised herself and Patty.

"I don't knowed what adoption or illegal or kidnapping means. I jus' knowed I want to go with ya, but I'm scared of what pa'll do if he catches us."

"Then, Patty, say yes! Don't worry about your pa. I'll take care of you."

"I knowed I can trust ya. I've always dreamt of a better life, an' ya make it sound so-ooo good.'

"Does that mean yes?"

"Yeah," Patty grinned.

Tuesday hugged her. "I promise that you won't be sorry. Get a few biscuits. We might need them. Can we drink from the mountain streams?"

"Yeah, th' water's clean," Patty said. No one had ever hugged Patty her in her entire life. For the first time she could feel safe and wanted a feeling she had never felt before. "Are we goin' now?"

"Yes, Patty, but don't tell anyone. We need to leave while Jacob's away. This could be our only chance. Get the biscuits. We can't carry much. Put this sweater on; yours is too thin."

Patty put the pretty yellow sweater on. She had never felt anything so soft, nor had she owned anything that looked so pretty. Before she went to get the biscuits, she put Joe's shirt over the sweater so her mothers would not have cause for suspicion. Her face glowed with happiness to have the pretty yellow sweater.

Tuesday was frightened. Not only was she taking a dangerous chance with her own life, she had involved a young girl. But she knew this was the only thing to do; she could not leave Patty to be abused by her father. She looked around for a way to leave the cabin. It was important that the others not see them leave. The less they knew to tell Jacob, the better. She knew if he found them she would not get another chance to leave.

*C*LIFF WOKE UP STIFF AND CRAMPED. WITH THE
heavy coat he wore, and the sleeping bag
zipped around him, he had not been able to move
his legs and arms during the night. He unzipped the
bag and crawled out. This was no easy job. His arms
and legs had gone to sleep and were numb. After he
managed to get outside his tent, he walked around,
looking for a place to take care of his toilet needs.

After he took care of the necessities, he ate his
breakfast inside the tent, sheltered from the bitter
cold wind. Afterward, he packed his gear, loaded it
in the back of the Blazer, and climbed inside. Carefully Cliff backed the Blazer through the brush that
hid the clearing from view, and made his way
higher up the mountain. Up ahead a cabin sat in a
cove below the highest peak of the mountain, and
smoke rose from the chimney revealing that it was
inhabited. Animal droppings were scattered
throughout the snow-covered yard, disturbing the
beauty of the white blanket of snow.

Tire tracks, where someone had driven close to
the cabin, went right up to the front door. Cliff

drove his four wheeler as far as the tracks went and turned off the motor.

The dirt road ended at this one small cabin. There were two roads leading to the cabin: the relatively unused road that he had just driven up and one that ran by another cabin continuing upward to meet the road Cliff had used. He had no way of knowing that, on the last fork, had he chosen the one to the right, he would be preparing to knock at Jacob's door.

The door opened and an old woman stared directly at him. She did not have the uncivilized look of the woman he had talked to at the edge of the forest. This woman's snow-white hair was naturally curly. She had a kind, sweet-looking face. She was about five feet tall and small boned. Her dress was homemade.

"What ya wantin' here? Don't knowed ya, so I don't," said the woman standing inside the doorway.

"Please don't worry," Cliff said, "I just want to ask you a few questions. Don't shut the door without talking to me a minute."

Three cats rubbed against her legs as she stood at the door.

"Ya look to be a nice sort, so ya do," she said. "I guess I can talk to ya for a spell, so I can. Can't imagine what you'd want with th' likes of me, so I can't. Don't often see strangers, so I don't. Come on in. It's cold out of doors, so it is."

Cliff smiled at the strange way the woman talked, confirming what she said each time she made a statement. The inside of the cabin was not as cluttered as the bizarre old woman's cabin had been, and much cleaner. The furnishings were rough, unpainted, and homemade. There was no electricity or water. As a matter of fact, there was no electricity anywhere this far up on the mountain. He had not seen any electric poles or wires since leaving the little town down at the foot of the mountain.

Two wooden rocking chairs were arranged in front of the potbelly stove. The cabin was only one room, but it was larger than it appeared from the outside. There were lofts on two walls, and where they met in the corner stood a wooden ladder. There was room for a dozen people to sleep in the loft.

She invited him to sit down and warm himself. The fire in the potbelly stove burned brightly.

"Who are ya, an' what ya wantin'?" She sat in a rocker and motioned for him to sit. "I jus' can't figure what ya could be wantin' from th' likes of me, so I can't."

"Can you tell me where Jeb or Jacob McCallister lives?"

The woman stopped rocking. "Why ya lookin' for him? Ya don't have no business askin' questions after him, so ya don't."

"I'm sorry, I should have explained why I'm here. My name is Cliff Moran. I need to discuss some business with Jacob. I have his address as General Delivery, Winding Ridge, but I need to know where he lives. I need to talk to him."

Aggie picked up a rusty tin can from the floor beside the chair and spit into it. She was holding two cats on her lap. Another cat rubbed against her legs, and two others were sleeping on the table close to the woodburner. Aggie set her makeshift spittoon back on the floor.

"What kind of business ya havin' with him? If ya wantin' to knowed where he's livin' ya have to tell me what kind of business, so ya do." Aggie wiped her chin with the back of her hand.

The cat that was rubbing against her legs decided to jump onto Cliff's lap. It walked around his lap, looking for just the right spot, then curled in a ball and went to sleep. Cliff allowed the cat to lie where it was.

"You know he has a business venture," Cliff said, raising his eyebrows. "I'm involved with him, and I need to see him."

"That don't tell me nothin', so it don't," Aggie said. She picked up her rusty can again and spit into it. Again, drops of brown spittle dripped down her chin. She did not bother to wipe them away.

"I really can't tell you anything more, except it's important that I find him."

Aggie stood up, a cat hanging over each arm, indicating that the conversation was over.

Cliff lifted the sleeping cat to the floor. Awakened by the activity, it looked up at him with sad eyes, not liking its sleep disturbed. Cliff stood. She had no intention of telling him anything. She was just interested in discovering why he wanted to find Jacob. The visit had not been a complete loss, though. He had discovered that she knew Jacob well and he probably lived close to her. He left her and parked out of sight so she would think he had gone. He walked back toward her cabin and waited behind the outhouse. If his hunch was right, she would soon be on her way to warn Jacob that someone was looking for him. Apparently she knew that Jacob's dealings were not legal; otherwise, the fact that a stranger was looking for him would not put unbridled fear on her face.

As he stood behind the outhouse waiting, Cliff petted the dogs. So far they had been quiet. After a few minutes, the back door of the cabin opened and closed again. The woman walked down a path. The dogs, preferring her company to his, followed her.

# *34*

*T*HERE WAS ONE SMALL WINDOW IN EACH ROOM of the cabin. They chose the window that was in the room housing the four-poster bed. Tuesday lifted Patty to the ledge and she jumped to the ground. Tuesday moved the heavy, homemade crib under the window. She stood on the mattress, climbed onto the sill, and jumped.

Tuesday took Patty's hand. With Patty leading the way, they ran toward a path that wound through the forest leading down the mountainside. Both were terrified of being observed. There was no turning back; they had sealed their fate. Jacob would be in a rage when he realized they were gone. They knew beyond a shadow of a doubt that he would show no mercy if he found them.

Their hearts pounding, they stopped to rest when they reached the cover of the forest. Tuesday had not realized how limb-numbingly cold, nor how dangerous, walking on the rocky, snow-covered ground could be.

"This's th' path I take to church," Patty said, after catching her breath. "There's a cave further down. If we get there 'fore dark we'll be safe 'til mornin'. I don't think Sara or Joe'd tell if they thought we'd gone there."

"Ya all right?" Patty startled Tuesday out of her thoughts.

The fire Patty had built burned brightly, pushing the darkness back, giving eerie light to their faces.

"Yes, Patty, but I'm a little worried that Joe and Sara will tell Jacob about this cave. He might even know about it."

"I don't think he does, an' if he did, he don't knowed I knowed about it," Patty said. "He'll think we headed straight to town anyways. Sara and Joe won't tell. They're afraid of me cause of my dreams. They think I can cause somethin' bad to happen."

"Patty, do you understand that Jacob kidnapped me when he brought me to the cabin?"

"Yeah, kidnap means ya didn't want to come to th' mountain with Pa."

Tuesday laughed. "I guess that's one way to put it."

"Tell me more about your house an' th' city an' 'bout the wonderful life off th' mountain. I want to forget all th' bad things I had until now."

Jacob came back to the cabin at eight o'clock.

He went into a rage when Annabelle told him that Tuesday was gone and had taken Patty with her. He viciously kicked the table against the woodburner. A bucket of hot water fell to the floor, splashing everywhere, leaving muddy puddles where tracked-in mud and snow had dried.

"I had not counted on Tuesday having an accomplice to find her way off the mountain," Jacob raged. "When I find them I'll sell Patty. I'll see to it that she's sold out of the country to keep her quiet. She knows what's going on, and if I don't take proper precautions she could make trouble for me."

Finally, Jacob sat at the table with his head in his hands.

"How long have they been gone?" he asked.

"It's been dark for a long time now," Annabelle answered. "It was nearly dark when I'd gone into the bedroom to get Tuesday for dinner, only to find out her and Patty was not there. I don't knowed what time it was. Ya knowed I don't keep track of th' time. I've no place to go nor plans to make."

"Well, it's useless to look for them in the dark," Jacob said. "They're probably holed up somewhere sleeping. There'd be no aid for them in town in the middle of the night. Everything's locked up for the night. One thing fore sure, Annabelle, I have the advantage. They're on foot, and I have a four-wheel drive truck."

Tuesday and Patty spent the night cuddled together near the fire. After a long, almost sleepless night, Tuesday could see daylight at the mouth of the cave. She gently shook Patty awake.

"We must go. Hurry!"

Tuesday tried to keep their fear at bay. She was well aware that if Jacob found them, he would not be kind when he rendered their punishment.

They each carried a handkerchief, the four corners of which were tied to one end of a small rope. In the homemade pouch they each carried crumbled biscuits and socks. Their hobo bags were tied to their belts with the free end of the short rope, thereby leaving their hands free. Each of them had an extra sweater tied around her waist.

"I'm thirsty. Let's get a drink of water," Patty said.

Tuesday squinted when she stepped from the dank, dark cave into the intense brightness of the snow. She followed as Patty walked toward a stream. "How long will it take us to walk to town from here?" Tuesday asked as they knelt to drink.

"Don't knowed how long, except maybe we can get there 'fore lunch time."

Tuesday shuddered at the thought of Jacob finding them. They left the stream and continued to walk down the path. It was difficult; the ground was no longer frozen and the melting snow was slippery.

Their feet were cold and wet. Neither of them had proper shoes for mountain climbing. Tuesday wore her sneakers. Patty had hand-me-down boots that had holes in the soles and were two sizes too large.

They came to a snow slide that blocked the path. "How are we ever going to get past this slide?" Tuesday asked, looking at it with huge eyes.

"We have to go around. It's too far to go back to the cabin and take th' road. An' like I said, Pa might see us," Patty answered.

The ground off to the side of the path was thick with briars and undergrowth. It was the only way. Patty picked a spot that looked passable and pushed through. Tuesday followed, and they made their way, with briars and twigs pulling at their clothes, down a more reasonable slope. They were well past the snow slide now as they moved east, so Patty changed their direction, making her way southwest toward where she believed they would meet the path at a point below the huge snow slide. They had been steadily climbing down the heavy brush covered slope for twenty minutes when Patty took a disastrous step.

With Tuesday following close behind, Patty went sliding and bumping down the rock face for eighteen horrifying feet in the small avalanche caused by their footsteps.

Patty scrambled from under the snow. "Where's Tuesday!"

She ran back and forth screaming, "Tuesday, where are you? I've got to stay calm an' find her." In the area where she had struggled from under the snow, Patty removed her cumbersome cotton work gloves and began digging furiously with her bare hands.

# 35

*C*LIFF PURSUED THE OLD WOMAN AS SHE MADE HER way slowly down the path, lagging far enough behind so as not to be discovered. She would not willingly lead him to Jacob. Obviously, she would protect Jacob, or she would not be struggling down this treacherous, snow covered path. After an hour of hiking, a cabin came into view, smoke billowing from a chimney. Someone was there. Cliff stopped at the edge of the clearing and paused until the woman disappeared inside the cabin.

Annabelle and Daisy sat at the table sipping coffee. Rose was in her rocking chair with a contented cat sleeping in her lap. Annabelle was surprised when Aunt Aggie stumbled through the doorway. She never came to the cabin unless she had been sent for. Annabelle got up from her chair, prepared Aunt Aggie a cup of coffee, and invited her to sit down.

"Where's Jeb?" Aggie demanded, huffing and puffing from her tedious trip down the mountain path. Her cheeks were red from the frosty air and brown tobacco stained her determined chin.

"Sit yourself down, Aunt Aggie," Annabelle said. "Jeb ain't here."

"Where's he at? I need to talk to him, so I do."

"If'n ya sit down an' calm yourself, I'm goin' to tell ya," Annabelle said.

Aunt Aggie sat at the table. "I don't understand why ya women live like this or how Jacob tolerates it, so I don't. I knowed with so many people livin' in th' little cabin it's a lot of work to keep th' place in order, so it is. Anyways I knowed I could do better. I remember when my father sold me to Ham Conrad. He had a sick wife an' ten children, so he did. T'was constantly pickin' up clothes, cleanin' and cookin', so I was. But I'd cleaned up after m'self and th' others, so I did," she congratulated herself. "I don't like a mess, so I don't."

"Jeb's looking for th' city girl," Annabelle said, refusing to get into it with Aggie. "She's run off'n took Patty with her."

"I need to talk to 'im," Aggie said. "There's goin' to be hell to pay with that city girl, so there is," Aggie said.

"I told ya, Aggie, he's out lookin' for th' city girl an' Patty," Annabelle said, watching as Aggie sat there twisting her hands. Soon, the old tomcat jumped onto her lap. It never came near anyone else except the children, Rose, and Aggie.

Aggie jumped at the loud knock on the door.

Annabelle hurried to find out who it was. She was surprised at having two visitors in three days. First the deputy, and now who could it be? She opened the door and a stranger filled the opening to the outdoors, obscuring her view of the back porch. This was so out of the ordinary, she stood there with her mouth gaping open.

Cliff did not wait to be invited in. He walked past Annabelle and confronted the old woman he had followed there.

"What ya wantin' here? Don't knowed you," Annabelle said.

"I'm a detective with the Wheeling Police Department," Cliff answered. "Where's McCallister and Tuesday Summers?"

Getting no answer from the women, Cliff turned and moved toward the next room without invitation. He swallowed his breakfast back down when it threatened to come up at the sour smell in the cabin. Cliff walked through the curtained doorway into the living room.

"Where ya think your goin'? Ya can't go in there," Annabelle yelled when she found her voice.

Ignoring her, he walked through the next curtained doorway into the second room. A huge four-poster bed dominated the room. Cliff spied a suitcase that was ridiculously out of place in the primitive room. He opened it. "This belongs to Tuesday," he said. "I'd bet the farm you women don't own such garments."

There was a third curtained doorway to his right. Pushing back the musty material, he walked into the room. Mats and quilts lay scattered on the floor. Clothes were piled in the corners, and some hung on nails around the walls. Other than clothes and bedding, the room was bare. There was no furniture. To his right was a fourth doorway. He parted the tattered cloth and was once again standing in the kitchen with the women.

Annabelle knew they were in trouble with Jacob. He would not bother to hear an explanation. It would not matter that the man, without invitation, had walked in and made his way through the cabin without their consent. Jacob demanded they do his bidding and would not accept any other behavior.

"Where is she?" Cliff demanded in a no-nonsense voice.

Accustomed to obeying the opposite sex, Annabelle said, "Tuesday's gone an' ran away. She's took one of our kids with her." She wished to get him to leave before Jacob came back. She had no idea if Jacob would return in a minute or hours.

"Tuesday must have taken the child with her to help find her way to town. Which way did they go?" he demanded.

"Don't knowed," Annabelle answered, her stubborn chin protruding out, unwilling to tell him more.

"When did they leave?"

"Don't knowed what time it was when they left," Annabelle answered.

"McCallister's out looking for Tuesday and the girl. Isn't he?" No one answered.

"If you know what's good for McCallister, I must find them first," Cliff said. "If only she had waited, I could have taken her away from here now."

"Well, she ain't here," Annabelle said.

"McCallister will be desperate to find her and stop her from talking. Her life's in danger if he finds her first. If you don't want to see him up on murder charges, you'll tell me where to find him," Cliff threatened. "Now I know McCallister must be the driver of the black truck involved in a boy's kidnapping."

Annabelle had no idea what he was talking about.

"No sense in wasting any more time here," Cliff said, leaving the cabin and heading up the mountain for his Blazer. Cliff had to use all the resources he had available to him, for McCallister had the advantage. He had grown up in these mountains and knew where to look for Tuesday.

"It's time to send for help," Cliff said to himself. "If I take the time to drive into town it'll give McCallister the leverage of a head start; time that's crucial. But on the other hand, I could look for days and not find Tuesday and Patty. If I don't find them on my way back down the mountain, I'll call for help when I reach town. They were certainly headed there, and the girl would know her way. It's possible that they could make it before Jacob has a chance to stop them."

The women gathered at the table talking, except for Rose who sat and rocked to and fro, oblivious to the rare events occurring around her. The women would starve without Jacob, unless another mountain man took them in. That was unlikely. It was difficult enough for them to feed the families they already had.

"We have to tell Jeb th' detective was here," Annabelle warned. "He goin' to knowed, in time, anyways. I should've told 'im 'bout th' deputy lookin' for 'im."

"What deputy? Ya didn't tell me 'bout no deputy, so ya didn't," Aggie accused.

"It was just Deputy Willis, ain't no never mind." Annabelle denied its importance. "We're goin' to have to tell Jeb 'bout th' detective, though."

"I'm gonna try to get Jeb to go away till this mess is forgotten," Aggie said.

Annabelle's main concern was that if he had to go away to hide from the law, they'd go hungry even more often than they did now, perhaps even starve. They could not grow enough food or kill adequate meat to last them through the long winter that would follow the brief mountain summer. They did not have the resources to bring in the necessities from town. They could not do without supplies such as flour to make bread, gravy, and biscuits. They needed salt for curing meat and many other items, staples they would have to do without if he took Aggie's advice and left the mountain. "Aggie ya go on an' talk Jeb into leaving, an' where ya goin' to get ya snuff?" Annabelle taunted

The women's lives were hardly worth living now. What would their lives be like without Jacob?

$\mathcal{N}$OPE, AIN'T SEEN ANYBODY LIKE THAT 'ROUND here," was the answer McCallister got every time he stopped and asked: "Have you seen a little girl who has a birthmark on her face? She would be with a pretty blond woman." McCallister walked up and down the lone street that ran north and south through town. He asked everyone he saw if he or she had seen the woman and girl.

McCallister had driven across every dirt trail he could maneuver the truck over. Snow slides had cut him off many times, forcing him to turn and go back the way he had come.

"Are they already on their way to Wheeling?" Jacob said aloud in frustration. "I must find them. I'll not allow anything to interfere with my neat little business of baby-selling."

McCallister turned and drove back toward his cabin.

Sheriff Moats sat at his desk. Through the window he could see Main Street. He had just watched McCallister walk up and down the street, stopping anyone he passed. He appeared to be asking questions. After a while, he saw him get in his truck and head up the mountain. "Willis, get out here," the sheriff called.

"What you want, Sheriff?" Willis asked, coming from the back, where he had been pretending to be busy.

"What's McCallister up to?" The sheriff got nervous when kidnapping was mentioned. Through the grapevine, word had come to him that his brother, Aubry, and McCallister were involved with baby brokers in Wheeling.

"I told you there was no one except McCallister's women in the cabin. I checked the entire cabin and saw nothin'."

Sheriff Moats got his large frame out of his comfortable chair and walked to the front door. "McCallister's out around town askin' questions. He's stoppin' everyone he passes. He ain't one to stop and chat. I want you to find out what he's up to. I want to know the questions that he's askin'."

Like a dark speck working in the immense, white landscape, Patty furiously dug to uncover Tuesday in time. At last, Patty uncovered Tuesday's face. She lay motionless, partially buried in the snow at the bottom of the steep rocky slope, looking like a disjointed rag doll.

"Are ya hurt?" Patty asked in a fear-filled voice, digging away the snow that covered Tuesday's lower body.

As they had climbed down the mountain the snow had served as a blanket, hiding the hazards of the mountain terrain waiting for the right step or sound to set off an avalanche.

Tuesday moved to get up, but could not. She had fallen onto a jagged rock hidden beneath the snow, breaking her right leg. "Are you okay, Patty?"

"Yeah, I'm okay. What about ya?"

"Patty, I either broke my leg or sprained it, and I can't walk. We are going to freeze to death. I shouldn't have brought you with me. It was selfish. I could've sent for you after Jacob was put in jail where he belongs." Tuesday knew they were in bad trouble now that she could not walk.

"We have to find another cave. We need to get dry an' warm," Patty said. "It's th' only way we're goin' to make it. Goin' back is not possible now."

"How? I can't walk. You go for help and leave me here."

"Nope, ain't goin' to leave ya here. Ain't no help for us now. Pa'll kill us if he finds us now. There's a cave on down the mountain. I'm sure we're close to it. I can drag ya to it. It's not far from here, and it's betta than th' other one."

The pain in Tuesday's leg kept her from passing out. *How did I get into a situation like this?* Tuesday wondered. *Are we going to die in this wilderness? We only have a few biscuits to eat.*

"Okay, let's go," Patty said. "I'm glad ya not big like Annabelle. I could never pull her through th' snow."

Even though she was cold and in pain, Tuesday had to smile at the thought of Patty dragging Annabelle anywhere. "I'm afraid we can't make it, Patty. Go get help."

"I won't leave ya here. Ya knowed nobody's goin' to help us. I'm goin' to get a hold under ya arms an' pull you. I knowed ya cold an' wet, but it ain't far to th' cave."

Patty removed her wet gloves, and taking Tuesday under her arms, dragged her slowly down the path to the new cave. Every step Patty took, pulling Tuesday with her, sent a blinding pain through Tuesday's leg.

When Jacob came back unexpectedly, Annabelle was glad Aunt Aggie was still there. She knew if anyone could calm Jacob, Aggie could.

"They got away," he yelled as he hurried into the bedroom, not questioning the rare fact that Aggie was here.

"I'm going after them. They will sorely wish they had stayed here where they belong."

Aggie followed after him. "I hate to tell ya that a detective was lookin' for ya, so I do. It's got to be told, so it does. He come right to my cabin. Said he's from th' Wheelin' Police Department, so he did. He's lookin' for th' city girl, so he is. He was here, too, so he was. Told ya not to bring her here, so I did. He looked all through th' cabin, so he did. Ya had betta go away somewhere till this is forgotten, so ya had."

"What the hell is going on? I'm sure the detective you're talking about is Cliff Moran," Jacob said to himself as much as to Aggie. "What would make him think that Tuesday's with me? How would he know to come here? He could not know anything. How could he?"

Jacob had not heard the news bulletin about Todd's kidnapping. He had no knowledge that in the course of the investigation, Cliff had learned his address. Nor did he know his truck fit the description of the one used in the crime, making him a prime suspect. Had he heard, he would have known who the kidnapper was. The sheriff's brother, Aubry, had a truck just like Jacob's own and he worked for Steven Lloyd, the owner of B A Parent Adoption Agency.

"You women know not to let anyone, and I mean anyone, in this cabin. Do I have to watch you all every minute? I don't have time now, but when I get back all of you will pay for this. I will see to it that you all learn to listen to what I say."

Jacob sponged off, not bothering with his shaggy growth of beard, and changed his clothes.

Annabelle had quietly brought a wash pan of hot water, a washcloth, a towel, and Jacob's box of city clothes from under the four-poster bed, while Jacob yelled at his aunt. It was best to anticipate his wants so he would not have to bother to ask. Jacob was ready to leave and walked back to the kitchen, with Aggie at his heels.

"Just what did you women tell the detective?" Jacob demanded.

"We didn't tell anythin' to him, so we didn't," Aggie said. "He'd looked all 'round th' cabin, so he did."

"I suppose he spotted the suitcase and recognized it as Tuesday's. I know he asked where Tuesday was," Jacob said in a deadly calm voice. "Now, tell me the truth. It's very important. What did you tell him?"

"I wanted to get shed of him," Annabelle said, "so I told 'im she ran away an' took Patty with her."

"This is the last straw. Not only did you let a stranger in, you told him everything you knew and let him make himself at home in my cabin." He slapped Annabelle so hard that she fell backward. She caught herself with her right hand on the hot woodburner, causing a nasty burn. She cried out in pain.

"Keep your mouth shut in the future," Jacob yelled. "I've had enough of you all. I'm going to Wheeling to find Tuesday and Patty. I'm going to bring them back here. I will lock them in the cellar house. They need to learn a lesson. You women take a couple mats and quilts out there. You can move things around and make room."

He slammed the back door on his way out.

# *37*

*O*N HIS WAY DOWN THE MOUNTAIN, CLIFF COVERED every navigable road. Unknowingly, within a quarter of a mile, he passed the location where Tuesday had fallen.

At the same time, Tuesday and Patty were making their way to the new cave.

Meanwhile, on an adjacent road to Cliff, McCallister had headed up the mountain to change his clothes and continue his search in Wheeling.

Cliff had talked to Aggie in her cabin for half an hour (counting the time he waited to follow her). It had taken an hour to trail her to Jacob's cabin; he was there fifteen minutes. It took forty-five minutes to walk back to the vehicle. He made better time going back because he was not following the slow old woman. The time spent gave Jacob two hours' headstart on him.

Cliff encountered the same problem McCallister had when he drove down the mountain looking for Tuesday and Patty. He would come to a snow slide across the road and would be forced to turn and go back.

When Cliff found himself at the foot of the mountain, he stopped at the only gas station the town had and filled the tank with gas. He also used the only pay phone to call Hal. "I've found Jacob's cabin; he's the one who took Tuesday. We were right. I found where he took her, and you would have to see the place to believe it. I couldn't begin to describe it to you. Anyway, Tuesday escaped and took a little girl with her. I haven't found Tuesday and still don't know how he managed to get her here. I'm certain Tuesday wanted the girl with her to guide her to the town."

"What can I do to help?" Hal asked.

"The weather's bad. Almost impossible to get around off the beaten paths. I need help to find Tuesday. It wouldn't take long for someone to freeze in this weather. They could even be stranded by a snow slide. Bring dogs. Dogs are the best chance we have," Cliff said.

"No problem, Cliff. It won't take long to get the dogs and our supplies together, but it will take us five or six hours' travel time. Hang in there," Hal said.

"Just hurry," Cliff pleaded. "I'll continue looking. I can't sit and wait. Call Cora and let her know what's going on. Ask her if she can give you something of Tuesday's for the dogs. They'll need a scent. Put an all-points bulletin out on Tuesday and the girl. They may be heading that way. I have no idea what McCallister's doing. I suppose he's here, but he might have decided she made it back to Wheeling, and he's looking there. Make sure the all-points bulletin on Jacob is still active; have him picked up on kidnapping charges if he shows. Bring four-wheel-drive vehicles. You can't get around otherwise. The mountain trails are really bad, not to mention the road leading up to Winding Ridge.

There'll be slides and high water coming from the mountain streams now that the weather's warming a few degrees."

After talking to Hal, Cliff paid for his gas and went to see the sheriff once more before driving back up the mountain.

Cliff climbed from the Blazer and barged into the sheriff's office. The scene was the same as before. The sheriff sat behind his desk looking at a *Playboy* magazine. When he heard the door, he slipped the magazine under a newspaper.

"You again. What can I do for you now?"

"I need help. The woman I've told you about has run away and is on the mountain somewhere, lost for all I know."

"When I talked to you before, I told you I'd check on your complaint. I sent my deputy, just after we talked earlier, and no one's there except for his women. You're mistaken." The sheriff puffed up his chest with authority.

"I'm not mistaken. I just came from there; her suitcase is there and the women who live there admitted that she had been there. McCallister's child ran away with her. Like I said, I need help and I need it now!"

The sheriff stood up. There was no way around it; he had to deal with the mess. "Willis ain't here now, but I'm goin' to give him a dressin' down. He should have spotted those things."

The door opened and Andy Hillberry rushed in with Deputy Willis right behind him. "Sheriff, McCallister's goin' all around town askin' questions. He's lookin' for a little girl and a blond woman. I've been asking' Willis here what ya goin' to do 'bout it. I knowed McCallister's up to no good."

"Andy, if you interfere in this, I'm goin' to lock you up and keep you here until hell freezes over.

You're just stirrin' things up and interferin' with law and order. Now you have a choice: get out of here or I lock you up. I'm in a no-nonsense mood, an' you can just get out'a here and let us law officers do our jobs."

"What time was McCallister in town asking questions?" Cliff asked Andy. "Is he still on the mountain?"

"I don't knowed. Who're ya anyways?" Andy asked.

"I'm a detective from Wheeling. I'm investigating McCallister in a kidnapping matter."

Andy laughed. "McCallister ain't no kidnapper. He sells his own flesh an' blood."

Cliff took out a pad and pen. "What's your name and address. I'll have to call you for questioning."

Andy gave Cliff his name and told him where he lived, since his address was just a post office box. "It's 'bout time someone done somethin' about 'im sellin' his own. I've tried to get th' sheriff to do somethin' 'bout it for years."

"That right sheriff?" Cliff asked.

"You can't listen to Andy. He's jealous of McCallister's truck and lifestyle. He'll say anything."

"We'll talk about this later. Right now I need to know when you last saw McCallister."

"I saw him about an hour ago," Sheriff Moats answered. "I sent my deputy out to check it out and you just witnessed the results."

"There's a good chance that Jacob's still on the mountain," Cliff said. "It's imperative that we do everything in our power to find the woman and girl before he does."

"I guess I can't ignore you guys, as much as I'd like to. Willis can go with you an' I'll round up a search party. I'm in charge, an' it's best you city boys not forget it. This is still my town, after all. I'll get the search party together, and they'll be ready first thing in the morning. Can't expect to get one together this late in the day."

The sheriff did not have an appetite to go tromping over the mountain in the cold and snow. He would direct the search from his comfortable chair.

Jacob was a mile from the cabin when he suddenly stopped. "They couldn't have made it to town and caught a ride to Wheeling," he reasoned aloud in desperation. "No, I would have had a reaction from the townspeople. She didn't get to town. Tuesday's a stranger to the townspeople. They don't like strangers. They don't like strangers any better than they like mountain people. There would have been gossiping. Nothing happened in town. Maybe they're hiding in someone's cabin. No, the mountain people would not take in a stranger, unless it was someone who wanted a pretty woman. Now I'm talking to my self. Shows I've been on this time-forgotten mountain too long.

"My only prayer is to find them and hide them," Jacob continued his conversation with himself. "Under no circumstances can Cliff be allowed to speak to Tuesday. If Cliff doesn't find her, I can't be arrested for kidnapping her. I'll have a talk with Frank Dillon. It's likely that Tuesday and Patty passed by his place when they made their escape down the mountain. If I don't learn anything from Frank, I'll go back to the cabin, change into warm clothes, and start walking. I'm beginning to feel like a caged animal going around in circles."

Patty had managed to bring Tuesday to the relatively safe and warm cave. She had walked backward the entire distance.

Inside the cave, Patty put the extra sweater and

dry socks on Tuesday, and tossed her wet shoes aside. Tuesday's leg was swollen. Using the knife that she always carried in her pocket, Patty cut Tuesday's wet jeans to relieve the pain. Then she covered Tuesday's legs with her own extra sweater.

"I'm goin' to go fetch wood for a fire. I'll hurry," Patty assured Tuesday.

"I'm okay. Go on and do what you have to. I'm more comfortable without the wet clothing and you relieved the terrible pressure on my leg when you cut my jeans."

It had taken Patty half an hour to find and carry the wood, twigs, and dry limbs back to build a fire.

She arranged the wood and the pages from old catalogs that she had wrapped around the biscuits to keep them separate from the extra socks. She placed small chips that would burn easily under the paper and lit a match. The paper caught right away and soon Patty had a blazing fire going.

She slumped, warming by the flames, exhausted from the long, eventful day.

"When it gets dark 'nough, I have to go to th' cabin and find ya 'nother pair of jeans an' a quilt. Ya goin' to freeze if ya don't have nothin' to keep ya warm."

"Patty, no! It isn't safe to go back to the cabin. You'll be seen. We must make do with what we have. I will not let you take the chance."

"When it gets dark, I have to go. You need to stay warm an' ya need food. I'll be careful."

Frank stood at the cabin door as Jacob parked his truck near the pole bridge.

"Hi, Frank," Jacob called as he walked across the bridge that swung back and forth each time he took a step. "Need to talk to you for a minute."

Frank stepped off the lopsided front porch as Jacob climbed down the rope ladder.

"Sure," Frank answered. "Must be important, for you to come here."

"Have you seen a blond woman with my daughter?" Jacob asked. "The girl has a large birthmark on her face."

"Haven't seen them," Frank answered, "but a stranger was here looking for you."

"Why the hell's he looking for me?" McCallister asked.

"Didn't say. I told him I don't mix into others' business. That's why I live up on this mountain away from others."

"Thanks, Frank," McCallister said. "See you around."

He hurried back across the pole bridge and drove his truck toward his cabin to change into warm clothes and continue his search on foot.

After cleaning up from lunch, Annabelle mixed bread for supper and for the next day's meals. Even though her hand hurt badly, she was afraid not to do her usual chores, seeing that Jacob was already furious with her. Aggie treated Annabelle's hand with castor oil and lard. The remedy called for castor oil and egg whites, but having no eggs, Aggie improvised. She put the mixture on Annabelle's burn and then she wrapped her hand in an old, dirty rag. Annabelle was at loose ends because she did not know what to think. Her life had never had so many strangers in it.

Joe and Sara had not gone to school. No one had bothered to tell them what to do, so they lay in the hayloft. "What ya thinkin' goin' on here?" Joe asked.

"Don't knowed. Why ya think Patty went with th' city woman?"

"Patty likes th' city woman," Joe said. "I could tell. Don't knowed why, except she'd talk to Patty. Patty's always thinkin' nobody likes her an' stuff."

"It makes me nervous to talk to Patty," Sara declared. "She's always havin' dreams that happen, an' she stares off somewheres. It's like she done gone somewheres we can't see. She's crazy."

"I wish she didn't go," Joe complained. "It's more fun with all three of us."

"I'm glad she's gone," Sara mumbled so quietly that Joe did not hear.

"Pa's lookin' for 'em," Joe said. "Maybe they're on th' mountain somewhere. Let's see if we can find them. We knowed Patty's favorite places. Let's go!"

Jacob came through the back door and slammed it behind him. The four women stared at him with despair in their eyes. Annabelle had no idea why he had come back so soon, except maybe to lock them in the cellar house after all, just like he'd threatened.

# 38

*C*LIFF AND JESS WILLIS PARKED THEIR VEHICLES above Jacob's cabin out of sight. They contin-ued on foot, taking care not to be spotted. Jess, his body long and lanky, clumsily made his way down the path. He was not accustomed to mountain trails and could not gain sure footing as he stumbled and slid on the slick path. Cliff, on the other hand, seemed born to the rough hiking and moved steadily. They each had backpacks packed with flashlights, food, canteens, blankets, and matches. Cliff, at least, was prepared to continue the search as long as it took. They drew nearer to the cabin.

"There's Jacob's truck," Willis said. "How we knowed if Jacob's inside the cabin or out searchin' for th' woman and girl on foot?"

"I have no idea," Cliff answered.

They stood watching the cabin. In the distance, several paths led down the face of the mountain.

"We'll assume he's out looking. If we choose the right path," Cliff said, "we'll find Tuesday and the girl, if they're still on the mountain. If we choose the wrong path, we could pass by them without even knowing since the paths circle down the mountain only yards apart. It would be simpler if there wasn't so much brush."

"Yeah," Willis said. "It ain't goin' to be easy."

"Let's wait and see what happens, Willis. Can you see the paths below Jacob's cabin?"

"Not from here, but there are several goin' down toward town. I've always lived in town and am not really at home on th' mountain, I'm afraid."

"Great," Cliff said sarcastically. "You'll be a lot of help. Neither of us knows our way around."

"Hey, you're th' one wantin' help," Willis said.

"Yes. Sorry," Cliff said. "I didn't mean to offend you."

"I don't know the mountain much because Sheriff Moats doesn't want to bother with the people who live up here," Jess continued explaining why he had no knowledge of the mountain. "I've never agreed with him on that, though. We're supposed to keep the peace in all th' county, not just in th' town."

"Yes," Cliff said in annoyance, "I've noticed Sheriff Moats' prejudice. A lawman can't function that way."

As Cliff and Willis stood there waiting to see if McCallister would come out of the cabin, he opened the back door. They ducked behind a large rock and watched as he walked off the back porch. The floorboards gave with McCallister's weight. Exposed to the weather, with no roof over the porch and no paint for protection, the boards were rotten. McCallister carried nothing but a rifle. He was not prepared for darkness. He walked around the cabin, looking for tracks in the snow.

"Willis," Cliff nudged the deputy. "Look, McCallister must be just beginning his search. I feel for the first time that I have a good chance to find Tuesday and Patty first. It sure looks like McCallister hasn't."

Soon, Jacob appeared around the side of the cabin, walking toward the ridge, surveying each path going down the mountainside as he walked.

"Willis, back me up." Cliff said. "Hold it, McCallister!" Cliff's resounding command echoed up and down the canyon. "You're under arrest for the kidnapping of Tuesday Summers."

"Moran, you're dreaming if you think you're going to catch me or get Tuesday back." Jacob shouted. "I'll see you in hell first. As you can see I make my own laws." McCallister's gloating lulled Cliff and Willis into expecting a verbal confrontation, and they were caught off guard. Before they could react, McCallister, who had been standing near the edge of a ridge, leveled his rifle. Aiming, he fired a shot that cracked through the thin mountain air like a thunderclap. Then he jumped, with lightning speed, over the edge into the blanket of snow and rolled out of sight.

Stunned, Willis had not reacted when Cliff stepped forward and commanded McCallister to "hold it." He had stood, as the shot rang out, making as good a target as Cliff.

Cliff turned to Willis, "I swear," he said. "I'm going to get him. That egotistical bastard is going down—"

Blood stained the snow scarlet.

"Did ya all here that?" Daisy asked.

"Ya," Aggie said. "It was a gun shot, so it was."

"Where are the children?" Annabelle worried. "I don't knowed what's goin' on anymore. What's goin' to happen to Jeb?

"Nothin' goin' to happen to Jeb, so it ain't," Aggie said. He's goin' to go away for a while, so he is. Just until all this craziness stops. I'm goin' to talk 'im into it, so I am."

"Let's go out and see what's goin' on," Daisy said.

"No," Annabelle said. "There's nothin' we can do. We'll stay here and wait 'til we're needed."

"I'm goin' to look," Daisy said and went out the back way to the porch. The others followed. "Someone's down out there toward th' ridge," Daisy cried. "I can't tell who it is. Oh, I hope it's not Jeb."

The women stood on the back porch ringing their hands. In the distance a man was down and another bent over him. "I pray it's not Jeb layin' on th' ground with the deputy bendin' over him," Daisy said.

"I can't tell who it is, so I can't," Aunt Aggie said.

"I don't knowed about ya all," Annabelle said, "but I'm cold, an' I'm goin' back indoors. If ya stay outdoors ya may get more than ya bargained for."

"Yeah," Aggie said, "let's get indoors. We'll find out soon enough what's goin' on, so we will. I 'spect that detective from th' city got what he's askin' for, so he did. Shouldn't of come 'round botherin' Jeb, so he shouldn't."

Without warning, Joe and Sara appeared in the cave, horrifying Tuesday. Jacob must not find them. Disobeying him was the one thing he would never forgive.

"Please," Patty begged, "don't tell Pa. He's goin' to kill us if he finds us."

"We ain't goin' to tell," Joe assured her. "Don't want Pa to kill you."

"We really need help." Patty said. "Tuesday broke her leg. She's cold, an' I can't get her water to drink. I don't have anythin' to carry it in. We're hungry an' don't have food to eat."

"I don't want ya to leave the mountain," Joe said, "but I knowed there's no other way; not now. Pa won't chance ya runnin' away again. He'd lock ya in the cellar house or kill ya. We'll help ya."

"What about you, Sara? Will you help?" Tuesday asked.

Sara nodded.

"No one's botherin' 'bout us now," Joe said. "We can sneak ya food an' stuff. We have to be careful, so no one'll knowed what we're doin'. We're goin' to be back as soon as we can."

"Wait Joe," Tuesday called. "I can't walk, nor can Patty drag me off the mountain. By ourselves, we're trapped, but with the help of you and Sara maybe we can leave. I hate to involve the two of you, but you're in too deep now anyway. If you can find two poles about five or six feet long and an old blanket or quilt, the three of you could carry me off the mountain. It's the only way. Patty and I can't stay here long. Jacob will find us for sure."

Since that was the only strategy they had, they all agreed to it.

Joe and Sara left to carry out their plan.

The explosion from the thundering shot hung in the air.

"What the hell?" Cliff said, "Where'd he go? He caught me off guard. I thought he was going to mouth off and bait us for a while. Didn't seem like the time to shoot. You okay, Willis?"

"I've been shot," Willis cried. "You gotta get help."

Cliff looked from where McCallister had disappeared out of sight back to Willis lying in the white snow, surrounded by the purest red blood.

"What rotten luck," Cliff muttered as he walked toward the injured man. The chance to capture

McCallister had gone. He could not leave the man to bleed to death while he ran after McCallister.

"Take me to Aggie. She's a midwife," Willis said. "She can dress my wound."

They walked toward the cabin with Cliff half carrying Willis. When they made it to the door, Cliff knocked loudly.

"What ya wantin'?" Annabelle asked.

"Deputy Willis has been shot," Cliff explained. "He needs help."

"We heard th' shot," Annabelle said. "Scared us to death." She was weak with relief to know that it was not Jacob who was shot, after all.

"Bring 'im in." Aggie could never resist a chance for doctoring. "Where's he been shot?"

"In th' thigh," Willis whined.

"Get over here and sit down," Aggie said. While Aggie got Willis settled and cut his pants away from the wound, Annabelle and Daisy found rags and hot water for Aggie to use. Aggie applied pressure to the wound and stopped the bleeding.

"Th' bullet went through th' fleshy part of your leg, so it did," Aggie said. Although there was a great deal of bleeding, the bullet had passed through. It had put a deep gash in the deputy's leg. She cleaned the lesion and bandaged it. "Ya good as new, so ya are," Aggie pronounced Willis.

"Man, it sure hurts," Willis said.

"It'll feel better if you keep moving and don't let it get stiff. Like Aggie said, you're good to go. Thank you all," Cliff said. "Guess we can get about our business. Let's go Willis."

"I can't go on," Willis whined. "Can't you see I'm injured."

"Willis, you're fine. Let's go."

Unwillingly, Willis followed Cliff back outside.

"Let's follow McCallister," Cliff said.

"Okay," Willis answered, "but he's had a pretty long head start, and there's so many places where the path branches off. I'd say we lost him."

"There will be tracks. He didn't have time to cover them. Here's the place McCallister went over."

Cliff jumped and landed in the snow. Willis, in deference to his wound, sat and slid down the path newly made by Jacob and now Cliff.

"We're goin' to freeze," Willis said, brushing the wet snow from his clothing.

"Come on, Willis, we're wasting time."

They followed the tracks for about twenty yards until they disappeared into the heavy brush. "There's no way to track him now," Cliff said. "When McCallister walked trough the brush, the snow on the growth fell to the ground and covered the tracks. There's no way to tell whether it fell from it's own weight or from McCallister passing through."

After the detective and deputy left, the women prepared the cellar house for Tuesday and Patty as Jacob had instructed. They moved jars, feedsacks filled with flour and cornmeal, and wooden crates to one corner. They arranged two mats and two quilts on the dirt floor.

In the cellar, where no fresh air could reach, the smell of stale air and damp earth prevailed. It was cold and dark as a tomb in the underground storage room. Spider webs crisscrossed the room and rat droppings spotted the floor.

*W*AIT, SARA. REMEMBER TH' SNOWDRIFT THEY went around. Let's get rid of th' tracks where they went off the trail, an' no one'll know they've been there. If Pa sees th' tracks, he's goin' to knowed they got around it, an' he'll find the tracks on th' other side and follow them to th' cave."

They each found a branch, and they carried them to the drift. They smoothed the path from where Tuesday and Patty's tracks came to a dead stop at the drift to where Tuesday and Patty left the path just beyond the fork in the trail. To finish the job, they thinly spread dry twigs and dead leaves over the path to hide any evidence of their handiwork. They stood at the fork and proudly looked back. The path looked undisturbed and there was no sign of anyone leaving the trail to detour around the obstacle in the path.

As they walked up the path toward the cabin, they heard someone coming and quickly hid in the brush behind a large boulder.

Cliff and Deputy Willis passed without seeing the children. Soon they came to the fork. One path was littered with fallen dried leaves and twigs; the snow underneath looked undisturbed. They chose the path that was trampled. It would not be long before darkness fell and Cliff was growing more and more concerned.

The children quietly waited until the men were out of sight. When they could no longer see either of the men, they continued on their way to the cabin, knowing the men would take the wrong path, leading them well away from the cave.

Inside the cabin, as usual, Annabelle worked at the woodburner. "Where ya youngins been?" she admonished.

"We're doin' our chores like always," Joe lied.

He hurried past the women. Sara followed him to the room where the big four-poster bed stood. They passed through their room from the kitchen, so the women would not realize where they had gone. They threw clothes and quilts for Tuesday and Patty out of the window. Prepared to find food for Patty and Tuesday, they returned to the kitchen; the women were still gathered there. It was not the time to get food without the women's knowledge. Joe motioned for Sara to follow him.

In the backyard, Joe whispered, "We'll have to get th' food after everyone's sleepin'. We'll take th' clothes an' quilts now."

He put the badly dented tin cup they used for drinking at the well in his coat pocket.

"See if ya can sneak a couple of biscuits for them, for now. Then come to th' window an' help me carry th' things we threw out."

At the same time the children camouflaged the path, McCallister, against odds, trampled through brush, climbed over boulders, and unknowingly made his way toward the path above where they worked. Finally, he came to a path and stepped out of the heavy brush; he heard voices. He ducked back in the cover of the brush and stopped to listen.

It was Joe and Sara. They walked backward, spreading limbs and dry leaves.

He waited until the children finished covering their tracks. "They're hiding Tuesday and Patty," Jacob mumbled. "I'll take care of them for that, but first I'll take care of Patty and Tuesday."

There was a rustling sound, like someone moving through brush. Suddenly, the children ducked behind a boulder. They had heard it, too. He stepped farther back into the cover of the brush and waited.

"I guess I'm not a murderer. Damned if it isn't Moran and that simple deputy Jess Willis, limping along. Must have got him in the leg. Got to practice more, was aiming for Moran." Jacob said, his voice filled with irration, forgetting to keep quiet in his regret that he had not actually killed Cliff. Jacob did keep quiet, though, as Cliff and Jess moved toward the fork where the path branched off. He could not tangle with them now. He must find Tuesday and Patty before anyone else did.

Jacob stayed low as Cliff and Jess chose the wrong path. The path that led to Tuesday and Patty looked as if no one had used it recently. He could thank Joe and Sara for that.

"Hot damn," Jacob mumbled to himself. "They won't find Patty and Tuesday on that path. Those good-for-nothing kids just helped me find them, though. But they should have known this is my business and not to interfere in it. I'll deal with them later."

Cliff and Jess moved completely out of sight, while the children continued up the path toward the cabin.

Cliff and Jess continued down the path that dead-ended at a swollen stream. The water splashed and foamed as it rushed down the mountain, cutting through a thicket with a thunderous roar.

"We'll have to turn back," Cliff said in annoyance. "Even Daniel Boone couldn't cross here."

"Turn back an' do what? It's goin' to get dark before ya know it," Jess whined. "Then ya can't see your own hand in front of your face. Ain't no city lights here."

"We're not giving up until we find them; they may be in trouble," Cliff said with contempt. "I saw another path a hundred yards back. Let's check it out."

Lying beside the fire, Tuesday worried. *Will I ever see my home again? Cora? What's going to happen to Patty? Am I wrong, taking her from the only home she knows?* She fully realized they could die there in the cave. She shivered. *There must be another opening to allow the cold wind to blow through and find its way out the other side,* she thought.

"Ya all right? I knowed ya cold, thirsty, an' hungry," Patty said. "Joe and Sara'll be back soon with food an' th' quilt to keep ya warm."

"Don't worry. Everything will be fine," Tuesday assured Patty, although she didn't really believe it. She wanted Patty to have hope. "I will take you to my home. You will have your own room and never be cold or hungry again," she said, belittling her fears.

Their attention shifted as something blocked the feeble light from entering the mouth of the cave. They expected to see Joe and Sara with food and dry clothing, but it was not. To their horror, Jacob walked menacingly into the cave.

Cliff and Jess made their way back to the place where Cliff had seen a second path.

"It's about time Hal and his men and dogs arrive," Cliff said. "The sheriff's sure the hell's no help."

As they walked on, darkness slowly fell. Cliff had no intention of allowing that to stop the search. Cliff and Jess finally reached the place where Cliff had spotted the other path earlier. They turned and continued walking. They knew they had lost their sense of direction when they saw the two children hurrying toward the cabin. They waited until the children were inside before they moved farther into the open.

"Hell, Jess, we're back where we started from."

"I don't believe we can do anythin' in the dark. I'm calling off th' search until mornin'," Jess said.

"Go on back to town and take care of your leg, I'll keep up the search. You don't know this mountain any better than I do, anyway. It's pointless for you to stay."

Cliff could move faster without the injured deputy. Besides, the scrawny, timid man wouldn't be much help if they came to face to face with the more powerful Jacob again. The fact that Jess was near the cabin and could see his Jeep was the deciding factor in his decision to stop the search. It was obvious the deputy had spent most of the day feeling lost in the wilderness.

With Willis and his Jeep out of sight, Cliff examined each path, looking to find tracks or anything that would show him which way Tuesday and the girl had walked down the mountain. He found nothing to mark their trail. Cliff chose the path that began at a point closer to the cabin.

Annabelle did not notice Sara was acting strangely. Annabelle was too worried about what was happening with her husband and the detective. Sara had managed to take a few biscuits without anyone stopping her, and she tied them in an old rag. The children divided the cache from below the window between them and walked back toward the cave.

After delivering the dry clothes, quilts, and biscuits, they would search for poles to make the stretcher. There was not enough time to make the litter and carry Tuesday off the mountain before full darkness fell.

"So," Jacob's voice thundered in the confining area of the cave, "think you can run from me, do you? You both should know better. But since you don't, I'll teach you in a way you'll never forget."

Tuesday and Patty were stricken with panic. It was obvious Jacob was furious and meant what he said.

"Get up, Tuesday! We're going back to the cabin. I've had the women make a special place for the two of you."

"She can't get up," Patty cried. "She broke her leg an' can't walk on it."

"That explains why you're in the cave." Jacob laughed. "Tuesday, your broken leg is a good break for me. It kept you from getting to town. Looks like luck's on my side."

Jacob secured the gun to his back by the shoulder strap; he lifted Tuesday from the cave floor, causing extreme pain to her injured leg. She passed out.

"Let's go, Patty, and remember, walk directly in front of me where I can see you. If you go too far ahead, or walk in the wrong direction, I will drop Tuesday and come after you. Do you understand?"

"Yeah, Pa, I understand. I don't want ya to drop Tuesday. I don't have nowhere to go anyways."

"Patty, you and Tuesday won't run away again, I'm taking the two of you to the cellar house. You'll not talk to anyone. Cliff won't find the cellar house, anyway. What do you know? There's Joe and Sara."

In their haste to get back to the cave, they had not seen their pa in time to hide.

"Joe, that stuff you and Sara are carrying for Tuesday and Patty?"

"Yeah, Pa, it is." Joe tensed.

"I want you and Sara to take it to the cellar house," Jacob ordered. "That will be Tuesday's and Patty's new home. After you've finished, go to your room and stay there until I ask for you. You're not to talk to anyone. And if anyone asks, you had better forget that you've ever seen Tuesday. Don't cross me. I will not stand for any more trouble from the two of you."

Shaking with fear, Joe and Sara turned back to do as they were told. When they reached the cellar house, they placed the quilts, clothes, and biscuits inside and went straight to their room, not daring to do anything except what they were told.

Jacob went directly to the cellar and unceremoniously placed an unconscious Tuesday on a mat. Not bothering to revive her, he stormed out and slammed the door, deliberately locking it behind him, assigning the two to total darkness. Patty moved closer to Tuesday, gently resting Tuesday's head in her lap. Tuesday came out of her faint at the touch of Patty's hands.

"Patty," she cried, "where are we? I can't see anything at all. The fall must have injured my head. I'm blind!"

"No," Patty said. "We're in th' cellar house. It's underground an' with th' door closed it's pitch black in here."

Unexpectedly the door opened, allowing light to flood in. Annabelle came in carrying two plates. Daisy followed with two jars of water. Annabelle handed Patty a plate for each of them, with chunks of sausage and two biscuits on each plate.

"It's pitch dark in here when ya shet th' door," Patty complained. "We can't see nothin'."

"I'll tell Jeb. Ya knowed I can't do nothin' 'bout it. Have to ask him. He told me to look at th' city girl's leg."

Annabelle stooped beside Tuesday and removed the quilt that covered her leg. "Ya have a broken bone. It feels like th' bone has a jagged edge. Your leg's black and blue. Most likely it's bleedin' in there," Annabelle informed them.

She got up, abandoning Tuesday to her pain. There was nothing she could do for her. Annabelle and Daisy left the cellar house and closed the door, leaving Patty and Tuesday in total darkness to eat their biscuits and sausage gravy.

# *40*

*T*HE SUN HAD COMPLETELY DISAPPEARED BEHIND the mountain. Cliff watched headlights cut through the darkness. They jutted like giant cones from two vehicles that moved slowly up the ridge across the valley from where he stood. He could not make his way to the road before the vehicles would pass by, but he had a flashlight, and it was dark enough for the light to be seen. He reached in his backpack and found the light. He flashed it toward the headlights, praying that someone would see his signal. Soon the vehicles stopped. Hal had seen his signal.

Cliff looked for a way to cross the valley between the two ridges. The snow had drifted in the valley, erasing where the valley floor started and the snow stopped. It would be dangerous to cross the gorge. The snow was shallow in some areas and deep in others, hiding rocks and boulders. It was much too risky to cross the valley. He walked higher up the ridge where the two embankments met and the valley disappeared. He shone his light back toward the vehicles as he walked to show Hal the way. The headlights slowly moved up the road, keeping pace with his light. Before long, he reached the crest and they moved toward him.

"Cliff," said Hal as he opened the door. "I'm glad we found you. We had no idea where to start looking,"

The man in the back made room for Cliff. He climbed in, thankful to be off his feet. "Where's the sheriff? I thought he'd have a search party out helping you," Hal remarked.

"He's getting one up," Cliff said when he finally caught his breath," but he won't send them out until morning. When I spoke to him a few hours ago, he said that it was too late to organize a party and get them to the mountain. He sent his deputy with me instead. He was with me until a short time ago. McCallister got a shot off on him. The deputy doesn't know the mountain any better than I do, so it didn't matter much when he decided to call off the search."

"He okay?" Hal asked.

"He's fine, but now we know that McCallister won't stop until he kills someone. He's dangerous."

"I'm not surprised," Hal said. "Now you have real manpower behind you. We have Anthony Harris and his dogs in the vehicle following us. John Gibson's driving."

"Glad to see you brought Randy McCoy. I like him. He's a good detective, as well as a cheerful sort," Cliff said.

A friendly smile was Randy's usual expression, and people could not always determine when he was serious or joking. He was the kind of man everyone likes to be around. He was redheaded, freckle-faced, and had an olive skin, a rare color combination.

Bart Howard sat next to Cliff in the back seat. Working together, the ever-serious Bart and light-hearted Randy were ace detectives.

After Jacob sent the women to take care of Tuesday and Patty, he angrily ripped the ragged curtain from the spike nail and stepped into the children's room. It was time he reprimanded Joe and Sara. He intended to make sure they caused no further trouble.

"Neither of you are to leave this room unless you are told. No school, no chores, and no playing. If either of you disobeys my orders, I will lock you," he pointed to Joe, "in Aggie's cellar house alone. And you, Sara, will be locked in with Tuesday and Patty." The arrangement was to punish Sara. She was actually afraid of Patty and didn't want to be separated from Joe. Both children nodded in agreement, too overcome with fright to say anything.

"Remember, I don't want you to talk to anyone about what happens here."

He shook his finger in their faces, almost unable to keep himself from backhanding each of them. Jacob left them there, barely able to control his rage, but they were more valuable to him if they stayed healthy.

"There'll be no further trouble from those two," he said as he walked into the kitchen, startling the cat as it crouched on the table enjoying the leftover food. Jacob had lost interest in what the cabin looked like and paid no attention to the cat.

Annabelle had braced herself for the blow that would come because the cat was in the cabin again. *I never knowed what's goin' to please Jeb no more,* she pondered, seeing that Jacob did not take notice of the cat. *Just don't understand. First he threatens my life, wantin' th' cats out of th' cabin. Now he don't care if th' cats are in th' cabin or not.*

"They need a light in th' cellar," Annabelle reported. "It's dark in there."

Ignoring her whining, he asked, "How is Tuesday's leg?"

"Real bad. It bleedin' inside," Annabelle answered. She resented the fact that he did not ask how her burned hand was. He just cared about Tuesday. Annabelle's burn was severe, and pain shot up and down her arm every time she used it.

"I'd betta have a look at her leg, so I had," Aggie declared. "If'n she'd die you'd be a murderer, so ya would."

"You're no damn doctor!" Jacob shouted. "What can you do? I'll tell you if I want you to look at her. They don't need a damn light in the cellar, either. They have to learn not to cross me. They're not supposed to like it in the cellar. I've had all I can take of you women!

"I'm leaving for a while. I'll see what the hell's going on in town. If anyone comes here, you're not to say anything. If you do, I'll cut your tongues out and you'll never be able to speak again. Do you understand?"

Jacob stomped out the back door and slammed it behind him before they could react. He climbed into his truck and drove down the mountain. His truck swerved at every turn, only to hold to the rocky, rutted trail.

Patty helped Tuesday to a sitting position, using the stone wall to support her back.

"I can't see my own hand," Patty said. "I'm handin' your plate to you. I need to find ya hand."

They felt around in the air until their hands touched. Patty kept hold of Tuesday's hand and reached for the tin plate with her free hand. Tuesday did not eat; she was too nauseated. But Patty managed to dip her biscuit in the gravy and ate, getting more food inside than on herself. After Patty finished eating, she struck a match to find where Daisy had put the water. Just as the match burned her finger, she saw the water. She managed to swallow her cry of pain. The burned-out match fell on the damp dirt floor, leaving them once again in total darkness.

The scream from Tuesday sent chills creeping up Patty's spine. "Patty, what's crawling up my leg?" Tuesday dropped her plate, still filled with uneaten food, on the cellar floor.

# *41*

KEEP MOVING AND TAKE THE ROAD TO THE RIGHT at the next fork. There's a clearing through those trees," Cliff pointed to a wooded area. "I camped there last night. No one will see the Jeeps there, and we'll walk from here."

After the Jeeps were parked safely out of sight, Anthony unloaded the dogs. He gave them Tuesday's scent, and they moved up the mountain, eager for the pursuit. Randy, Bart, and John paced ahead with Anthony and the dogs in the lead as they walked deliberately up the narrow mountain trail.

"What do you make of this mess, Hal?" Cliff asked. "I'm sure Tuesday and the girl never got to town. Someone would have seen them. There would have been gossip."

"I don't know, Cliff. Maybe she got to town and found a ride. You're a stranger here. The townspeople wouldn't tell you even if they did know something. You said yourself that they don't care for strangers."

"No, the townspeople wouldn't talk to me. But they would have been buzzing with gossip if they knew a young woman and child had run away from a mountain man. Most likely, she's still on the mountain. Is she hurt or freezing somewhere? Or the worst thing, did Jacob find her?"

"Don't worry, Cliff, with these dogs we'll find her."

"Yeah, we have the advantage now, that's for sure," Cliff said.

The dogs were well trained and walked quietly up the path, not making a sound. In the distance a low rumble vibrated in the still air. Then, with a thunderous, earsplitting roar, an avalanche of snow came crashing down the mountainside. Mushroom clouds of pure white filled the air and bullets of ice expelled from the sky. Frightened outcries from the men and startled, yipping dogs could be heard amidst the explosion. They frantically ran for safety.

Silence . . .


All the regulars were in the town bar. Jacob stood just inside. He didn't notice Andy Hillberry sitting at the end of the bar on the corner stool, watching him with hate in his eyes.

No one knew why Andy ran a hate campaign against Jacob. If the truth was known, Andy Hillberry didn't know himself, but deep in his heart there was a jealousy that would not die. He envied Jacob's new truck, his fancy clothes, and his frequent trips to the city. Andy was hellbent on getting Jacob into trouble for having the very things that he desired for himself.

Frank Dillon turned as Jacob took the stool beside him. "Hi, Jeb, how's it going?" he asked. He did not question what was going on with Jacob. Jacob's business was Jacob's business.

"Just fine," Jacob answered. "Frank, I may have to

leave the mountain indefinitely and my women will starve without me. Daisy's going to have another child. Joe's fourteen now. I'm sure you know I keep him because it's hard to keep up with so many women and I like to spend most of my time in the city. I'm sure you could use him, too. My two daughters are twelve and thirteen and will be old enough to have children soon. I'm sure Joe's already broken them in. If I go, I may not be able to come back for years. If that happens and you want them, they're yours. The price is taking Aunt Aggie too. She's a good midwife and knows some doctoring." Jacob got up and walked out of the bar, not bothering to wait for an answer. Frank would decide in his own time.

"It's okay. It's nothin' to hurt you." Patty comforted Tuesday. She would not frighten Tuesday more by telling her that it was probably a rat that had crawled up her leg. Patty put her arms around Tuesday in an attempt to keep her warm as they sat on the cellar floor. It was coal black in the cellar house; they would not have known the difference between night or day, imprisoned as they were ten feet below the earth's surface. There were no windows for daylight to shine through. The only door stood in its own shadow.

Tuesday's leg throbbed with pain, and she was frightened for herself, but most of all she was frightened for Patty.

"I only wanted to help you, and I made everything worse for you." Tuesday sobbed. "I'm so sorry, but I just don't know what we can do. There's no way out of here. Even if there was, I can't walk."

"Ya are th' only one who ever care'd 'bout me," Patty said. "We had to try to get away. Pa won't keep us in here forever. Everythin's goin' to be fine."

The men let out sighs of relief until they realized that Anthony and the dogs were nowhere to be seen. Had they been twenty yards farther up the path, the whole lot of them would have been buried under thirty feet of snow. Bone-chilling silence filled the air as they realized what had happened. They were stunned and stood stock-still in the eerie, quiet aftermath of the thunderous avalanche.

The hair stood up at the nape of Cliff's neck. He knew that there was no way to rescue Anthony or the dogs. Just the same, Cliff and Randy ran high stepping, clumsily in the deep snow, toward the spot where they had last seen them. They frantically dug with only their gloved hands to work with, desperately trying to save one of their own.

"Cliff," Hal shouted as he and John rushed toward the recklessly flying arms that created a cloud of snow and ice chips. Hal pulled at Cliff while John grabbed Randy. "You'll never find Anthony in time to save him. There's thirty feet of snow to dig through."

"That's right!" Bart bellowed. "And we had better get out of here before there's another avalanche! I hear a low rumble up above. We need to get the hell moving down the mountain!"

"We got to try!" Randy said.

"Anthony was right about there when the avalanche came down," Cliff said. "Let's try to find him. He could be alive." The two of them started digging and the others joined in to help. They kept it up until finally Randy discovered Anthony's arm. "Over here," he said. "I found him."

Anthony was dead. He had suffocated as he lay buried under the heavy snow. With heavy hearts, the others dug Anthony from under his snowy grave, and Randy carried him as they all made their way down the mountain toward the Jeeps.

"The loss of Anthony and the dogs could result in the loss of Tuesday's and the girl's lives as well. I've been all over this time-forsaken mountain and haven't seen anything except an inconceivable abundance of snow," Cliff said, defeated.

"Let's get the Jeeps. We're losing time. We've got to get to the sheriff, report the accident, and get help for our search," Hal said. "Time's one thing we can't sacrifice."

"Let's go," Cliff said. The sheriff promised a search party by morning. Somehow, we have to send for replacements for the dogs we lost. We don't have a chance in hell without them."

Ozzie Moats approached his office at his usual time. Two unfamiliar Jeeps were parked outside his door, and several men waited beside them. One was the detective who had come to him the day before demanding a search party.

"I was hopin' I had seen the last of him. I suppose he's a wantin' that search party he's so set on," Ozzie muttered to himself.

The men stepped away from their vehicles to greet the stubborn, bigoted sheriff.

"Hi, Sheriff. You have the search party ready?" Cliff asked.

"Not yet, but won't take no time." The sheriff slammed the door of his Jeep.

"We just lost a man on the mountain," Cliff informed the sheriff; saddened to the marrow of his bones about the loss. "There was an avalanche last night. He and his dogs were our best hope of finding Tuesday Summers. Now they're gone. Anthony's in the back of the Blazer. Need you to call the coroner."

"Sorry to hear it," Ozzie said with sincere sadness in his voice. "But you should'a asked when you was here if ya wanted dogs. We have dogs. Have the best. It'll take a'couple of hours to get'em here. Old man Keefover over at Centerpoint has 'em. Use 'em to find men trapped in the mines."

Cliff felt like slugging the sheriff. Had he mentioned having the dogs the day before, most likely the tragedy would not have happened. He'd never dreamed the sheriff actually had access to trained dogs.

Deputy Willis pulled in behind the sheriff's Jeep and got out, curiosity written all over his face. Obviously he was alarmed to see the five men. The one he had spent yesterday with, a miserable day, had brought four others.

"Willis," Ozzie ordered, "go find old man Keefover and bring him and his dogs to me. We have an emergency."

Jess Willis climbed in the sheriff's Jeep, mumbling under his breath with contempt. "Didn't think it was an emergency yesterday. Gettin' scared so many city detectives on your mountain."

Cliff and Hal stayed at the office with Sheriff Moats and Deputy Willis, waiting for Morgan Keefover. Randy, John, and Bart went for supplies. While they waited, the sheriff called in men for the search party. By the time the sheriff had exhausted his list of men for the search, Randy, John, and Bart had returned from The General Store.

During the pre-dawn hours, while waiting for the sheriff, the men had eaten the last of the food Cliff had packed in his backpack at the start of his search.

Minutes after the coroner left with Anthony, the door banged open. A gust of frigid air rushed in just ahead of Morgan Keefover and his unkempt dogs. The dogs made an annoying click-click sound as they briskly pranced on the tile floor, as

far as their leashes would allow them. They skidded to a stop.

"Brung th' dogs like ya wanted," old man
Keefover said, proudly nodding his unshaven,
tobacco-stained chin. "They kin find anyone ya
wantin'."

"Thanks for comin', Morgan. These men are detectives from th' big city," Ozzie said in introduction.

"How're ya," Morgan said and extended his
hand to each man in turn. "See ya have quite a
search party gathered outside. Don't need 'em, ya
knowed. I got my dogs. Th' dogs're enough to' find'
whoever ya wantin'."

The twenty-five or so men who had answered the
sheriff's call were gathered outside, awaiting
orders. They all carried rifles and backpacks. Sheriff
Moats motioned Cliff and his men outside and held
up his hands for order.

"We're lookin' for a city woman. She's blond, and
I understand she's a pretty one. She's with McCallister's kid. If ya run across McCallister, bring him
in if ya can. Don't shoot him. Don't have no call to,"
Moats looked at Cliff for agreement.

"Search in groups of four." Cliff took over. "If you
get McCallister, assign two men from your bunch to
bring him in and lock him in a cell. Use whatever
force you have to. The sheriff will assign each group
a search area. My men and Keefover will go directly
to McCallister's cabin. The dogs can pick up the scent
from where the girls left the cabin. I'll leave two men
guarding McCallister's cabin in case he returns. In
the event you find Tuesday and the girl, bring them
to the sheriff's office and leave a man with them for
protection. Have a man drive over the trails and fire
a shot every few miles to call the others in."

"Let's go," old man Keefover shouted.

"When Pa let's us out an' ya get betta, we'll get away from here," Patty said as she sat with Tuesday's head in her lap.

"I hope so, Patty," Tuesday answered to please Patty, but she could not hide the hopelessness in her voice.

"You'll see. We can't give up hope. Please don't give up. Th' life we talked 'bout when we was in th' cave sounded so wonderful," Patty said wistfully.

"Patty, what's that sound?" Tuesday tensed. "It must be the creature that crawled up my leg earlier."

Patty had been listening to the scurrying sounds for some time as Tuesday floated in and out of consciousness and prayed she would not notice. Patty knew it was rats attracted by the leftover food on the plates. Their fear of humans was forgotten in their overwhelming hunger. In the dead of winter their food was scarce at best.

"It's rats." Patty told Tuesday the truth. The rats would get out of control. They were crazed with hunger by the smell of their leftover food. She felt around for the plates with her right hand and pushed them as far as she could across the dirt floor, hoping to keep the rats away.

"I can't believe Jacob would expose us to this horror." Tuesday sobbed.

They huddled closer, the eternal minutes of their imprisonment slowly becoming hours as they shivered in the damp, tomb-like cellar. The scurrying noise, mingled with squabbling squeals, grew louder as the rats fought over the food and more rats invaded the small space in the cellar. The sounds were ominous as rat claws scraped at the tin plates being used as a battleground. Patty and Tuesday cuddled closer as the rats forgot their fear of the humans. In their greed for food the rats scur-

ried at will to and fro across Tuesday and Patty's
legs and feet.

Patty kicked violently at the offending rats, praying all the while that Annabelle would be sent back
to the cellar. Her entrance would scare the devious
rats away. They were not afraid of Tuesday or Patty;
they could smell the impotent fear that invaded the
cold cellar.

"Patty, find a weapon, a club or something,"
Tuesday demanded. "I'll be damned if we give up
to a pack of hideous rats."

"Lean back against th' wall, an' I'll find somethin'," Patty said and stood.

Carefully, Patty lit a precious match. The light
startled the rats, and they scurried backward. Their
mean, beady eyes reflected the light as they stood
their ground at the moss-covered stone wall of
Tuesday's and Patty's prison. The feeble light
revealed at least a dozen menacing rats.

"Patty, we're getting out of here," Tuesday said,
finding new courage. "We got away from him, and
we are not going to be taken by him again."

"What're we goin' to do?" Patty asked.

"Find something to pry the door open. Everything I've seen so far in and around the cabin is rotted. I imagine the door to this hell hole is rotten,
too." Patty lit another precious match.

"Look, Patty, what's that behind you against the
wall?"

"It's only Pa's tool box," Patty said.

"Open it. There may be something in it we can
pry the door open with."

Patty opened the box and she and Tuesday felt
inside. There were wrenches, screwdrivers, and
other tools in the box. Tuesday pulled out the
largest screwdriver and handed it to Patty. "Take

this and wedge it between the door near the latch. It should pry the door open."

Patty wedged the screwdriver between the door and the doorjamb and twisted and pried until she heard the wood splinter. She used the screwdriver to get maximum leverage, and as she pushed against the screwdriver and pulled on the door with all her might, the door miraculously opened, pulling the hardware with it.

"We're free," Tuesday said with relief.

"Let's go," Patty said.

"Help me and I can make it. There's no way I'm going allow Jacob to get his hands on you again." The thought gave Tuesday the strength she needed.

As they left the cellar, they heard men's voices.

"Where can we hide until the coast is clear?" Tuesday whispered in desperation as she pulled the door closed behind them.

The men noisily made their way to the window where the two had originally jumped out. Tuesday knew they did not have much time. Patty was obviously frightened by the commotion the search party made.

"Patty, stay calm. We made it this far in spite of the rats. Think! Where can we get out of sight quickly?"

"Well, if ya can make it, there's a small dugout on th' mound above th' cellar. When I was a little girl, I used it for a playhouse. We can wait there until th' coast is clear."

Tuesday followed Patty to the side of the cellar. Although the pain was great, she was able to put a little weight on her leg now that Annabelle had bandaged it tightly to hold the bones in place. Patty found the rock steps and climbed up. The brush and rocks gave good footing. At the top Patty took Tuesday's hand and Tuesday pulled herself up to the top. Patty crawled into the opening of a small cave-like chamber, dragging Tuesday as she went.

"If we get out of this mess, I'll never speak to a stranger again," Tuesday said, knowing Patty had no idea what talking to a stranger had to do with their dilemma.

When Cliff, Hal, Randy, John, Bart, and old man Keefover got within sight of the cabin they parked the Jeeps and unloaded the dogs.

At Cliff's direction old man Keefover led the dogs to the window that Cliff guessed Tuesday and the girl had escaped from. They allowed the dogs to get the scent from Tuesday's scarf.

Old man Keefover released the dogs. He whistled and ordered, "Hunt."

The dogs picked up the scent right away and ran toward the path that Cliff had first gone down. The dogs sniffed the area around the path then, to every-one's surprise, turned back toward the cabin. The dogs headed directly to the cellar house that was located just to the right of the cabin. The dogs became excited and sniffed at the ground below the door. They jumped excitedly, as if trying to reach the top of the door. Cliff had not noticed the cellar house before. All that was visible was the door and part of the front stone wall. The door was secured with a padlock.

"They're in there," Old man Keefover declared.

"Let's break the lock," Hal ordered.

"Look," Cliff said, "there's no need. The lock's intact, but the hinge has been pried from the door-jamb."

Tuesday and Patty heard the sound of muffled voices down below the mound at the entrance to the cellar.

"Who could that be?" Tuesday whispered. "Why the dogs?"

"I don't knowed," Patty said in a quivering voice.

The snarl of the dogs reminded Tuesday of the chaos that had erupted in the cellar when Patty had found an old fence post and clubbed the more aggressive rats to death. The others had hidden in fear.

Someone opened the door down below. Tuesday knew that it was not Jacob or Annabelle at the door. The dogs could only mean a search party. She could feel heart beating rapidly in her chest. But what if it wasn't? Maybe Jacob had enlisted help in his search.


"There's no one here," Cliff said as he flashed his light around the cellar." The rats that had survived the massacre retreated further into darkness. There were soiled quilts, mangled tin plates, and dead rats. Their mutilated bodies lay in a pool of blood. "

They've been here, but they're gone. What could have happened? Jacob must have learned we were close and taken them to another location."

"That don't make sense. The dog's led us here. They have to be here," Randy said.

"You're right 'bout that," Morgan Keefover said. "If th' dogs says they're here, they're here."

"Why are they jumping around the cellar door, then?" Cliff asked.

"Don't knowed, but they're here somewheres," Keefover said. "Let's go back to th' cabin an' see what they do."

The men walked back toward the cabin and stood on the back porch. The dogs didn't follow. With their noses to the ground they went to the right of the cellar door and jumped up the embankment and slid back down. Each dog tried to scramble up the knoll and slid back to the ground.

"The dogs are trying to get to the top of the bank, and there's too much snow for them to get a good foothold," Cliff said. "Let's get up there."

"Who'd ya think's out there?" Patty whispered.

"I don't know," Tuesday answered, "but we're trapped like the rats you killed earlier."

They both cowered as flashlights were shone in their faces, blinding them.

"Look, whatever you want get it and leave us alone," Tuesday demanded, worn down from the entire situation.

"Tuesday," Cliff said, "don't be frightened. It's me, Cliff Moran."

Tuesday could not believe her ears. "How did you know where to look for me? I believed that I was trapped on this mountain for the rest of my life."

Cliff went to her and took her into his arms. She cried out in pain when he pulled her to him and caused her weight to shift to her right leg.

"Be careful," Patty said. "She'd fell an' broke her leg."

Cliff shone the light around the small cavern. "Tuesday's hurt. We need blankets to warm the girls. Have Randy bring a car up close."

"Remember the twins you found and could not trace?" Tuesday asked Cliff.

"Yes, we found them. They're with Hal's wife," Cliff answered. "How did you know about the twins?"

"Patty told me that Jacob sold his twins, a boy and girl, and an infant just recently. Apparently he has three wives and sells their children." Suddenly overwhelmed by the events in the past days, Tuesday began sobbing, unable to say more. Cliff held Tuesday close, warming her with his own body heat.

"Now I understand why the children had not been reported missing. I'm going to get enough evidence to hang McCallister and his cohorts, after all."

Cliff turned toward Hal. "The clinic is where the children are taken first. Sam Johnson matches them up with the parents he has diagnosed as infertile. Jacob doesn't merely kidnap children; he also breeds them to sell for profit. When we confiscate the records from the clinic and law firm, who knows what we'll find?"

"I never dreamed that we would get a break like this when we came up here to find Tuesday," Hal said.

"Cliff," Tuesday said. "Patty must go with me; she's in danger from her father now. I must protect her."

"Don't worry. We'll have you in a hospital soon," Cliff reassured her. "Patty can ride with you."

After Randy and Bart left for the hospital with the girls, Cliff and Hal went to the cabin to question the others. John drove down the mountain signaling with gunshots, letting the others know that the girls had been found.

## *42*

$O$N HIS WAY TO THE CABIN TO PACK, JACOB SAW headlights up ahead. They moved slowly in the direction of the cabin. He pulled his truck out of sight in heavy brush and waited.

He lay back against the seat, watching out the window, mumbling to himself. "I'll take up with Steven Lloyd. He'll pay big money for the kids I get him. It'll be a while before I can produce children of my own, so I'll find Aubry Moats. He's an expert at picking up children. The no-account drives a truck like mine. Flattered he admires me so much, but that's got to stop. Might be what got me in hot water this time. He must have messed up a kidnapping and his truck was spotted, same description as mine. Damn, that's it!" Jacob banged his fist against the side of the cab. "The sheriff's no-account brother. No help for it now, but as soon as I set myself up with a few women who'll be more than happy to bear my children, he can set me up with a broker.

"I'll take Tuesday with me. I can't take a chance on her talking. She's not strong like my mountain women, but I bet she can make babies just the same."

He fell asleep.

Annabelle did not know what to do. There were two men at the door. One she knew as the detective who had followed Aunt Aggie in order to find Jacob. The other man was a stranger. Annabelle had heard the men breaking into the cellar earlier. She felt that if not for the detective's interference, there would be no trouble now. It never occurred to her that Jacob had brought it upon them and himself.

Aggie dropped the can that she had just spit into. "What ya wantin' now?" she demanded of the men, wiping her mouth with the back of her hand. She succeeded only in smearing the brown spittle over her chin. "Ya caused 'nough trouble, so ya have."

"You all know Jacob was holding a woman and a child against their will," Cliff said. "He locked them in your pitch-dark, rat-infested cellar with no heat. The woman has a broken leg and is suffering from shock. If you don't cooperate, I can jail you all as accessories to his crime."

This news terrified Annabelle, although she did not know what he meant by "accessories." She could tell that he was not talking just to hear his own voice. He wanted answers, and she knew he would take no nonsense. No matter what the women did, Annabelle realized, they were in trouble.

"I want to know what is going on here," Cliff demanded. "Tuesday tells me Jacob sells your children. We have twins in our custody who may be yours."

The mention of her twins and the fact that these men knew where they were loosened Daisy's tongue. "How are they?" Daisy wanted to know. She was happy to be hearing about her babies, and she was too naive to realize she was implicating Jacob further. "Can I see them? I'm wantin' to see them," Daisy said.

"Are they yours?" Hal asked.

"Yeah."

Annabelle wondered which would be worse, Jacob's rage or these men putting them in jail. She realized Aunt Aggie would do anything to keep Jacob out of jail. She would rather go herself than see him go.

"Daisy, ya shet ya mouth," Aunt Aggie said. "Ya don't knowed what ya talkin' about, so ya don't."

Rose spoke the first meaningful words she had spoken since Jacob sold her baby. "He sold my baby, too. I'd only just brung it into th' world."

"That would have to be the child McCallister took to the clinic," Hal said. "We're actually going to nail those bastards—McCallister, Cunningham, and Doc Johnson."

"Something just came to my mind," Cliff said. "During the interrogation of Norman and Lea Wright, they revealed an overheard conversation in George Cunningham's office. 'I'm wantin' bigger money for th' kids I bring ya. If ya don't, I'm goin' to call Lloyd an' work for him from now on.' Another voice said, 'Get the hell out of here, Aubry. This is neither the time nor the place to discuss the matter.' George had called the man, who spoke like the people from Winding Ridge and the mountain area, Aubry. Do you women know a man by the name of Aubry?"

"Yeah," Annabelle answered, "He's Sheriff Ozzie Moats' brother. Th' no good left th' mountain a long time ago. Left with his tail between his legs right after th' mine explosion. He'd been in it hisself if'n he'd not been layin' drunk that night. Told his brother, Ozzie, he'd not step one foot in them mines ever again. An I guess he ain't."

"I'll be damned. The sheriff's brother is the man who kidnapped Todd, the one who drove the fancy black truck matching Jacob's," Hal said.

Cliff nodded. "It's falling into place. Also accounts for the sheriff's aversion to outside law enforcement. Afraid his brother's going to get caught at what he's doing."

McCallister was awakened by a gunshot. He vaulted forward bumping his head on the rearview mirror.

"What the hell?"

Headlights bounced in the darkness as they moved closer. He started his engine. Grinding gears in his panic he pulled out of the brush with his rear-end fishtailing from side to side.

McCallister's headlights pierced the darkness, shining in John's eyes for a second, and hastened down the mountain. John saw that it was Jacob, who had no way of knowing the shot was a signal for the men to stop the search for the girls. John threw his rifle aside and concentrated on his driving. He was gaining on Jacob's truck.

Up ahead, John saw that Jacob was in trouble when his truck bounced violently out of the deep ruts and skidded sideways down the rutted road. Abruptly jammed in a rut, the truck came to a standstill. Unprepared for McCallister's sudden stop, John saw that he would hit the truck broadside. He was going too fast to stop on the icy incline. His body tensed, preparing for the impending collision. McCallister threw his vehicle into reverse. His wheels spun and gained traction, and abruptly the truck recoiled over the rutted road into the brush, just as John's vehicle came jouncing past.

McCallister pulled onto the road and drove the opposite way, fishtailing from side to side, his tail-lights moving out of sight. There was more than one way off the mountain. He turned his headlights off. The moon was bright and he could see well enough.

No one knew the mountain trails as well as Jacob McCallister did.

Frank Dillon sat on the barstool next to Rosily; they discussed Dillon's conversation with McCallister. Neither Dillon nor McCallister knew that the other had an affair going with Rosily.

"What's going on, and why's the law looking for Jacob McCallister?" Dillon asked.

"I can't tell ya cause I don't knowed," Rosily answered.

"Whatever it is, I like the idea of having Jacob's women and children. That will double my income. Besides, Joe can look after my women when I'm in the city."

"I knowed ya and Jacob like to spend time in the city. Ya like th' fancy women ya knowed there. Us women on th' mountain bore ya. If ya want to keep seein' me, ya have to take me to live in th' city with ya."

"Now, Rosily, you know I enjoy being with you," Dillon humored her, "but I can't take you to the city."

"That's what ya always say," Rosily said.

"I got my mind on something else now. I don't have time to listen to your foolishness."

"Well, then, what ya goin' to do? Ya goin' to take Jacob's women?"

"I'll wait and see what happens first. It don't sound good for McCallister, you know. He wouldn't leave his profitable little setup if he weren't in big trouble. I'll not take a chance on getting involved just yet, though. I've plenty of time to wait until things cool down. I've got too much of a good thing going myself to take a chance on jeopardizing it. I'll wait," Dillon explained to himself as much as to Rosily.

Tuesday was relieved to finally arrive at the tiny hospital located in the mountain town. The ride in the bouncing four-wheeler had been painful for her. Randy and Bart carried her inside, leaving Patty to follow behind. It was not at all like the bustling hospitals she had gone to in the city on occasion. She was more than a little worried.

The men placed Tuesday, still strapped to the litter and inside Cliff's sleeping bag, on a hospital stretcher. Bart went to check her in and talked to the nurse who stood behind the desk. Randy reassured her that Cliff would be there to check on her as soon as he could. With nothing more to do for the woman and child, they headed back to Jacob's cabin.

The nurse wheeled Tuesday into one of the examining rooms, and Patty followed, wide-eyed. Tuesday could see that Patty was amazed by the clean, cozy, warm hospital. The nurse unzipped the sleeping bag and slid it from under Tuesday, causing pain to shoot up her leg. She then secured the straps to the portable stretcher, leaving Tuesday until the doctor came in and checked her leg.

The nurse instructed Patty to sit on a second examining table and picked up a clipboard. Just as the nurse finished questioning Tuesday about her medical history, the doctor came into the room. He looked as if he should be dressed in a chef's hat. He had a huge belly overlapping his belt, large fat cheeks, and bright red hair.

"Now, what happened to you, young lady? Looks to me like you've been out in the cold too long."

"Feels like a week, but I've been out at least two nights. I fell and landed on jagged rocks buried under the snow."

"Let me look you over." The doctor noticed her face and hands were bright pink. "Your leg looks nasty, young lady. We'll do an x-ray and see what's going on in there."

It was ironic, Tuesday realized. This whole experience had started because she had been afraid of being exposed to the freezing weather. Thus, she had accepted a ride from a handsome stranger only to end up suffering from frostbite of her hands, feet, and face.

After Tuesday came back from x-ray, the nurse and doctor put her and Patty in tubs of water at room temperature to treat their frostbite. There was no internal bleeding as Annabelle and Cliff had suspected. Later, the doctor set Tuesday's leg and put splints on it until the swelling went down. Only then could a cast be put on her leg.

After the splints were in place, the nurse, with the help of an orderly, put Tuesday and Patty to bed in a room together.

With the exception of Aunt Aggie, the women, following Annabelle's lead, had decided to cooperate with Cliff and Hal and had answered their many questions. Annabelle feared they would be sent to jail if they did not. She did not realize it could not be worse than living in poverty in the small cabin and going hungry most of the time. She had no idea that Cliff would not actually put them in jail.

Annabelle did not fully understand why the men asked so many questions. Mainly the questions concerned the children who no longer lived in the cabin. Annabelle was drained when Cliff and Hal finally left.

"What're we're goin' to do now?" Annabelle asked. "I don't even understand what's happenin'."

"I do, and it ain't good, so it ain't," Aggie said. "I knowed one thing. I ain't leavin' until my boy is back here and safe again, so I ain't."

"We'll never trace all the children McCallister's sold," Cliff said. "But the twins, the infant, and the kidnapping of Tuesday give us enough evidence to put him behind bars for a long time."

"You know, Cliff," Hal said, "I thought I'd heard everything, but I'm shocked by what the women told us."

"Yes," Cliff agreed, "I understand what you're saying, I'm astonished by the many children McCallister's fathered and sold, despite the human misery we see almost daily."

"We'd better get moving. John, you and Randy wait here in case McCallister comes back to his cabin," Hal said. "I'll send the others to bring you food."

"I'm anxious to discuss Aubry Motes with his brother, the sheriff," Cliff said. "Sheriff Moats must have known what Aubry's been up to. I have little hope that the sheriff will admit he knows where his brother is."

"Aubry will be taken in by the net that's now engulfing the baby brokers," Hal said. "We can't put up with any bigoted crap from the sheriff. His cooperation is imperative. The time has come that the sheriff can no longer protect his brother from the arm of the law."

"The sheriff has to be on the lookout for McCallister as well. He could be holed up on the mountain somewhere," Cliff said.

John found a place he could turn around and drove back up the mountain in pursuit of Jacob. He soon realized he had lost him.

"Guess I'd better finish my job," John muttered to himself in disgust. He picked up his shotgun and turned, driving down the trail.

# *43*

*T*HE DARKNESS WAS THREATENED BY THE MOON-
light shining through the window. Tuesday
and Patty were both asleep.

The doctor had told Cliff that it was safe for Tuesday to travel to a hospital in Wheeling. He sat by
Tuesday's bed and waited for morning and the
ambulance from Wheeling. It would be too uncomfortable for Tuesday to ride in a small four-wheeler
that distance in her condition.

She opened her eyes.

"Tuesday, you look like someone who's seen a
ghost," Cliff said. "Are you feeling okay?"

"Will I ever be able to forget the horror of living in
that cabin and being locked in the dark, damp cellar
with those horrid rats?" Tuesday asked with tears in
her eyes. "Can't I even trust my own judgment?"

She did not tell about the rapes.

"It's over now," Cliff comforted Tuesday. "I
promise you that you'll never have to worry about
him again. I'm going to put him behind bars if it's
the last thing I do."

"Why is Cliff so determined to find me?" Jacob asked himself as he drove through the night. He glanced repeatedly out his rearview mirror in paranoia. "He has to know more than I thought. One day I will pay George back. He has to be behind this. Maybe he's trying to make a deal to save his own hide. The women are so stupid. They probably told Cliff that Tuesday and Patty are in the cellar. That sure would get me a long jail sentence.

"I can't even go back to the cabin for my things or for Tuesday. I'll have to let the chips fall where they may. As far as I'm concerned, a kidnapping charge is my word against Tuesday's. Hell, she wanted to come to the mountain with me, then got snooty about it.

"I'll head for the southwestern part of the state. I have money to buy what I need. When I'm settled, I'll contact Steven Lloyd and Aubry Moats. I'll make a deal with Moats to provide the kids, and I'll sell them to Lloyd. Old George Cunningham has seen the last of Jacob McCallister. I'll take my business elsewhere. I still have most of the money from Rose's baby and Daisy's twins tucked in a secret compartment in my truck. That'll keep me going for a while. By the time I run low, I'll be in business again." Jacob laughed loudly.

"How I hate that stupid sheriff, and he hates me back for getting his brother involved in the baby-brokerage business," Jacob grumbled. "It serves Ozzie Moats right, thinking he's better than the mountain men are.

"The southwestern part of the state is a good place to start over. Everyone will think I'd get as far away from West Virginia as I could. No one will think to look in my own backyard."

The women sat around the rough wooden table. Annabelle was afraid for Jacob and for the others.

The children would not leave their room and refused to come to the kitchen. Annabelle carried their food to them.

The men were outside, waiting for Jacob's return. "Jeb'll not be back," Aunt Aggie said, "as long as them men are out there, so he'll not. Sure hopin' he'd gone away somewheres, so I do. Ya all shouldn't otta told them men 'bout Jeb's business, so ya shouldn't."

Annabelle knew that if she did not prepare food for the next winter, they would starve. She did not understand what had happened or why, and she could not move herself to do anything. Annabelle could not make decisions on her own. She was accustomed to following Jacob's orders.

Since Joe would not come out of his room to chop wood or to hunt, they would soon run out of food and wood. There would be no fire for cooking or for warmth.

The old cow had run away again. She had gotten out of the barn where several boards were missing at the back wall. Annabelle imagined the cow went looking for food, preferring food to shelter. There was not enough hay stored in the barn to satisfy the cow's daily needs, nor to feed the cow through the winter, or she would have stayed put. Annabelle prayed the cow would find her way back after she realized there was no grass under the heavy snow cover. At least secured in the barn she got a fourth of a bale of hay each day.

To look the situation over, Frank came by and brought food and supplies he figured they needed. Annabelle was surprised, but grateful. She did not realize he was biding his time as he decided if it would be in his best interest to take them for his own.

Aunt Aggie sent the children for her cats and dogs and her supply of snuff. She would not return to her own cabin until she knew that Jacob was safe.

Jacob found a small mountain town about ten miles outside the city of Authurdale, West Virginia. It was a coal mining town with a population of 1,320. His new home, Ten Mile Creek, was further from Wheeling and the baby brokers he dealt with, than Winding Ridge was.

He would not forget Tuesday or Cliff. His burning desire was to get revenge. He planned the many ways to get his vengeance as he walked down Main Street, noticing the people stared at him. Judging from the way they glared at him, they did not like strangers.

It was his kind of town. He didn't cotton to outsiders either.

## THE END

## CABIN II RETURN TO WINDING RIDGE
### will follow

C. J. HENDERSON WAS BORN ON CHRISTMAS DAY. Her father, a coal miner, was a storyteller who kept his listeners spellbound. Raised on stories about C. C. Camp, Ponds murder farm, and other fearsome tales that came straight from her father's mind, C. J. began telling her friends stories of her own, oftentimes getting into trouble for frightening the other children.

After high school C. J. married and became the mother of two sons. During the marriage she attended college, and at her father's urging, studied real estate and became an agent. The knowledge gained from her real estate career led to a position with a utility company in which she leased property. That work took her into the remote mountainous areas of West Virginia, where she met many colorful characters. Often C. J. had to wait in her car for property owners to show up for appointments. As she waited, appointment by appointment, the novel came alive on her legal pad.

C. J. is now a real estate broker operating her own company and working on more novels.

## Order Form to Purchase
## Your Autographed Copy(ies)

## The Cabin-Misery on the Mountain
## Cabin II-Return to Winding Ridge
*Pre-Order Now. Available Mid-October.*

METHOD OF PAYMENT

☐ Check or money order enclosed. Make payable to:
MICHAEL PUBLISHING CO.
PO Box 778
Fairmont, WV 26555-0778

☐ Charge it to:

    ☐ MasterCard     ☐ Visa

    ☐ American Express   ☐ Discover

Card Number: _____

Expiration Date: _____

Signature: _____

Address: _____

_____

| | | | |
|---|---|---|---|
| Copy(ies) of *The Cabin* | @ $7.99 ea | $ _____ | |
| | Order at wholesale price: | | |
| Copy(ies) of *Cabin II* | @ $7.99 ea | $ _____ | |
| WV sales tax (if resident) | @ 6% | $ _____ | |
| Shipping & handling | @ $2.49 | $ _____ | |
| Additional Copies for S&H | @ $1.13 | $ _____ | |
| | Total | $ _____ | |

Note: Canadian price is $9.99. Ask for them at your local book store (ISBN 0-87012-633-4). Thank you for your order.